ETHICS

OF A

THIEF

MARY GALE HINRICHSEN, PHD.

iCrew
digital publishing

with love
Mary Gale

Ethics of a Thief

Copyright © 2015 Mary Gale Hinrichsen

Published in the United States of America.

iCrew Digital Productions is an independent publisher of digital works. We support the efforts of authors who wish to publish in the digital realm

ISBN:978-0692388402 (iCrew Digital Productions)

Chapter One

On her drive to the yacht club, Abigail Wilson had a sense of impending doom. But once she turned her attention to the road, she noticed the tall eucalyptus trees and radiant flowers along the winding road, and thought, "What a beautiful day."

At that moment, she determined to put the glooming feelings to rest. *Think positive and enjoy the ambiance of a new day.* Quickly she loosened her death grip on the steering wheel and rolled down the window. *Oh, how I love the ocean air.*

While taking in deep breaths, she glanced in the rearview mirror at her niece, Lisa, and nephew, Danny. Both seemed happy and content. *I'm glad they adjusted so quickly to their parents vacationing without them.*

Wide-eyed Lisa turned to Danny, who was still moving to the sounds emanating from his iPod.

In an attempt to relax, Abigail filled her lungs, held her breath, and slowly exhaled. After reaching the parking lot, she pulled into a space. "We're here kids."

After opening the back door, Lisa jumped out and stood. She took her jacket off and tied it around her waist. She noticed that her brother was still sitting, so she yelled, "Danny! We're here!"

The boy removed his earphones, slowly placed his iPod in its carry case, and hopped out of the car to join his sister.

"I'm hungry," he whined while glancing at his aunt.

With a snip in her tone, Lisa said, "You're always hungry".

Abigail rubbed the boy's buzz haircut. "Let's walk around before we eat, okay?"

After adjusting his jeans for comfort, he bent to tie his tennis shoes. When he looked up, he called out to his sister, "Hey, let's look for sea lions."

Lisa grinned and nodded. "Let's race to the pier!" While running, her hair swished as she gripped her jacket. When she glanced back, she noticed her brother was catching up. When he was about to reach for her, she started giggling.

"Hey you two, pay attention!" Abigail yelled. "Thank God no cars are around."

After stretching her long legs, and twisting at her waist, she headed toward the pier. When the ocean breeze kicked up, her strawberry-blond hair blew into her eyes, so she quickly put on her visor, and dug into her handbag to retrieve suntan lotion. She rubbed it onto her Scandinavian face and arms.

The sun felt good. Once she reached the dock, she stood on her left foot with her right hand on her hip. As the sun reflected on the water, it looked like sparkling diamonds. When she turned her attention to Lisa, the girl was hopping around like a playful kitten. When she saw Danny, his hand was over his eyes to block the sun while looking for sea lions.

Just as she started to relax, she noticed a well-built man walking up to Danny and starting a conversation. When she moved toward them, the man glanced her way, and cocked his head, with his mouth slightly open. His eyes were inspecting her tight black jeans and snug tank top.

Soon, the man turned his attention to the water, and asked Danny, "What do you see out there?"

"Nothing yet, but I want to find a sea lion."

The stranger leaned against the metal rail. "Have you actually seen them here before?"

Danny shrugged his shoulder, and said, "A few times."

Lisa skipped over to her brother and stopped. "Find anything?"

"No."

Abigail noticed the man's eyes sparking as he smiled at Lisa. He said, "Have you seen sea lions here?"

"I saw one, I really did," the girl squealed.

As Abigail came near, the stranger glanced at her. She stopped and stood between the children, and quickly placed her hand on Lisa's shoulder. She stared at the man without a word.

"Does it bother you, me talking to your children? I know some parents are pretty sensitive."

"The boy's my nephew, and she's my niece. And yes, I am protective. Sorry for making it so obvious."

It surprised her when the man's face went from a smile to sadness so quickly. His voice lowered. "I know from personal experience, you can't be too careful." His forehead revealed lines, and his hazel eyes looked away. But soon he faced Abigail and said, "Never apologize for being protective. If you ask me, adults need to be more aware of what's going on with children." They were both silent for a moment.

Abigail wondered what caused his sudden emotional change and the depth of his empathy. *Something must have happened to him or someone close.* Not wanting to pry, she said, "Thanks for understanding."

The man turned his attention to Danny as the boy was still searching the water.

While he was talking to the boy, Abigail noticed the man's Tommy Bahamas shirt, and slacks. *Most men prefer shorts on a warm day near water.* She liked the man's distinctive square jaw line and Roman-shaped nose. His appearance was appealing. She hadn't dated for a year, but he would be a consideration if she were in the dating mood.

When she glanced at his face, his incredible hazel eyes were focused on her in a way that revealed his interest. It caused her stomach to flutter. Although she felt good inside, she was grateful when he didn't make further advancement. *I'm just not ready to date.*

He bent down and sat on his heels. "I don't think you'll find too many sea lions out there today. Sorry."

The boy looked up and stared, "Why not?"

"They normally stay out farther."

Soon Abigail called out, "Well, you two, let's get a wiggle on it. Let's go eat."

Just the mention of food, Danny's smile became broad.

While walking to the restaurant, Abigail turned to give the man a goodbye smile.

When their eyes met, his smile revealed his beautiful white teeth. Their attraction to each other was so obvious, causing her to feel vulnerable. When they turned to leave, she reached for Lisa's hand, but quickly the girl let go when they were on the brick pathway. She yelled to Danny, "Watch me! I'm jumping over all the dark colored bricks!"

"But, you just missed one," her brother teased.

"I did not!" she yelled.

Once Abigail's nose caught the smell of food, she realized how hungry she felt. She reached for the door and held it open for the children. The large bay window drew her attention. It would be soothing just to sit and enjoy the scenery.

Soon Betty, their petite gray-haired hostess, walked toward them. "Well, if it isn't Miss Abigail. Where have you been, girl? We haven't seen you in these parts for a long while. And, you, Mr. Danny, you look more like your daddy every day. You have his charming green eyes and thick brown hair. So, tell me, how old are you? You're twelve, right?"

The boy's chin and eyes lowered. He preferred people to guess he was older.

Betty lightly touched Lisa's shoulder. "Look at those big, brown, cow eyes." She pinched the girl's cheek. "Goodness, you must be ten by now, right?"

"Soon, in two weeks," Lisa said, while she snickered at her brother.

The woman said, "Are you staying with your aunt?"

The children nodded.

"That must be fun."

Danny stood erect, with his chin high. "We just came from Santa Barbara."

"Oh." The woman grinned. "So, you're a world traveler, huh?"

The boy awkwardly squirmed while he stared at his shoes.

Betty grabbed one adult's and two children's menus and led them toward a table. "Abigail, you're the only blue-eyed beauty in the family, aren't you?"

Abigail smiled, and snickered, "Must have been the milkman."

When Betty let out a loud chuckle, her chin rose.

While looking for a table, Abigail noticed the seating was plentiful. Around the walls were many red-leather booths, and in the middle were many tables with black upholstered chairs. The metal portholes and sea paintings gave the feeling of being on a vessel. Her favorite picture hung over the mahogany bar. It was of a man on a boat in the middle of the ocean being overcome by waves. It reminded her of her own vulnerability -- like last year, when her heart was broken at the corner booth. She pushed the thought away. *Remember, Abigail, today's a new day.*

They heard a familiar voice call out, "Hey! Is that you, Abigail?"

She spun around and saw a family friend, Larry Kilgore. His hand motioned for them to come. His petite, blond-haired wife, Sandra, and he were at their favorite booth.

Abigail's family often referred to them as the mystery couple. Both were in their mid-forties, neither worked nor offered much personal information. They spent most of their time traveling the world. Her family found them both pleasant, and everyone enjoyed their interesting travel stories. Her dad suspected that one of them inherited their family's fortune while her mother, with her vivid imagination, teased about other possibilities. It seemed that not knowing just added to the couple's intrigue.

Larry said, "Could that be Danny and Lisa with you?"

The man approached the children and gave them a big hug. His beard scratched Lisa's face. "Don't," she said, while giggling.

His slender frame wore casual linen pants and a shirt.

Sandra pushed herself from the booth and stood to greet the children. Her short frame was Danny's height. As usual, she wore a colorful dress and high-heeled sandals, which had shiny stones and were most likely from Neiman Marcus.

"Come sit with us," Larry said. "We have plenty of room. Goodness, the last time we saw you, let's see -- wasn't it at your parents' Christmas party?"

Abigail nodded, "I thought you were off traveling someplace exciting on your new yacht?"

Sandra waited until Lisa was seated next to her before sitting. She glanced at Abigail, "We just got back."

Lisa gawked at Sandra's necklace. "I like those green stones." When Lisa saw the woman's four-carat matching emerald ring, she said, "Wow. When I get big, I want one just like that."

Sandra said, while smiling, "I'm sure you'll have nice things, too, when you grow up."

Lisa sat closer to Sandra and gazed up at her. "Mommy and Daddy just got married."

"Oh, they're together again, that's nice."

Lisa grinned and nodded.

Danny sat between his aunt and Larry. "Did you really buy a bigger boat?"

"We sure did."

"How big?"

"Very big, want to see her?"

Danny's eyes brightened, "You mean, go on it?"

"Sure." Larry's grin became a chuckle. "After we eat, you can check her out for yourself."

At that time, their waitress had arrived and smiled broadly at Larry. "Ready to order?"

"Is it too late for breakfast?" Abigail asked.

"You can order anything on the menu," she replied.

Larry and Sandra ordered lunch dishes while Abigail ordered eggs and toast, and the children asked for blueberry pancakes.

Sandra asked, "Lisa, where are your parents now?"

"In Hawaii."

"Hawaii? How come you didn't go?"

"Silly. They're on their honeymoon."

"That's right. That's a very good reason for not going." She smiled, showing her perfect teeth. "I bet you're happy they're back together."

The girl nodded.

Danny looked up at Larry. "Me too! I don't like them split up, but they yelled too much together. Daddy wants Mommy to work, and she doesn't want to. She wants to stay home. Now, he said she can stay home, but she wants to work."

The adults laughed.

Danny grinned as the waitress placed pancakes before him. He dug in. The juice from a blueberry ran down the right side of his mouth.

As Sandra watched him, she asked, "So, young man, was your aunt starving you?"

Lisa scowled. "He always eats like that." The girl took her fork and picked at her food before taking her first bite.

"I can see why you're so skinny," Larry teased the girl. He turned to Abigail. "So, what's going on with your parents?"

After putting down her fork, she said, "They're both doing pretty well. They're in good health. They had a wonderful time on their trip to London and their quick visit to France. Speaking of trips, I heard you both went to the Middle East."

His eyes looked down and away. "Yes. We did."

"Weren't you afraid, with all the unrest?"

"Yes. But, we avoided dangerous spots." His head cocked. He was silent for a moment and then said, "With the suicide bombers, no one felt safe for a minute."

"What made you decide to go to the Middle East?"

Larry didn't answer. Instead, he hurriedly changed the subject. "So, tell me Abigail, why was it that you left such a great career? Weren't you the district manager of some large corporation?"

She stared at her food and nodded.

"Your dad bragged about your success. Wasn't your district the most successful in the country?"

Abigail studied her food and then connected with his eyes. "It was a great career, but I have no regrets for leaving. I like being a teacher. But, to answer your question, I left because I felt as if I was competing against myself."

"Why's that?"

"I spent months training my staff, and then they would leave to compete against me."

"I see. So, what grade do you teach?"

"Sixth."

"So, do you pass along your high moral standards?" he mocked.

"I don't put up with much, if that's what you mean. Especially if a child is mean to another, he's in big trouble, then."

"Well, aren't you the tough one," Larry snickered.

After the meal, their full-figured waitress returned. She leaned forward to give Larry the check, and revealed her ample cleavage. When he handed her his credit card, he also gave a twenty-dollar tip.

As they prepared to leave, Danny asked, "Can we see your boat?"

"I didn't forget, young man. Besides, I want your aunt to see our wheelhouse."

Abigail touched Larry's arm. "Are you sure you have time for this?"

"We have all the time in the world, missy."

Sandra glanced at Lisa. "Want to see our new yacht?"

The girl clapped her hands, and her eyes sparkled. She squealed, "Yes!"

While walking, Abigail said, "We sure appreciate your kindness, Larry."

When they got to the walkway, she noticed the same man from earlier talking with someone. She was glad he didn't see her. Even if he was charming and attractive, she wasn't ready for any complications.

Chapter Two

While walking to the yacht, Lisa playfully hopped over the dark-colored bricks. Each time she missed, she giggled because Danny didn't notice. He was too busy trying to figure out which yacht belonged to Larry.

Danny yelled, "I see one!" Lisa glanced to where he was pointing. From afar, it looked like two young pups bobbing their heads.

Everyone's attention quickly changed direction when Sandra announced, "There's our new yacht."

The girl put her hands to her mouth. "Oh my, it is big!"

Abigail gasped. "Couldn't you find a larger one?" The couple laughed.

Sandra said, "It is quite big. It is more than ninety feet long and has three levels."

As Danny examined the vessel, he said, "Check out the small boat at the back."

"It's used for shore visits," Larry said, while looking over the boy's shoulders.

Abigail looked around and said, "Why so many life preservers? I guess you don't want to be like the Titanic."

Larry's head went back as he laughed in amusement, "We thought the same thing. But, they were included, so we didn't argue."

The boy glanced up at Larry, "Can we check out the galley?"

Lisa smirked, "Is that all you think about -- food?" But, the boy was too excited to be annoyed by his sister. Larry's hand touched Danny's head, guiding him. "Come, we'll go there first."

When they entered the galley, the boy's eyes opened wide. "Wow! This is bigger than our kitchen."

The girl peeked into the galley. "Gee, it is big. Look! The refrigerator has two doors."

After Sandra opened a cupboard door, she took out a package of cookies. When they were offered, Danny immediately grabbed two.

Suddenly, Larry tapped Abigail's shoulder. "Let's go topside."

She grinned, and her eyes became bright while she swiftly followed him up the ladder.

When they reached the wheelhouse, she observed the metal-framed glass enclosure. On a hot day, the glass rotated to allow for cool breezes. "Goodness, Larry. You have every imaginable electrical and mechanical device possible. Do you know how everything works?"

"No. It's too new."

She noticed the area behind the wheelhouse. At once, she saw a Jacuzzi. It seated six and had drink holders around the deck. Nearby was a small bar, which she was sure was fully stocked.

Larry watched her inspect the grown-up play area.

"They didn't forget a thing, did they?" she said.

"That's part of the fun of showing it off." He grinned.

"I bet."

As they walked back to the wheel, she smiled broadly. "Being here is wonderful. I wish Dad could see this. You know how he loves to check out yachts. And, he would enjoy being out at sea on a day like this."

Larry nodded in agreement.

They turned when they heard jubilant voices coming from the ladder. Danny boldly marched up to Larry. "Wow! Will you take us out sometime?"

After placing his hand on the boy's shoulder, he said, "Sure." He winked.

The girl exposed her biggest smile while looking at Sandra. "Can we go out today?"

Abigail's face turned red. She squinted with a glare at the girl. "Young lady, it is not polite to ask such things."

"The child can ask anything she wants." Larry smiled at Lisa.

"She needs to learn not to impose upon others. It is not right to put anyone on the spot like that. It is just not polite," Abigail said.

Sandra stood in front of Lisa, then bent down to her level and asked, "Is it truly your desire to go out to sea today, little one?"

"Can we? Can we really go? Today?" Lisa's face lit up. She jumped up and down clapping her hands.

After Abigail's face turned a brighter shade of red, she stared at the child. "No, not today, Lisa!"

"But, why not?" Larry piped in. "Do you have better things to do?"

Before Abigail had a chance to respond, Sandra said, "It'll be pleasant having you three on board." She surveyed her husband's face. "Abigail can help you at the wheel. Can't she, dear? Knowing her, it won't take long for her to get the hang of it."

"Sure, it'll be fun." He then faced Danny. "Want to spend the night out at sea?"

By then, Danny was so excited he hugged Larry's neck without letting go.

Abigail shook her head in disbelief and quickly folded her arms tightly. *Everything is happening too fast,* she thought, staring at the children. She looked at Larry and Sandra. "I can't believe you're giving in to the children -- really, overnight?"

"Our replacement skipper was due to come today," Larry said. "I'll have him meet us at sea after faxing him our navigational chart. Sandra, we still have our clothes on board. It'll be fun. Abigail does learn quickly. I'm sure she won't mind helping me navigate this thing."

Abigail's head throbbed. *How did I get us in this mess, and how can I get us out?* Her arm felt tight after recalling her earlier warning while driving from Santa Barbara. Each time she had a premonition, she feared it might come true. While feeling the pressure to say yes, she really wanted to say no, but hesitated when she saw the children's jubilant faces.

"Pleeeeease," Lisa begged.

"We still have our clothes in the car," Danny said. "Remember?" His eyes danced with delight. "Can we go get them, can we?"

Although her instincts wanted to say no, those happy faces broke down her defenses. She turned to Larry. "Are you sure you want to put up with us overnight?"

"It'll be delightful."

Soon Sandra placed her arm around Abigail's shoulders. "Don't worry. It will be fun for all of us. So, go get your things. When you return, I'll show you to your cabin."

Quickly, Larry disappeared and then came back with a luggage carrier. "Use this. It'll be easier."

On the way to the car, Abigail was still upset with the children and herself. At that moment, she wished she wasn't responsible for them. And, she desperately wanted to be alone to think. Everything was moving too fast.

Why am I so upset with the children? She questioned herself. I love the sea. Why am I resisting the idea? She stopped. It's that fear again. I must let it go. While walking to the parking lot, she told herself, we're on vacation, aren't we? I'm just being silly. Perhaps, I should apologize for not being more appreciative. And, it's too late to back out now. I might as well enjoy myself. She put on a smile for the children and decided not to scold them.

When they reached the car, they quickly got their bags onto the carrier and grabbed the smaller items. Danny's face was beaming with anticipation. "I can't wait to tell Dad. He won't believe we were on a yacht. I wish he were with us."

Lisa was grinning while saying, "We'll have our own cabin. Won't it be fun?" She glanced up at her aunt.

Abigail grabbed the girl's ponytail. "Yes. This will be an adventure to remember."

When they returned with their bags, Sandra gave them a choice between two cabins. Danny said, "Can we stay in this one? It has a couch. We can all be together."

"Can we?" The girl said, with her chin held up, blinking. "Pleeease?"

"Sure. That'll be fun," she said, while thinking, I desperately need alone time, just to think. My mind can't catch up with what's happening. Not being in control is not one of my favorite things. I feel defenseless over what others want. Everything is out of my control right now.

After they got settled in and changed clothes, the children went to the main salon and played cards with Sandra, while Abigail joined Larry topside. He was moving the vessel from the dock and it needed his full attention. She remained silent as she watched him steer the yacht away from the pier.

Larry saw her and waved her closer. "Where are the kids?"

"Playing cards with Sandra, is my guess."

"It's a beautiful day. I'm glad you decided to join us. Or, did we decide for you?"

While smiling, she turned away. She was grateful that at least one person knew her true feelings. It felt good to be away from the children, even if for a few minutes. She had developed a greater appreciation for stay-at-home moms.

I must stop worrying. It is a beautiful day.

After he successfully moved out of the harbor, Larry said, "Come take the wheel." While he showed her the fundamentals at the helm, he also showed her how to shut down the engine in case of an emergency or to take a break.

"Where's Captain Majors?"

"On leave. He is in Mount Dora."

"Where's that?"

"Not too far from Orlando. Bill was raised there."

"How long will he be gone?"

"Just a few weeks."

"The person coming later today is his replacement."

"How will he find us?"

"He'll take a smaller boat."

Abigail's attention turned to the children, who were yelling. "What's the problem with you two?"

"I won, "Lisa said, tearfully," but he said I cheated

"You did cheat," he said.

"No. I did not, Danny." She pushed him.

"Stop teasing your sister," Abigail demanded.

Danny's chin lowered. "Okay." The boy turned his attention to the wheel and watched. "Can I help drive the boat?"

"Sure," Larry said. "Come here." For twenty minutes, Larry stood behind the boy patiently teaching him how to handle the wheel.

"What's Sandra up to?" Larry asked.

"I don't know," Danny said.

"I'll go check on her." He faced Abigail. "I need to speak to Sandra about something important. Are you okay at the helm?"

After giving him a reassuring smile, she nodded.

"Will you two promise to stay with your aunt? I don't want her alone."

"I can help her drive the boat," Lisa said. Larry smiled and kissed her forehead.

As he walked away, he stopped and spoke to Danny. "Come get me if she needs me, okay?"

The boy nodded.

While she stood behind Danny at the wheel, Lisa checked out the ship-to-shore equipment and noticed the radio. She turned it on and found a station. After ten minutes, the girl was bored. "It's my turn!" she yelled at her brother.

After Danny vigorously objected, Abigail said, "Let him be. You can have your turn later."

Within five minutes, Lisa let out a loud breath. "Can I drive the boat now?"

"Let your sister have her turn." This time, Danny didn't object. While stepping away from the wheel, his face lit up. "Let's look for whales."

"No! It's my turn." Lisa grabbed the wheel. Abigail placed her hands on Lisa's.

"Are you looking forward to going to school?"

"No. I don't like my new teacher. She's mean."

"How is she mean?"

"She just looks mean. She never smiles. No one likes her."

"Perhaps something bad happened, and she is sad. Maybe your smile can make her feel better."

"I don't want to drive anymore," she said. She blissfully skipped toward her brother. Together, they searched for creatures living in the sea.

Abigail enjoyed the sun on her skin, but knew she needed more lotion. She wondered how they went from having a late breakfast to being on a fantastic yacht at sea—and all within hours. *Everyone knows I'm a control freak, so how did I suddenly give in to two small children? It must be love.*

Danny and Lisa stepped into the wheelhouse to visit their aunt.

"Hi, kids. Having fun?" The girl smiled, causing her teeth to show and her eyes to squint. The boy nodded.

"Hey, young man," Abigail said, "is it true you were in a fight a few months ago?" He nodded.

"Did your dad find out?" "Yes. I said that the boy hit me first. Daddy said, 'Kick him in the butt if he tries it again.'"

"That would be your dad," Abigail said, while holding back a laugh.

Lisa yelled, "I see something. It's a whale."

He stared at where she was pointing. "No, it isn't. It's only a school of fish—that's all."

The children sat down. "What do you think Mommy and Daddy are doing?" Danny asked.

"Snorkeling?" Abigail guessed.

"No, they're sightseeing," Lisa said.

"You don't know that!" Danny sneered.

The boy stood and marched up to his aunt. "I'm hungry. Where's Mr. Kilgore? He didn't come back."

"Yes, I know, Danny. Maybe he is still talking with Sandra."

"But, I'm hungry."

"After eating all those pancakes?" Lisa said loudly.

"It's been forever since then!"

"You're right, Danny. Larry's been gone for hours. I'm starting to get hungry, too."

"Can we go now?" he asked.

She nodded and shut down the engine. As they moved toward the ladder leading to the main deck, they decided their priority was the head.

The first to return was Danny. He entered the galley and started opening cupboards to check out the food supplies. Within minutes Lisa and her aunt joined him. Quickly, he grabbed the bread and peanut butter and searched for jam. After the sandwiches were made, they went into the main salon and relaxed while eating sandwiches.

"Where are Sandra and Larry?" Lisa asked.

"Well, they must be on the lower level. Either the master suite or the engine room, I would guess." Because she felt exhausted, she wanted to kick up her feet for a while. But, for some reason, she felt uneasy about the Kilgores. She hoped everything was okay.

Chapter Three

While Abigail and the children searched for the Kilgores, they reached the engine room. Quickly, Danny opened the hatch and stepped in. "Not in here."

"Maybe they're in their bedroom," Lisa said.

"It's a sleeping cabin," Danny responded.

"It might be a sleeping cabin, but it has a bed, too. So, it's a bedroom."

"Don't argue, you two," Abigail said, while smiling at the girl's logic. "Let's see if Lisa's right."

They continued and saw a hatch with a gold plate that said, *Master Suite*. Abigail promptly knocked. No response. Again, she knocked, still nothing. So, she called out, "Sandra, Larry." No reply. After slightly opening the hatch, she called out their names again, but still no response.

"Well, that's strange. What's going on?" Suddenly, her stomach was uneasy and her arm tightened.

"Let's check the other cabins," she said. The three of them continued until they reached the last cabin.

After opening the hatch, they entered. Soon, they heard alarmingly loud voices. At first she was excited, she thought it was Larry greeting the new captain. That until she heard a stranger shout, "I'll search the lower deck."

Another yelled, "I'll start in the main salon."

Neither voice was Larry's.

Instantly, she knew something was terribly wrong. She heard footsteps coming closer, so she quickly grabbed some blankets for hiding and whispered, "Cover up. Lie still. Don't say a word." Hiding under the blankets was not a great idea, but it was her only option.

While she listened to the sound of her heart pounding in her ears, time seemed to stand still. Slowly, she rubbed her arm hairs and thought they felt like porcupine pointers. She thought she was alert enough to hear a needle drop three cabins away. She desperately hoped they would not be discovered.

After waiting for what seemed like an eternity, the sound of footsteps stopped. She held her breath as the latch turned. She cringed when the hatch connected with the bulkhead. The footsteps came closer and abruptly stopped. She heard what sounded like a blanket being pulled away. A man said, "What are you, a stowaway?"

Quickly, she removed her own blanket and stood next to the boy. Danny's eyes were wide, and his mouth was open, gawking at the stranger. Abigail immediately recognized him from the dock. "Why did you follow us?" she demanded.

After looking into her eyes, his face softened. "You're the woman from the pier, aren't you?"

When she didn't respond, he moved his attention toward the closet. "Is someone hiding in there? Who's in there?" he said, louder.

He moved swiftly to the cabinet and threw open the door. "Nothing." He swiveled and briskly moved to the bench seats. After pulling the blanket off Lisa, he said, "Can you stand up and step away?" He lifted the bench, but after his examination, he found only supplies.

"Who else is here?" he questioned. "If someone else is hiding, I want to know now! Do you understand?" They were silent, so he moved toward the hatch, and walked out of sight.

Lisa pulled on Abigail's arm. "Why is he here? Why is he so mean?"

"I'm not sure," she said, while being mortified that earlier she enjoyed his attention.

Danny looked to his aunt. "How did he get here?"

"I don't know, Honey." She thought, *Well, isn't this great! We can't very well hide or run. So, what else can we do?* While she squirmed and tapped her fingernails on the bulkhead, she felt distressed and knew lines were forming on her brow. *If this keeps up, I'll need Botox before I'm forty, but I guess that's the least of my problems.*

The Kilgores were missing, and strangers had taken over. As she rubbed her temples, she heard a loud bang, as if someone slammed another hatch against the bulkhead. The man returned -- his face drained white.

"What's wrong?" Danny asked.

The man stood in silence for a moment with his chin low and arms hanging at his sides. He grabbed Abigail's arm and pulled her into the passageway.

While trying to resist, she said, "Who are you? What are you doing here?"

"Look, miss, you need to come with me, right now! Understand?" He pivoted and advanced down the passageway, half dragging her.

When Abigail heard Lisa crying, she yelled back at the children. "Everything will be okay. Please stay in the cabin with Danny."

The man pulled her to the master suite, stopped at the hatch and waited.

"What's going on?" she asked, while glaring.

Although he was silent, his eyes showed horror. "Who are they?" he demanded. He placed his hand on her back to guide her into the master suite.

She tried to resist his push, but lost. She faced the bed as she entered. There was no way she could have been mentally prepared enough. On the bed were the dead bodies of her hosts. After covering her mouth to hold back a scream, she leaned into the man. She stared at the bullet hole on Larry's forehead. Blood dripped from his mouth. Sandra laid half on the bed, with her blonde hair hanging off to the right and blood covering the carpet.

She started hitting his chest with her fists. She yelled, "Why did you do this? Why did you kill them?"

He grabbed her arms and pushed her away. Glaring at her, he said, "I'm not a murderer. I didn't do this!" He quickly led her into the passageway.

She suddenly became weak, doubled over and used her hands to cover her face. When she fell to her knees, she yelled, "No! This can't be happening. It just can't be real. Oh my God, how can this be?"

The man closed the hatch when he saw Danny and Lisa running to their aunt. "What's wrong?" the boy called out to his aunt.

I have to pull myself together, she told herself. She tried to take in air while she grimaced at the thought of what she just witnessed. She was desperate to get the images out of her mind that were tearing at her heart. She slowly moved herself up the bulkhead, looked at the children and leaned forward with her arms open wide. After their embrace, Danny pulled away, but stood with his body still touching Abigail.

"Don't worry, you two," Abigail comforted. "Everything will be okay." She knew that Danny wasn't buying it.

"Who were those people?" the stranger demanded.

While looking up at him, she choked back her tears. "Our friends, Larry and Sandra Kilgore. They were our hosts."

Finally, she was able to stand up. Once she was standing, she yelled, "Who are you, and why are you here?"

She noticed that his face was still pale, and his shoulders were slumped. He said, "My name is Matt, miss."

"Why are you here?"

"We're looking for something."

"Who invited you?"

"Look, lady. I have my own questions, so why are you here?"

While staring at him with contempt, she yelled, "We're invited guests, unlike you -- I'm sure!"

"Did you hear the gunshots?" he whispered.

"No," she said, and then she wondered why. She glanced at him. "Maybe they used a silencer. We didn't hear anything at the wheelhouse."

I hope I'm wrong about him, Abigail thought. He did seem genuinely surprised. Perhaps, he didn't kill them, but does it really matter? The killer is still on the vessel, just waiting to kill again.

While Matt spoke, she was unable to hear his words because her mind was consumed with how to get the children to safety. After feeling powerless, her fear became pure panic. Her only comfort was to see that Matt was as distressed about the murders as she.

"I'm sorry about your friends. Please know we had nothing to do with it. We are only here to find something the Kilgores took. We thought our friend, Captain Forelli, was on board, but he isn't here yet."

At that moment, her heart sank, knowing that even the new captain was someone she'd have to contend with.

"We thought Forelli would be alone on the vessel. They were to stay ashore. Forelli faxed us the course and didn't mention they would be here." He stared at her. "Why did they change plans?"

Suddenly, his words cut like a knife. Her stomach felt ill as she hung her head. My God, if we didn't run into them, they would be home—alive. Now, they're both lying dead. Guilt engulfed her. Why did I say yes? I should have said no to their invitation. Everything happened so fast. I had no time to think. My God! They would still be alive. Suddenly, she was unable to hide her emotions and her tears fell. While covering her face with her hands, she bent down and sat on her heels and wept.

Instantly, Danny fixed his eyes on his aunt and said, "What's the matter? Why are you crying?"

While wanting to respond, she couldn't. After a time, she barely spoke out, "It's nothing. So, don't you worry, okay? Everything will be fine." "But, you don't look fine. Your face is all sad. You're crying."

Lisa sat next to her aunt, hugging her. Suddenly, her tears flowed. "I want to go home. Can we go home now?"

Although desperately wanting to reassure the girl, she fought back tears. She finally managed to say, "I'm just concerned, that's all, everything will be fine. God will take care of us, don't you worry." She lifted Lisa's chin, kissed her forehead and pulled her closer to comfort the girl and herself.

The boy stood, glaring at Matt. "So, you're the man from the pier. I liked you, but not now. Why did you make my aunt cry?"

As Matt stood looking at the boy, he said, "Young man, I have no intention of hurting you or your family. I came here to find something, that's all. Once it's found, we can all go home safely."

Sure, Abigail thought, as if I could believe you for a minute.

The boy stood snug against his aunt. "What're you looking for?"

"I'm not sure. All we know is it's valuable and hiding on the yacht, but no one knows what it is exactly."

The girl glared at Matt while holding onto her aunt, "But, how can you find something if you don't even know what you're looking for? That's silly."

"Good point, little one," Matt said, grinning. "This much I know: It's smaller than a breadbox -- that is, if they still make them." A wide smile spread across his face and revealed his perfect teeth. Color finally returned to his face. Warmth flowed through Abigail, she thought that perhaps he wouldn't hurt them -- but she quickly reconsidered. Even if he didn't, someone murdered her friends, and it could have been one of his cohorts.

"Let's go," Matt said. He rotated toward the ladder leading to the upper level.

Abigail told herself, This is not the time for this, stop wallowing in self-pity and guilt. You can do that after the ordeal is over. These children need me. I'm all they have. She put Lisa in front of her and followed.

When they reached the main salon, they noticed another man. He had a medium build with dark hair and was standing and shaking his head while his piercing blue eyes drilled right through her. He scowled at the children. "What the hell! Where did you dig up the woman and kids?"

The intensity in his tone scared Abigail.

"Calm down, Robert," Matt said.

"Don't tell me to calm down. Where in the hell did you find them? You said only Forelli would be on board." "I know. It does cause problems."

Robert's voice was louder. "Why are they here?" "Hey! I'm not too happy about this either," Matt yelled back. While the men argued, more footsteps were heard. Abigail whirled around so fast that her hair flung to one side. As another man entered the area, she noticed that his build was similar to Robert, except he had blond hair and sported a beard.

"Now, what do we have here?" he said, calmly. His smile turned into a snicker.

"Hi Brent," Matt said. "I found them on the lower level."

The man grinned. "Won't Jack be thrilled? You know how he loves surprises." Brent's eyes sparkled, as he played with his beard.

"Forelli isn't here yet," Matt said, in a low voice.

"Who's manning the vessel?"

"That's a good question."

"It's on autopilot," Abigail said. "Before leaving the helm, I shut it down."

When Matt moved toward Robert, Lisa and Danny started talking to each other -- the first time since the ordeal began. The children glanced at the men and whispered.

Abigail felt shaky inside, not knowing what to expect, but wanting to appear secure. To calm herself, she decided to use a technique from grief therapy. Each time she felt overwhelmed, she made herself aware of her surroundings. In the past, the technique helped, she hoped it would again.

While the men conversed, she gave the main salon a careful inspection. The cabin was large enough to entertain twenty people, and the large portholes allowed the sun to light the area. The furniture varied; a few pieces of modern, lots of contemporary and a sprinkle of antiques. That was one thing about the Kilgores -- they did their own thing when it came to decorating. She had to admit everything did come together with an atmosphere of comfort and intrigue. There was a thirty-foot wrap-around couch that appeared comfortable, and a magnificent cherry-wood coffee table. Near the galley was a glorious dining table.

After taking a few deep breaths, she held it for a count of ten and slowly let it out. Once relaxed, she quickly shifted her thoughts to finding a way to escape without causing havoc with her abductors. One thing was for sure -- she had to find a way to be alone. After stepping near Matt, she stood with her weight on one foot and the other hand on her hip. "I'm going to get drinks for the children."

Matt touched his chin and observed her before he grinned and nodded his approval.

She grabbed the children's hands and advanced toward the galley. Robert yelled, "Stop! The kids stay here. If there is even a hint you're up to something, you'll regret it, lady. Understand?"

She spun around and scowled at the man. "Yes. I understand."

She studied the children's faces and gave a reassuring smile. As she stepped toward the galley, she overheard Matt say, "The kids and woman stay with me. I'll be responsible. I found them." Abigail could almost hear a sigh of relief from Robert and Brent.

Abigail entered the galley, passed the stainless-steel island and refrigerator, and stopped at the sink. For the first time, she noticed a vessel from the porthole. Suddenly, it hit her -- signal for help. She hoped her days in the Girl Scouts would pay off. She glanced over her shoulder to reassure the vessel was still in sight; it was, of course. Frantically, she opened the cabinets to search for a flashlight. She had no luck. *It must be in the wheelhouse.* She quickly scanned around for matches and candles, but found none.

After grabbing a shiny pot, she decided she could angle it so the sun would help signal for help, but before she tried, she saw Matt from the corner of her eye. He was silent and stood with his arms folded leaning against the hatch with his hazel eyes looking down.

Suddenly, she felt a tinge of guilt mixed with fear, as if caught doing something wrong and hoped the pot in her hand didn't give away her intent. Swiftly, she placed it down and busied herself by getting drinks. *Well, isn't this great! I just missed my first opportunity to get help.*

Chapter Four

Abigail then looked around for a tray on which to place the drinks. She heard a robust voice. Matt was by the hatch. Next to him was a large, potbellied man with a high forehead; his pants and shirt were too tight. His forceful voice matched his large frame. The man scrutinized her every move. His hateful eyes caused her to shiver.

"What's going on here?" the man bellowed. "Is this some kind of sick joke? Where did the woman and kids come from? The last thing we need is another distraction."

"Calm down, Jack. I didn't plan this. I found them hiding in a cabin."

"Hiding? Why where they hiding?"

"They must have heard our voices and were frightened."

Jack glared at her. "Why were they alone on the vessel?"

"They weren't alone. The Kilgores took them out."

"My God, they're here, too?" Jack started to pace.

"Their dead bodies are."

The man stopped abruptly. "You must be shitting me. This is absurd. You're telling me we have dead bodies on board?"

"I'm afraid so."

"For God's sake, how did they die?"

"Both were murdered."

Jack threw his hands up. "You're jerking me around? You can't be serious. If that's true, then why in the hell are we still here?"

After listening to the man's reaction, Abigail's concern was increasing by the minute. The edge in his loud voice was troubling, but it was the fire in his eyes that was terrifying. She couldn't believe her ears when the man asked, "Did the woman kill them?"

"No."

"How do you know Matt? Were you thinking below the belt – 'cause she's pretty?"

"Of course not! It was because she became hysterical at the sight of their dead bodies. She couldn't have faked that."

Abigail felt invisible as they talked about her as if she wasn't there.

Jack got in Matt's face. "Things aren't right. We have to get off this vessel -- now! Do you understand? We're talking about murder. I've taken enough risks for you, but this is too much."

"Yes, I know Jack. I'm sorry for insisting you come."

When she saw Jack's face soften, she knew the two men must have been close.

Brent strolled up and stood behind the other two men, but didn't add to the conversation. The three men stood silently, staring at her. Brent was checking out her curves, Jack was looking straight at her eyes, and Matt was solemn. At that moment, she wished she could have just pushed some magical button and disappeared. But that wasn't possible, so she mustered up enough courage to carry the drinks past their watching eyes -- she pretended not to be terrified. After she had placed the drinks on the magnificent table, the men came over. She felt the tension in her bones. She knew the men must have been trying to process the news of finding dead bodies, two children and a woman.

It was at that moment, she discovered the loudness of silence. It was scarier than Jack's forceful voice. Her hands perspired as she calmly gave her nephew a root beer. She tried to break the icy silence. "Lisa, would you like an orange drink?" Her words fell on deaf ears. Even Lisa was unresponsive. The girl fumbled with her braids.

Abigail stood with her weight on one foot and her hand on her hip. She waited for someone to speak. She was questioning how in the world she got the children and herself into such a mess. Yet, she knew the answer -- it was from ignoring God's warning. She resolved to pray with her eyes open, *Dear God, help us through this ordeal. Please give me wisdom and direction on how to get the children to safety.* Again, she took a deep breath, held it for ten counts and slowly let it out. She noticed Danny was inspecting his captors and standing perfectly still.

Suddenly, one by one, the four men came and selected a drink.

Lisa finally grabbed the last orange soda. *Stress does cause thirst,* Abigail thought. Her mouth felt like cotton, so she, too, grabbed a soda. While drinking their refreshments, the children sat and talked. Before long, Matt stood with his head cocked and watched his three comrades march out of the main salon with purpose.

Matt faced Abigail. "I think it's best for you three to stay with me. Look, none of us want this. We're as troubled as you are. We just want to finish what we came for, and go home. At this point, we can't risk letting you go. That's why you must stay with me. After the item is found, we'll all leave."

Abigail shifted her weight uneasily. She listened, but she doubted all was well.

Matt touched his chin. "At this point, you have two choices." He glanced down as he ran his fingers through his hair. He looked up. "You can help me find what we're looking for, or you can hinder our search. If you decide to help, you will go home sooner. Do you understand?" He took a long study of Abigail's face. "Hey, what we came for is extremely valuable. We'll not leave without it."

Silence, then filled the room. Abigail scowled at her captor. She wanted to get the children to safety, but he had just told her she couldn't. Someone killed her friends; if not one of these four men, then who did it?

As Abigail followed Matt into the library, she vowed to do anything to get the children home safely. She placed her arm around Lisa. "You're so quiet; are you okay?"

"I want to go home," Lisa said, with tears welling up. "I want my mommy."

"I know, Sweetie. The man said we can go home once he finds what he's looking for. Do you want to help him?"

"Promise we can go home?" Lisa asks.

"Sweetheart, that's what the man said." Abigail glared at Matt. To her astonishment, he came over, sat on his heels and spoke to Lisa.

"Look. This must be hard on you, but I promise you'll return home safely. Do you believe that?"

Lisa silently gazed into his eyes for several seconds. His warm smile caused her to stop crying. She reached over and hugged his neck. Neither spoke a word. Her tears started running down his shirt. Lisa pulled away and moved next to her aunt. *How amazing,* Abigail thought, *the same man keeping her hostage is now comforting Lisa and making her feel safe.* Abigail reached down to brush a curl away from Lisa's eye, as they watched their captor.

Although Danny was adventurous, he, too, was afraid and wanted to go home. After watching the four men, he knew they were in control, and he must do what they said. Earlier, when he saw Matt on the dock, he was okay, but after seeing how mean he was to his aunt, he had doubts.

While he adjusted to the situation, he tried to think of some happy memories. His whole life seemed to come into his mind.

When they lived in Pine Valley, he and Lisa spent many hours exploring the land near their home. On one occasion, they spied a caravan of gypsies on the bank of a nearby stream. He and Lisa would hide and watch the tribe cook meals and visit together. One day, he eyed a young, black-haired beauty a few years his senior. Lisa mercilessly teased. "You want to marry her, don't you, Danny?" His denial was ferocious, yet it didn't stop him from staring at the girl.

He had heard stories about gypsies, but was still amazed to see women wearing dresses and jewelry, yet barefooted. One time, Lisa started to get a closer look, but he pulled her back, afraid of getting caught.

Daydreaming, his mind went to another time of exploits. They waited for the old ice cream truck to slowly make its way up the steep incline. Lisa would ask him to get ice cream. He would jump on the fender, open the back door, grab a few ice creams and toss them into the bushes. After the truck was out of sight, they would sit and eat. They thought the ice cream tasted better than at home. As young Christians, they were taught that stealing was wrong, but they had too much fun to feel guilty.

Danny recalled the times he walked Lisa home from school. The poorly paved road they traveled had weeds on each side. Their mother wanted them to pick up the mail for her friend Gordon Snyder. He was a large, sickly man and was unable to walk down the steep, long driveway to fetch his mail.

His sister and he were often out of breath while walking up the winding, dirt path to his modest abode. Around the house were weeds and a few shrubs. Gordon's two ferocious Doberman Pinschers greeted them with angry barks. The only thing separating the feared dogs from them, was a flimsy screen fence.

He feared that one day the animals would escape and attack. Somehow their fears only heightened the adventure. One day, Lisa bravely walked up to the dogs and yelled, "Calm down, you two." To the boy's amazement, the dogs obeyed.

When the front door opened, Gordon stood tall over them. He was six-foot-five, weighed four hundred pounds and had large, swollen legs covered with sores. A strong, unpleasant odor came from his overalls. They referred to him as a gentle giant. Gordon always offered him and Lisa a reward for bringing his mail. They had a choice of a nickel or a glass of Kool-Aid. On hot days, they preferred the refreshment.

While they visited the old man, Danny would sit and observe everything -- the cement floors in the living room, the chipped paint on the walls and the sparse furniture in need of replacement. The house was one large room with a dividing wall separating the living area from the bedroom.

Danny had had many adventures, and, as he sat in the yacht's library, he realized he had a different adventure ahead of him -- to get home without harm! He didn't see the Kilgores' bodies, but he heard them talking about gunshots. Something happened, and he feared the worst after seeing the terrified expression on his aunt's face.

The fear he felt was similar to having those angry, loud Doberman Pinscher dogs bark at him. He felt like the gypsies -- watched by strangers. Danny started to wonder if God was punishing him for stealing ice cream. He decided to pray, *Dear God, please forgive me for stealing. I promise never to do it again.* Much to his surprise, he felt more at peace; the short prayer had worked.

Danny knew the four men were not invited guests, and that he, his sister and aunt were not safe. He wasn't afraid of Matt as much as the situation. He wanted his parents, and to go home.

When he looked up from his thoughts, he watched Matt examine books. He took one at a time -- he would open it and fan the pages, then read the first page and put it aside.

"What are you looking for?" Danny asked.

"Hidden compartments and the date it was published."

"Why?"

"Sometimes people buy look-a-like books that are hollow and place valuable items in them."

Danny watched for a few minutes, and thought, *If I can help find what he is looking for, we can go home.* "Can I help?"

Matt turned to face Danny. "Tell you what. If you find it, you'll get a reward."

"What kind of a reward?"

"How about five thousand dollars?"

Danny's eyes sparkled, his lips turned up into a smile.

Matt cocked his head. "What do you say?"

"That's a lot of money," Danny said.

Matt glanced toward Abigail. "That goes for you two, as well. Understand?" Abigail didn't respond.

"Where do you want me to start?" Danny asked.

"Any place you wish."

Lisa broke her silence by asking her brother, "What do you want with your reward money?"

"A telescope. With five thousand dollars, I could buy the best in the whole world. At night, I could see faraway stars and planets."

Lisa turned to face her aunt. "He wants to be an astronaut, you know."

Abigail nodded.

Danny grinned. "I won't ask Mom or Dad for one. They argue about money too much." He fixed his eyes on Lisa. "Are you going to help?" She looked down, turned her head and touched her cheek with her finger.

The boy asked his sister, "What do you want?"

Lisa squinted. "I don't know. Could I look through your telescope?"

"Sure!"

Lisa said, "This is weird. We don't even know what we're looking for." Lisa shrugged her shoulders. "It's stupid."

Danny noticed his aunt seemed calmer. He turned to watch Matt methodically examine each book. He decided to make his experience another adventure, as if he was on some scavenger hunt. Yet, he knew it was one adventure they could do without. He glanced at his aunt and saw her rubbing her temples. A few strands of her strawberry-blond hair covered her hand. Danny hoped Matt would keep his promise, so they could all go home after they found the stupid treasure.

Abigail stood on a brilliantly colored rug near a porthole. She walked up to the cherry-wood desk that sat in front of the bookshelves and watched Lisa.

The girl put her hands on her hips. "How can we find something when we don't know what it is? That's dumb."

Danny said, "We all heard you the first time, Lisa."

"So, I said it again. So, what!"

Abigail walked to the desk and picked up an exquisite ceramic square container, shaded green with a sprinkle of gold, which gave it depth. It stood on four lion's feet. Both sides had two small, jeweled handles. She pulled off the lid by a beautiful gold figure of an angel that topped it. "Maybe this is it! It's small enough to fit into Matt's breadbox."

Abigail turned it over, and glanced at the bottom. It was made by a manufacturer that was still in business, and she knew it couldn't be worth even the five thousand dollars Matt offered.

A small bud vase caught Danny's attention. After picking it up, he turned it over and handed it to his aunt. "Is this worth anything?"

"I don't think so, Honey. It doesn't seem valuable enough to have four grown men searching for it, but you have the right idea."

Abigail knew they could find it only by chance. She watched Lisa. Each time she found something, she quickly brought it to Matt and asked, "Is this it?" That time, she had a small painting by a famous artist. When she showed it to Matt, his head shook back and forth.

After searching for a few hours, Danny became weary, "Can we get something to eat?"

Matt dropped a book on the desk. "Sure. We could all use a break."

As they headed for the hatch, Abigail placed one hand on Danny's shoulder while holding Lisa's hand. "Danny, everything will be okay." He then noticed that she no longer stood tall, she had lines on her forehead, and her cheerful smile was gone. To him, it meant she was unsure of their fate.

Chapter Five

Abigail felt the movement of the sea while she watched Danny and Lisa as they sat under a porthole. *How am I to protect them and keep them safe?* she wondered.

Each time Matt's eyes glanced her way, as if to soothe her, she turned away. *How can I trust anyone keeping us hostage?* Her captors huddled and talked in whispers. Jack's eyes glared in her direction. Matt's eyes were on the overhead, as if in deep thought. The men's discussion subsided, and Jack stepped away. *Great,* she thought. *What are they up to now? If Jack had his say, he would throw us overboard.*

The children's eyes followed Jack's movement. "He looks like Gordon." Danny whispered to Lisa.

She shook her head. "No. He is smaller, but his voice is loud."

When Brent grinned at Lisa, she whispered to her brother, "He's cute."

Abigail pondered. *What are my options?* She glanced out the porthole and noticed the touring vessel still a few hundred yards away. *Signaling it, might be our only chance for help,* she told herself, *but how can I do it without being noticed?* Her body froze. *The captain Larry Kilgore hired. He must be at the helm. Perhaps he had already called for help, and the Coast Guard is on their way. Okay, Abigail, stop it. You're just being your old, optimistic self. Find a way to signal for help. That ship may be your only chance.* The water movement started to stabilize, and she felt more sure-footed.

As Matt watched her every move, it was difficult to do anything. "I need to use the head." She spun around so fast she felt her hair swish over her shoulder.

She glanced toward the children and moved her fingers toward her -- signaling them to come. They glanced at Matt. "You two stay here!" He glared at Abigail. "They just used the head. You know that."

"You two stay, and I'll be right back," she said. When she reached the head, she searched under the washbasin, and rummaged through two drawers. She found a compact with a mirror and placed it in her pocket. Her heart beat faster, and her palms were moist as she slowly walked back into the main salon. As she entered, she saw a tall, thin man with a pockmarked face. When he glanced her way, his eyes examined her curves.

Captain Forelli's eyes shifted and stared at Matt's feet. "What's with the broad and kids?"

Matt folded his arms and his lips tightened. "They were here when we arrived."

"I don't like it. Luke will be furious." Forelli's shoulders slumped.

"Look, we're not overjoyed either -- especially when your beloved boss, Luke Percy, said, "No one will be on board except you!"

Forelli started to circle, and proceeded to leave. "I'm taking a break. I'll be in the crew cabin." He walked toward the galley.

Jack stood next to Matt. "There's something creepy about that man. He always appears to be hiding something."

Abigail dropped her head. I guess Captain Forelli won't be helping us, she thought.

Jack stood and watched Forelli step though the galley hatch, while Matt said, "I'll go ask Forelli some questions. I can't wait to get his reaction to the murders." His smile rose up on one side.

Matt stepped toward the galley and stood at the hatch. "What's up?"

"Nothing," Forelli said, while he looked in the refrigerator.

"How do you know Kilgore?" Matt asked.

"Larry called Luke. He needed a captain for a week or two. Later, Larry sent me his navigation course and asked me to meet him at sea. By the way, where is Larry?" Matt was silent. He looked down for a minute and then glanced up.

"He and his wife are dead."

"What?! They're dead?" Forelli became silent, while his eyes darted from side to side.

"Do you know anything about their murders?" Matt asked.

"Murders? They were murdered?" Forelli's mouth dropped, while his eyes stared at the floor. Both men were silent.

"Who might want them dead?" Matt asked.

"Why ask me? I barely knew the man."

"Well, none of us did it. Was someone else coming aboard?"

"You mean like that woman?" Forelli said. "It had to be her."

"No."

"How do you know, Matt?"

"I just know."

"Who found their bodies? The person who finds a body is often the prime suspect."

Matt ran his fingers through his hair. "I did. You know I wouldn't do it."

"Where did you find them?"

"In the master suite, on their bed."

Forelli's voice rose. "Did you even question the woman?"

"I forced her to identify their dead bodies. Her reaction was enough for me."

"Where did the woman come from?"

"She is a family friend of the Kilgores. She and the kids were hiding in another cabin when I found them."

"It had to be her, why else would she hide? She had the opportunity." Forelli's forehead wrinkled, as he scratched his head. "Does Luke or any of the Top Dogs know?"

"No. Not yet."

"Luke needs to know. He arranged this gig."

"Yes, yes, I know," Matt said. "But, first let's figure out who murdered them. Have any ideas?"

Forelli's eyes were hyper focused -- revealing nothing.

Matt cocked his head. "Well, what do you think? Want to tell Luke and the others, or wait until we figure out who did it?"

"Frankly, I don't give a crap." He slammed the refrigerator door and quickly walked out of the galley.

Matt followed him out of the galley and watched him descend the ladder leading to the crew cabin. Once out of sight, he returned to his cohorts.

"What did he say?" Jack asked.

"Not much. He's putting on a convincing act that he knows nothing. Well, at least, we know he won't blow the whistle on us. It wouldn't be in his best interest with his federal criminal record. Besides, his boss, Luke, will be furious when he finds out."

The men were silent. Jack's eyes were vigilant.

"But, what if you're wrong about Forelli? What if he does alert Luke? Do we want to take that risk?"

"What are the options here?" While looking down, Matt touched his chin. Everyone was silent as Matt glanced at Abigail. She seemed to be in deep thought.

"Let's just go about our business," Matt said. "See if anything looks fishy with our captain." The men stared at each other. Matt continued, "By the way, no one touch those bodies! The fewer fingerprints found, the better for all of us."

"Won't your prints implicate us?"

"Hey, the only thing we're guilty of is overtaking the vessel, and robbery. None of us carry weapons, do we? How much trouble could we be in? All we have to say is that the Kilgores invited us. They're dead, so they can't deny it."

Jack stared at Matt. "How about kidnapping? We're holding the woman and those kids against their will. That, alone, places us in deep trouble."

"But, we're not holding them at gunpoint."

"That doesn't matter, Matt. We're still holding them against their will. If one of us is convicted of murder or kidnapping, we all go to prison."

Matt turned to Jack. "Look, I'll take full responsibility for holding them. If you want to leave, go."

Abigail's fear increased, while listening to the men.

"I'll take over the helm," Robert said.

Matt shook his head. "I'll do it."

"What about the woman and kids?"

"They'll come with me. Fresh air will do them good."

Robert turned to leave, Brent followed.

Abigail was alert when Matt turned toward her. "You three come with me." He turned and stepped up the ladder to the helm.

She took her first deep breath and let the ocean air fill her lungs while she lifted her face to the sun. Just for a moment, she felt better. The children were off playing. They seemed oblivious to any danger. Matt checked the controls panel and grabbed the wheel. In the sunlight, his eyes seemed greener, and his sun bleached hair seemed lighter. *Stay focused,* she told herself. *If I can take over the controls I might be able to signal for help.*

"My father owns a boat," she said.

Matt gave her a blank stare for a moment. Then, his expression softened, as he smiled.

"I loved helping my dad at the wheel. Do you mind if I take over for a few minutes?"

He backed away to let her hold the wheel, and came so close their bodies touched. The electricity between them was noticeable, and she started to pull away. The last thing she needed was to fall for some thief keeping her hostage. When she felt his eyes fixed on her, her stomach fluttered. *Okay, Abigail, stay detached,* she told herself.

Just for a minute she considered using her femininity to manipulate him, but quickly decided against it. It would have only served to complicate things. She was already fretful that her body responded to his touch. She knew she must guard her heart, for that first attraction to him never left.

Chapter Six

After Abigail took in a few deep breaths, she pondered how to get the children to safety. Matt stood too close for her comfort. Being at the wheel just wasn't working. *Having sexual tension with a thief is something I can do without.* She backed away from the wheel. "You take over."

His eyes focused on her. "I know this is hard on you, but no one's going to harm you. Not as long as I'm around."

Everything within her wanted to yell, "Then, let us go home!" but she thought better of it and bit her tongue. *Don't be fooled by his charm,* she told herself, not wanting to become like other women who bond with their captors. *Don't let your guard down for a minute,* she told herself. *They may not have intended to harm us, but in order to protect their own necks, that might change.*

Lisa's eyes looked down. She said to Danny, "What do you think Mommy is doing right now?"

Danny glanced at his sister. He cheerfully said, "Sightseeing."

Abigail lifted the girl's chin. "You miss your mom, don't you, Sweetie?"

Lisa nodded and a few tears fell down her cheeks.

"We'll be home soon, and, in a few days, your parents will be home, too."

Abigail tried to relax, but knew the minute Larry and Sandra went missing, her ability to relax ended.

She watched the touring vessel maintain their same course.

The men on that ship must have some connection with Matt and his cohorts. Thank God, I failed to get their attention.

I must notify the Coast Guard, she decided. If I toss a few life preservers overboard, it might catch someone's attention. The Great Discoverer was on them, so it was likely it would be reported, if found, she hoped. No, that won't work. The touring vessel might see them first. It came to her. She beamed with excitement. I need to find the EPIRB. There must be one on board. All large vessels are mandated to carry the three-inch-by-eleven-inch orange mechanism that calls for help. It should be easy to spot. All I have to do is find it, turn it upside down, and it automatically notifies the Coast Guard. Its warning signal is unique, much like a fingerprint. But, what if the thieves hid it from me? No. They would never think a woman would know about an EPIRB.

Her finger touched her chin, and she lowered her head. She glanced at the storage bin behind the wheel. Matt hummed some tune and faced forward. She backed up until her legs touched the storage bin. Matt turned and beamed. "What a great day to be out here." They both turned their attention to the stairs and saw Forelli walking in their direction with his chilly personality intact. After rotating away from the wheel, Matt's arm touched hers. *That energy,* she thought and quickly moved away. Her heart wanted to be his ally, but her intellect told her it was childish thinking.

An eerie cold breeze kicked up as Forelli grabbed the wheel. Lisa held her arms around herself. "I'm cold."

"Me, too," Danny said.

They headed back to the library. The next time we're at the helm, I'll have the children distract Matt so I can find the device and alert the Coast Guard. She sighed. I lost my opportunity.

When they returned to the library, Abigail asked Lisa to stay with her. She and the girl sat near each other on the floor, away from Matt.

"The next time we take a break, will you sit with Matt? I need to talk to Danny, okay? Can you do that for me?"

Lisa's eyes widened. "Like your secret agent?"

"Yes, Sweetie." She gave the girl a hug.

After a few hours in the library, Lisa asked for something to drink. Danny wanted to go with her.

Matt stood abruptly. "No. We'll go together."

Once they arrived, they walked into the galley. Matt strolled over to the refrigerator and opened the door. The children peeked around him for drinks. Lisa chose apple juice. She reached around him and grabbed one. Danny saw a Coke and grabbed it.

When the children returned to the main salon, the boy sat near the porthole while his sister sat on a chair at the table. Matt followed and walked to the large table. "Can I join you, young lady?"

The child gave him a smile and nodded. "Do you have a yacht?" Lisa asked. "You know a lot about boats."

He fixed his gaze on her. "I have a sailboat. Her name is Firefly."

"That's funny." She blinked. "Why that name?"

"At night, when I'm at sea, I look at the stars. They flicker like fireflies."

"Oh. I never saw a firefly," the child said.

Abigail walked toward the padded seats near the portholes, far from Matt. "Come sit by me," she said, while motioning for Danny to come. He sulked as he walked toward her and sat. "It's hot over here."

"I know. But, I want to talk to you so Matt doesn't hear. Danny, I need your full attention. This is very important. Do you understand?"

His eyes became alert as he nodded.

"Right now, while we're talking, act as if we're saying something funny, okay? But, please listen carefully."

Danny's eyes widened, "Sure, Aunt Abigail."

"The next time we go to the wheelhouse, I want Lisa to act sick. I need for you to ask Matt to help her. It'll give me a chance to signal for help. Do you understand?"

"We're going to escape?"

"I need to alert the Coast Guard, so they can come for us. But, first I need for you to distract Matt."

"Okay." Danny nodded and grinned, as if on another adventure.

As Abigail watched and listened to Lisa talk to Matt, she was surprised at his kindheartedness while listening to Lisa say, "I was a flower girl at my mom's wedding. She married my dad again. They're in Hawaii on a second honeymoon, but they'll be home soon."

It saddened Abigail to think that she placed her niece and nephew in such danger. She wondered how she would explain everything to Alisa and David. They would be horrified to learn that thieves had held their children hostage.

Brent and Robert weren't having much luck finding the treasure on the lower level. "Why are the Top Dogs following us?" Brent asked.

"I guess they want to be the first to get their hands on the treasure when it is found." Robert looked at him. "Do you think Forelli is the murderer?"

Robert sat on a stool. "Wouldn't surprise me, but he wasn't here until after we arrived."

Brent reached down and picked up a box, opened it and examined the contents. "What's the deal between the Kilgores and Top Dogs?"

"What do you mean?"

"There's something going on, some business deal."

"You mean you haven't figured that out yet?" Robert said.

"The Kilgores smuggle for them."

"So what we're searching for was smuggled?" Brent stopped. "Then why don't the Top Dogs know exactly what we're looking for?"

"Because Larry Kilgore only told Luke that the treasure fit in his carry on and was worth a fortune."

Robert stood. He peeked into a storage compartment. "It must be priceless if the Top Dogs are offering us ten million dollars. What's in that box?"

"Nothing of interest." Brent tossed the box to one side and kicked at the wall. "Why would Forelli kill them?"

"Luke likely arranged for him to do it."

"But, why would Luke want them dead?"

"The Kilgores ripped him off on their last deal."

"How?" Brent asked.

"Luke found out that Larry withheld an extra hundred thousand dollars from what was to be a fifty-fifty split."

"That must have ticked him off. How did Luke find out?"

"Someone he knew from an underground auction house. He said the Kilgores took seventy percent, and forged the receipt."

Brent's eyes stared just ahead of him. "How stupid of Larry. No one gets away with ripping off Luke."

"You're right. I heard Luke say Larry would live to regret it, that's why I think he arranged for the couple to be murdered."

Robert said, "If Luke arranged for the hit, he would ask Forelli to do his dirty work. That might be the reason he sent Forelli as captain."

Brent folded his arms. "Why kill them? Wouldn't taking a priceless treasure be punishment enough?"

"Perhaps they hadn't planned on it, but when Forelli reported they were on board, Luke gave the order." Robert let out a long breath. "I bet having the Kilgores on board would stand in the way of us confiscating the treasure." Robert walked to the hatch and looked around before facing Brent. "Luke is in some financial trouble and needs the money from the artifact to bail him out."

"I wouldn't put it past Luke or any of the Top Dogs to arrange the hit. Each man is pretty cold-hearted. Last month, they made some deal with a widow and ripped her off for a half million. They did it just because they could. The poor woman was too despondent to think straight."

Both men silently continued their search, discarding each item they ruled out.

Robert stopped and stretched. "Have you ever been on the touring vessel while it was used to gamble?"

"No. Have you?"

"Once. You wouldn't believe their setup. The legs of the tables lifted so the tops could be turned for gambling. If the Coast Guard ever made a surprise visit, they could turn it back to its original position."

"How would they hide the chips and cards?" Brent asked.

"They had foam and plastic that clipped over the gambling top. It was ingenious. No one knew about it except the Top Dogs and crew. I don't think their spouses even knew."

"How come you never told me?"

"Sworn to secrecy." Robert cocked his head. "All crew members agree to keep their secret."

"How did you hear?"

"I dated a food server, and one day, she needed a replacement -- I showed up."

Luke Percy leaned against the bulkhead to steady himself from the sway of the touring vessel. He saw his reflection in a porthole. He didn't look as bad as he felt. Although short in stature, he could easily pass for a male model. He had blue eyes, black hair and a refined style of dress. *I feel queasy*, he thought.

Luke knew women were attracted to him, so he spent time with many beautiful, wealthy women; one became his wife. Linda was a petite, natural blond with expressive gray-blue eyes. He liked the fact that she seldom dressed in high heels.

He missed not having her on his arm. She complemented him, but last year things changed between them. He needed to get his hands on money quickly, so he arranged for her diamond and ruby heirloom necklace to be stolen for insurance money. She suspected him. Its disappearance coincided with his payoff to his pregnant girlfriend.

Early in their marriage, she caught him seducing a family friend. Linda agonized over divorcing, but decided against it. He crossed the line when he took her family heirloom given to her by her father on her wedding day. She screamed, "You have one week to return my necklace! If you fail to deliver, I'll tell Dad. You'll be ruined! You'll never get away with stealing from me. I'm filing for divorce."

Luke depended on her for his social standing. If they divorced, he would have little to show from the marriage. She forced him to sign a prenuptial agreement -- he would get nothing.

There was no way of retrieving the stolen necklace because it was sold in a silent auction without a paper trail.

Linda could easily destroy Luke, socially and financially. Once crossed, she became more ruthless than he. Luke had no choice. He had to do something quickly. He called Forelli. The man owed him. No one would hire Forelli because he had a federal criminal record. Luke offered him a job. It was payback time.

The deed was done within a few days -- Luke became a widower and inherited her estate worth millions. Linda didn't have an opportunity to tell her father, and Luke remained in good social standing with his father-in-law. Forelli made it look like a car accident, so no investigation took place.

Chapter Seven

After Alisa pulled back the drapes, she watched the ocean waves crash on the rocks. "What a beautiful view. The kids would love it." She spun around to face David.

He patted the bed. "Come here. We need to talk."

While walking toward him, she searched his eyes hoping to see the cause of his seriousness.

After sitting beside him, David took her hand and kissed it. "I meant what I said. You never have to work again. We'll find a way, financially. We always do. The children need you. Look how great they're turning out." David gazed into her tear-filled eyes. "I'm glad you stuck by your convictions. It was stupid of me to ever leave you." He gently took his thumb and wiped away the tears from her cheeks. "Please forgive me for being such a fool."

"You're not a fool. Oh, David, I forgave you long ago." They hugged, kissed and came together as never before -- they gave of themselves completely.

While returning from a trip to a volcano, David and Alisa held hands in the back seat of their taxi. She glanced up toward the mountain they just visited.

David squeezed her hand. "We made the right decision to get back together."

"We sure did," she said, while turning to kiss his cheek.

"We'll bring the children on our next visit, they'll love it here."

"Yes, David, but now it is our time."

He beamed. "I bet Danny would have been halfway down the volcano before we could stop him."

Her eyes twinkled, "He's a lot like you."

She looked out the car window. "It looks like we're going to have a downpour."

David watched the dark clouds coming closer. "It sure does." Then he turned his attention to the driver. "It appears you got us out of there just in time."

The driver nodded. "It seems the weather turns bad daily at this time. I try to take my passengers before or after our wet weather."

The nameplate on the dashboard read Jessie Rodriguez.

"How long have you lived on the island?" David asked.

"I don't. I have a place near UCLA. I'm with my parents to save money for next semester."

"What's your major?"

"Law," Jessie said, while turning on the windshield wipers. "Wow. It's really coming down."

When the road became slippery, David tightened Alisa's seatbelt. He told the driver, "You need to pull over."

The young man tried to comply, but he hit his brakes too hard and caused the car to spin. The driver lost control of the car, and, within a second, the car rolled down the thirty-foot embankment and landed on the rear driver's side.

Officer Jim Robinson drove as fast as he could to respond to a reported car accident, but it still took twenty minutes before his rescue team could reach the scene. Several cars were parked near the place the taxi disappeared off the ledge. His partner, Randy Drake, jumped out of the van and stood at the edge, staring below. "This won't be easy, Jim. You better get the gear." For a 200-

pound man, Randy moved quickly. His eyes carefully watched for loose rocks and safe places for his feet. Soon, he reached the taxi and peered through the window. He turned his head and yelled, "I see a woman."

"Is she alive?" Randy called out.

"Don't know yet." After he tried to open the back door without success, he tried the front. It took time, but he finally got it open enough to climb into the front seat. He reached for the woman's pulse. After retreating from the front seat, he yelled, "She's alive, but unconscious. There are two males, a driver and passenger." Randy reached for the pulse of the driver. He smiled. "He's alive." He took the male passenger's hand and checked his pulse. Randy took a deep breath. He bowed his head and silently prayed.

Within a short time, Jim reached the taxi with a stretcher. They pried open the back passenger door and carefully pulled out the limp body of the woman. They secured her in the stretcher and slowly moved up the mountain. When they reached the street, a new van was there waiting. They placed the woman inside and watched as the paramedics quickly started an I.V. for her.

Randy moved fast, back down the wet, slippery mountainside. When he returned to the taxi, he re-checked the pulse of the male passenger -- there was still no pulse. *No matter how often I do this job, I hate this part.* His throat felt tight.

When Jim came down to the taxi again, Randy shook his head as he crawled out of the back seat.

"Well, this one's gone. We need to call the coroner."

Jim asked, "Was he wearing his seatbelt?"

"No, but I noticed that the woman's belt was on tight. That's what saved her life."

Jim shook his head, slowly. "They never learn, do they?"

Randy quickly returned to the front seat. "My God! He is so young, he's just a kid. His legs are pinned, hand me a crowbar."

"Can we get him out?"

"I think so. When I pull up the dashboard with the crowbar, lift him out.

"Randy, you need to move the seat back as far as possible. It'll give us more room to release his legs."

"Good idea. That might help." Randy reached around the young man and lifted the lever. The back of the front seat lowered. He reached under the front seat and then pushed the seat as far back as he could.

"He looks pretty bad. He's in shock, his eyes are open, but he's not responding."

Together, they worked by moving the driver, inch by inch, away from the metal pinning his legs. Finally, he was free, and they lifted him to the stretcher. Once secured, they slowly carried him up the hill. Randy's footing slipped so he dug the side of his work boot into the ground. Once back in control, they advanced up the mountain. When they reached the van, Jim called the coroner.

Jim drove as fast as weather permitted while the paramedics did their job. When they reached the hospital, the young man was taken into the emergency room. The doctors worked on the driver for hours before he was placed in the recovery room, but he remained in critical condition.

Randy found the admitting doctor to inquire as to the progress of the woman. He said the CAT scan didn't reveal any severe internal signs of injury, but she still remained in a coma.

The coroner's office found the man's wallet. His name was David Glover. They also found the woman's purse and her wallet. Her name was Alisa Glover, but the two passengers had different addresses. The police department arranged to notify the nearest of kin. They discovered that the woman had an address book. They called the phone number next to Mom.

Steven Wilson sat comfortably in his parents' living room, talking with his father, John, when the phone rang. John got up, went into the kitchen and grabbed the phone. "Hello."

Steven heard his father say, "The police department? What happened? Are you sure? When? Are you sure it's my Alisa Glover?" John dropped the phone and leaned against the wall.

Within seconds, Steven grabbed the phone. "Who is this? You were speaking to my father. What's going on here?"

"I'm sorry. But, we have unpleasant news," the policeman's voice was solemn. "There's been a tragic car accident. It occurred in Hawaii. Mrs. Alisa Glover is in a coma."

"Where's David?"

"I'm sorry, but Mr. Glover didn't make it." Steven doubled over and was unable to speak. He forced himself to regain his composure and asked, "Are you sure? My parents just spoke with her. When did this happen?"

"Eleven o'clock this morning."

"Where is she?"

"At the Hawaii Memorial Hospital," the officer said, and then he gave the phone number, address and the admitting doctor's name and phone number. "You can call and receive updates." He felt as if the life had been sucked out of him. It was hard for Steven to breathe.

"My name is Sergeant Thomas Loo. We need to reach David Glover's family. We noticed he had a different address; were David and Alisa sister and brother?

"No. Husband and wife. They just renewed their marriage after being separated for a while."

"Can I get the name and phone number of his parents?"

"Yes. I'll have to call you back. My mother isn't here, and she has their phone number." Steven wrote down the sergeant's information.

It took a while for Steven to get his father settled down in the living room. John sat, his eyes low as he whispered, "I can't believe it. It can't be true. We just talked to her last night. Now, he's dead and she's in a coma." He looked up at Steven and stared.

They heard the back door open and close. "It's Mother. You have to tell her. I can't move right now. Please, Steven. Go talk to her."

Slowly, he walked toward the kitchen. He saw her short, heavy frame holding an armful of flowers from her garden. She wore her favorite sundress with her apron over it for protection. When she saw him, she smiled and revealed her dimples.

Elizabeth placed the flowers in the sink. She looked for and found a vase. "How long have you been here?"

"Not long."

After putting water in the vase, she carefully arranged each flower.

She searched her son's face and said, "Are you all right? You look dreadful."

He sat on a kitchen chair and motioned for her to join him.

"What's going on? Are you okay? What's wrong, Son? Is Dad alright?"

"Dad's fine. He's in the living room. But, Mother, please come and sit. We need to talk."

Her eyes were as round as her face. "Are the grandchildren okay? Did something happen to Lisa or Danny?"

"They're fine. Mother, please, come sit."

"You're scaring me, Son." She wobbled toward the table, pulled out a chair and sat. "Now, tell me what's going on."

"We just got a call from the police department."

"Did something happen to Abigail or Alisa? What happened?" Tears started to well in her eyes. "Oh my God, what happened?"

Steven told her about the car accident, Alisa's coma and David's death.

"But, that can't be. We just talked last night. Everything seemed fine. My God. How could she be in a coma? That's not possible -- it can't be so. When, Steven?"

"Today, late morning. The sergeant said it happened around eleven."

His heart hurt to see his mother's anguish. At the same time, he felt guilty for being glad it wasn't Alisa who died. He wondered if his mother was having the same thoughts.

Tears streamed down her face. Steven stood and walked behind her to embrace her.

"I just can't believe this. David's dead? Does his mother know?"

"The sergeant asked for her phone number, so I doubt she was notified. I'll call the police department later with her number."

Quickly, she stood. "Does Dad know?" Steven nodded. Elizabeth staggered into the living room weeping. "John. I can't believe our Alisa is in a coma." She knelt on the floor before him and placed her head on his lap as she cried. He patted her head without speaking. His tears ran down his cheeks as he listened to his wife sob.

Not knowing what to do to help, Steven decided to find his mother's personal phonebook. First, he checked their bedroom without luck. Then, he looked in the living room and saw it on a table. He looked up the number for David's mother, wrote it down, went into the kitchen and called the police department.

When he returned to his parents, he said, "I called the police. David's family was notified. So, I called David's brother, Bruce. He said his mother didn't know yet. She's still at work."

Elizabeth got up and walked to the phone, called and spoke to her pastor. "This is Elizabeth Wilson." Silence. "Not good." Tears fell as she told the man what happened. "Please ask our church family to pray for Alisa and David's family." Silence. "Thank you." She placed the phone back in its cradle.

Next, she phoned the hospital. Steven stood by his mother's side during her short conversation. She hung up. "There's no change in Alisa's condition." Her sad eyes glanced at her son. "The doctor on duty will call back within an hour."

For the first time, Steven knew what it felt like to be powerless.

When they returned to the living room, Elizabeth paced. "Were there any other cars involved? What did the policeman say?"

"The sergeant didn't give me any details."

John looked down at his hands. "All I know is they were in a taxi. Bad weather. The driver hit his breaks. They saw the skid marks. Apparently, the driver lost control, and they rolled down a mountain."

They sat in silence.

"Mom, when I spoke with Bruce, he said he didn't want to be alone when his mother heard about David. He was crying. He asked if we would go over before she gets home." He searched his mother's eyes.

"I'm not sure. John, are you up to that? I don't want to leave you home alone. Do you think you can make it?" She turned to her son. "What time is Ruth expected home?"

"Around five-thirty."

"John, what do you think? Want to go?"

"I can't be alone right now." He stood and slowly walked toward the hall.

Elizabeth called Bruce and told him how deeply sorry she was to hear about David. She said they would be there by five o'clock with dinner. Before hanging up, she said, "You must be crushed to hear about your brother. You were so close."

When John came back into the room, he sat next to Elizabeth on the sofa.

"It's all set," she said. "We're bringing dinner. He expects us over by five."

"Is Bruce living with his mother?" Steven asked.

"Yes. He was trying to save money -- wants to buy a home."

Elizabeth stood abruptly and said, "My God, has anyone called Abigail and the kids?"

"Are they back in town?" Steven asked.

"Yes. Yesterday. I'm expecting them for dinner. I'll call her." Elizabeth looked weary and sat back on the couch.

"How do we tell the kids?" John asked.

"I'll call," Steven said and jumped to his feet. He went into the kitchen, grabbed the phone and dialed. "I hate to tell her," he said, as the phone rang.

When she didn't answer, he felt relieved and disappointed at the same time. "She's not home, so I called her cell. I left a message on both phones."

"That's odd." Elizabeth's forehead had lines, she looked at the floor. "They should be home by now." She looked up. "If she's driving, she can't answer. Maybe they're on their way over."

"When did you last hear from her?"

"Yesterday. They were on their way to the yacht club to eat."

"Do you think she changed her mind?"

"No. She was in San Diego when she called."

His sister's predictability annoyed Steven. "Don't worry. I'll track her down."

Her dimples revealed to him her gratitude. Within minutes, she stood and walked into the kitchen to start working on the evening meal for the Glovers.

"Can I get anything at the store?"

"No, but thanks. I have what I need."

He saw the sadness in his mother's eyes. He walked over, turned her around and held her. She wept.

Elizabeth pulled away and returned to dinner preparation.

"I love you, Mom."

She choked with emotion and nodded.

He started his search for Abigail. First, he called Carry English, her best friend since childhood. She wasn't home, so he left a message. "Mom, what hotel did they stay at?"

"Don't bother calling." Her voice rose, "I told you! Abigail's in town. She was taking the children to eat at the yacht club yesterday."

Chapter Eight

When they returned to the library to search for the mysterious object, Abigail noticed Matt's brow lines and saw his mouth turn down. She wondered if he felt upset about being a murder suspect, or becoming a kidnapper. He glanced up and noticed her eyeing him. Her eyes darted away.

After looking at him again, she saw a blanket of weariness come over him. He seemed almost sad, as if he was longing for something. *Get a grip! Abigail, you can't read his mind.* She bent to pick up a book. "Well, I'll be --," she said.

Matt turned to watch her. "Did you find something interesting?"

She chuckled, "This book might be a treasure to me, but it's not what you're looking for. I know the author, that's all. He was a personal friend of my grandfather, so it brings back memories."

"Are they alive?"

"My grandparents? No, I wish they were. I miss them terribly. They were wonderful people." She scanned the book. "My grandfather was an evangelist. At times, my grandmother traveled with him and played the piano and sang."

"Did you visit them much?"

"Often, my grandmother and I would sit side by side for hours playing the piano and singing, mostly from the Psalms."

"Psalms. What are Psalms?"

She let out a loud laugh. "Most of my friends are Christians, so it didn't occur to me that you might not know what Psalms are."

He turned his back toward her.

"Please forgive me. I didn't mean to be offensive. Psalms are a poetic book from the Bible. They were written by King David."

Matt gave her a silent glare.

Later, Abigail sat on the sofa and glanced over at Matt. He seemed mentally preoccupied. "Is something wrong? Did my laughing offend you that much?"

"No. That's not it. Just racking my brain to figure out who murdered the Kilgores. Who do you think did it?" Matt walked over and sat on the couch next to her.

It surprised her he wanted her opinion, "I don't know. Perhaps your friend Jack?"

"No. He didn't do it. I'm certain of that. We go way back to childhood. He isn't the type to go around killing people. Plus, he has absolutely no motive; he is here only because I forced him to come."

"He seems pretty scary to me."

Matt glared at her.

Abigail turned her attention to observe Danny reading a book, and Lisa lying on the floor asleep.

"Why don't you like Jack?"

"I just don't trust him. That's all."

"Think what you want, but he's my best friend. I know his character."

"Why are you defending him?"

"We've been friends since junior high. We met on the baseball team. He was the catcher and, I, the pitcher. We work well together. Jack gave excellent signals; he knew exactly where the ball was moving. We spent hours practicing together."

"What does baseball have to do with him not being a murderer?"

"Nothing, I guess. Maybe I'm thinking out loud. The kids at school found him intimidating, too. With his deep voice and large size, he scared the other kids. But, he never scared me, and he knew it. That's why we hit it off. But, I noticed, even when we were kids, Jack kept to himself, he was almost shy."

"Nothing about him seems friendly; he's a cold man."

"Jack has never been the warm, friendly type, but he always had incredible instincts. He always knew when things weren't right."

"Like what?"

"Once, at the park, Jack needed to take a leak. Sorry. Use the restroom. When he returned, his face was as white as a ghost. He seemed terrified. He said, 'Some pervert looked at me funny and gave me the creeps. The guy tried to take a peek.' His eyes darted back and forth in genuine fear. 'Don't go in there alone,' Jack said, and made me promise. I told him, 'Don't worry, I get the point. The last thing I want is some pervert checking me out.' Well, the next day, we heard that some kid was killed. His body was found the same day in the same restroom. We were too terrified to tell anyone, afraid he might come kill us, too, if we told."

"Do you regret not telling your parents, or the police?"

"Later on, as adults, sure, we both wished we spoke up."

"That experience must have made an impact on two young boys."

"It wasn't as dreadful as another occasion."

"What?"

"We were hiking up a hill, near our homes. When we reached the top, we saw a parked car. Jack said, 'Hey. Something's wrong. Cars shouldn't be up here.'"

"We heard noises coming from under the car. We both were trying to get a better look, so we laid flat on the ground to get a better look. It was then that we saw two naked bodies going at it. Neither of us had even seen a Playboy, so, what a shock! At first, we were concerned the woman was being hurt." Matt went silent.

"So, what did you do?"

Matt stood up, visibly upset. "I never told anyone about those incidents before. Thinking about them gives me the creeps." So he quickly returned to searching.

Matt's mind raced -- he didn't want to tell her the rest of the story.

The woman under the car started weeping. When they were about to go for help, the man said, "Now, Sally, don't go and do something foolish and tell your husband. You know, he'll kill me if he finds out."

"If he doesn't kill me first," the woman said, between sobs. "What have I done? What on earth was I thinking? If he finds out, he'll kick me out. I will never see my kids again."

"Pull yourself together," the man said harshly.

After she calmed down, they got up, got dressed and drove off.

It was then that we noticed the bleached blond hair on the woman. "My God, she looks like your mother. Oh shit! Her name is Sally! That's your mother's name." We were in shock, horrified and speechless. We both watched his mother having sex with another man, how awful!

Soon Jack became physically ill. While sobbing he said, "How could she?"

I was unable to move, say a word, or to comfort. It took years before either of us spoke about what happened. One day, out of the blue, Jack asked how it affected me.

It was crazy, right up there with the man in the park who murdered that boy. Seeing his mother like that! I kept asking myself how I would feel. It would be too humiliating for words.

Jack never told his father or mother about that day. Soon after the incident, his mother started going to AA meetings. I think it was her wake-up call for what happens when she's drunk.

Abigail walked up to Matt. "What happened? All of a sudden you shut down."

"I told you. Talking about those things gives me the creeps. I haven't thought about those things in years."

"What you told me still doesn't eliminate Jack as a murder suspect."

"True, but I know he would never intentionally hurt anyone. Maybe in self-defense or to defend a friend, but that's it. He's a loyal friend. Someone I can count on. And, he's a man of his word."

"If he is a man of his word, then ask if he did it."

"No. I know he didn't," Matt said, flatly. "For starters, he and I arrived on the yacht together. He didn't have time to kill them." He moved back to the bookshelf to examine the last set of books.

She moved closer. "I need to ask you something. How did you and your men know where to find us at sea?"

"Forelli faxed us the yacht's course."

Abigail walked toward the children and whispered, "Did you tell Lisa about our plan?"

"No."

"If Matt and I talk again, will you tell her?"

"Sure."

In a normal voice, she said, "So, what have you been up to?"

Danny pointed to an object in the corner sitting on a pedestal table.

"What do we have here?" she said, as she picked up what looked like a Russian Fabergé egg.

"Come. Look what Danny found."

Matt dropped his book and walked over. After carefully examining it, he said, "Yes. It is a gem. But, why would they leave it in plain sight?"

"I thought the same thing."

He grabbed the jeweled egg to examine it more closely. His eyes opened wide during his inspection.

"I found it!" Danny yelled.

"We found it together," Lisa yelled back.

"If this thing is genuine, it is worth a bundle. This diamond looks to be two carats." He glanced toward Abigail. "Unfortunately, some good cuts of zirconium sparkle like diamonds. I'll have Jack evaluate its authenticity."

"But, why would the Kilgores keep it in plain view?" Then, she remembered what a good sense of humor the couple had. They would have gotten a kick out of having it out. "If it is genuine, you can bet Larry put it someplace safe before letting guests disembark."

Matt grinned. "This might be real. Let's say the diamonds, rubies and emeralds are each worth $200,000, plus the value of gold and workmanship, it could be worth a lot. If it's rare or has historical value, it is worth much more."

"What do you mean?"

"Let's say someone like Hitler or Stalin owned it -- the egg could be priceless. Who knows? It might be what we're looking for.

But, just as easily, it could be a good fake, worth little, or secondary to the real treasure.

Jack's a jeweler, by trade; he has a good eye. He can tell its value."

Abigail's mouth dropped open. "You mean you're planning on showing this to Jack?"

"Yes. We're a team. We split any money."

She was concerned at the thought of him showing the egg to Jack. He might trust his friend, but she surely did not. No matter how many stories he told her, she would never trust the guy. *Great! If the egg ends the search, the children and I might be in more danger. We're the only witnesses. I need to notify the Coast Guard, and quick!*

After walking to the hatch, Matt said, "Let's take a break. I need to show this to Jack."

As they climbed the ladder leading to the main salon, the children argued. "You know, we found the egg together," Lisa said. "You have to split the reward with me."

"No way. I found it first."

Matt stepped in, "Tell you what. If it turns out to be what we're looking for, you both get a reward."

They grabbed some snacks before bringing them to the main salon.

The children were motioned to sit by the portholes. "You two need more sunlight. Watch over your sister for me." She whispered, "Tell Lisa to act sick the next visit to the helm."

Danny grinned. She hoped he would remember to tell his sister about their plan and hoped he wasn't more interested in his reward money.

"How did you determine the egg's worth so quickly?"

"From Jack -- he owns a jewelry store in La Jolla. He specializes in appraisals. Even he finds it difficult to discern the authenticity of a diamond without an eyepiece. There's a lot that goes into an appraisal."

"Would it be okay if we go to the wheelhouse? The children need some fresh air. Perhaps our captain can use a break."

"No. He'll let us know when he needs us." Matt glared at her for a moment, as if trying to read her thoughts.

Her palms became clammy, and she was hoping he couldn't sense her anxiety. I desperately want to alert the authorities, but Matt just said no to going to the wheelhouse. Now what?

Chapter Nine

I should have made a dinner date with Carry, Abigail fretted. Everything would have been different. I would have said no to Larry's invitation. The couple would still be alive, and we would be home. She glanced over at Lisa. Carry and I were younger than she is now.

It seems like yesterday that Carry English and her family pulled up to their new home across the street. My dad helped bring in their heavy furniture and boxes, while Mom cared for the children and prepared dinner for both families.

Steven and Stan played in the front, while Carry and I visited in our backyard. Alisa was away with a friend, so I had Carry all to myself. I was thrilled to play with someone my age, and we both were going to start kindergarten in a month.

We stood under a large umbrella tree that covered the wood patio deck. A small table with child-sized chairs sat near the house. My dolls were on the chairs, and the table was set for a tea party. Carry didn't seem too impressed. I took my dolls off each chair and placed them on the deck. We sat on the chairs without speaking.

"I can't wait until school starts," I said.

"Why?" Carry asked.

"Silly, so we can play with other kids."

"I don't want to go," Carry pouted.

"Why?"

"I don't know anyone. Dad got a job here." Carry's eyes welled with tears. "I didn't want to come here." "But why?"

"I like my old house. I miss my friends. I want to go to school with them. I will never see them again." Carry's tears cascaded down while she said, "My dad made my whole life go away." Her eyes opened wide. "He told me his job is here, and the weather is great. No snow to shovel. But, I said, 'I like snow and helping him shovel. We have fun. We throw snowballs at each other.' When I said that, my dad looked sad. Now, I don't say anything." Abigail smiled. "I never lived near snow."

Carry looked up, "My mom said I have to support Daddy. No one wants me to talk about it," she said, with eyes filled with tears.

They both silently sat.

"Come eat," Mom called out.

Before entering the house, we could smell homemade cookies.

"Wash your hands, girls."

Carry and I hurried to the bathroom, quickly washed and ran to the kitchen and went directly to the cookie sheet.

"Eat your sandwich first, girls."

We picked at our food. When Mom left the room, we abandoned lunch, grabbed two cookies each and hurried out. We giggled on our way back to the table. Both of us had grins as we gobbled down our treats. We were glad my mom never came to scold us.

"Where's the school?"

"Over there," I pointed behind us. "It's across from the store."

"Do other children live close?"

"Mom counted eighteen."

"Any my age?"

I nodded. "Dick's seven. Lillie's five. They live that way." I pointed to the left. "There's a boy named Berry. He's older. He lives at the end of the street. No one likes him. He throws rocks at cars. He hits Steven. Mommy gets mad." "Let's pretend we're having tea with our cookies."

Carry nodded.

Remembering those days, it seems like another lifetime ago, Abigail thought. *I'll be telling her every detail of our ordeal.* She listened to Lisa tell Danny, "I want a tea set with my reward money." Abigail laughed.

"What's so funny, Aunt Abigail?"

"What?"

"You're smiling," Danny said.

"Oh, just thinking about Carry. We also liked having tea parties."

Lisa smiled. "I miss her. Can we see her?"

"When we get home, I'll call. Okay?"

Great, Abigail thought, I left my stupid cellphone in the car. Everything happened so quickly that I forgot.

*   *   *

In the early evening, Carry English arrived home. The answering machine light flashed. She pushed the button and listened. One message was from Steven. She hadn't heard his voice for a long while. She quickly returned his call. When he answered, he wasn't his cheerful self. "Can I call you back?" he asked. "My parents and I aren't home right now. Can I call you later?"

"Sure. Steven, are you okay?"

"Yes," he said. "I'll tell you about it later, okay?"

After placing the phone down, she stared at it for a moment. Her forehead started to form lines, and her smile disappeared.

I hate not knowing what's going on. I bet it's about Abigail. Why else would he be calling? She shrugged her shoulders. I hope I'm just overreacting again, she thought. But, Abigail should have called by now. She picked up the phone and dialed Abigail's home number. No answer. She called her cell -- no answer. She left messages at both numbers for Abigail to call back ASAP.

Hearing Steven's voice brought back childhood memories about the fort he built in his backyard.

Abigail was ill one day, and he invited me to join him and his friends in his fort. I felt glad he didn't know Abigail and I often entered his sacred place while he was at little league.

While in the fort, the boys and I ate crackers and drank water from a canteen. Everything was going well until fifteen-year-old Berry pulled out his penis. Everyone stopped talking, and didn't move. The boy reached for my hand and tried to force me to touch it. The other boys giggled and squirmed. Steven screamed, "Stop! What do you think you're doing?" Everyone went silent, their faces red.

I couldn't move or talk. I was glad when Elizabeth looked in just in time to see Berry quickly put his penis back into his pants.

"Get out," Elizabeth shouted. "Do it now! You disgust me, Berry. You're no longer welcome at our house. Your parents will be getting a call about this." Elizabeth stared at me for a moment, and yelled to all of us, "Go home, all of you, right now!"

While walking home, my head hung low, my mouth turned down and tears were forming in my eyes. Once I opened the front door, I couldn't hold back tears.

"What's wrong?" my mother asked.

"Berry grabbed my hand; he tried to make me touch him," I sobbed.

Quickly, my mother wrapped her arms around me and held me tight. Mom broke the silence. "Sit. Tell me what happened."

After I finished telling her everything, she said, "You did nothing wrong, Honey. What happened wasn't your fault. You're innocent. Berry did something wrong to you." Mom had tears in her eyes and, within minutes, she started sobbing.

"I'm okay, Mommy. Don't worry. Really, I didn't touch it."

Once my mom composed herself, she said, "When I was a teenager, a boy at school did something similar to me. That experience filled me with guilt and shame all these years. When I said to you that you are innocent, God comforted me. I now realize what happened to me wasn't my fault either. I, too, was innocent." Mother and I tearfully embraced.

Later that evening, Elizabeth called my mom. "I need to talk to Carry and you -- can I come over tonight?"

"Come around 6:30 p.m. My husband will be home. He needs to hear what you have to say."

When Elizabeth arrived, Mom placed drinks in front of us.

Elizabeth said, "I had a long talk with Steven. He set me straight on some things. None of the other children had any idea or warning that Berry would do such a thing. I believe my son." She turned to me. "I'm so very sorry you were exposed to such a thing. Please forgive me for not protecting you." Tears were now coming from her eyes.

My dad stood up, his eyes were fierce. He said, "I'll have a little talk with that punk."

"Let's not do anything rash." Mom reached for his hand.

"That boy violated our daughter. He'll pay for what he did."

"I called his parents," Elizabeth said. "They're expecting me to drop by at seven o'clock. Do either of you want to go?"

My dad walked back and forth while talking. "No need for you to go. I'll go by myself." He turned to Mom. "You need to stay here with Carry, I'll go."

Many years later, I heard what happened. When Dad had entered Berry's home, his parents, Mr. and Mrs. Holms, acted indifferent to how their son behaved. Dad noticed a Playboy magazine sitting on the coffee table. It angered him to see it out in the open.

Mr. Holms said, "Boys will be boys."

His wife said, "Most children their age explore their sexuality. It's no big deal. It's a natural part of their development."

"That's a bunch of crap!" my dad responded. "Your son violated my daughter. If you don't make Berry accountable for what he did, I'll call the cops."

Mr. Holms got up from his chair, walked over and picked up the phone. His eyes opened wide when Dad walked over and took it from him and called the police.

Within fifteen minutes, Officer Mitchell arrived. Although, he took a report, he told Dad, "Little or nothing will come of this. We're overloaded with rape and murder cases to solve."

The officer walked over to speak with Mr. Holms. In a low voice, he said, "If you want to keep peace in the neighborhood, get your son to apologize."

Mr. Holms called Berry into the room. He jerked the boy's arm, pulled him toward Dad and said, "Apologize for what you did. Do it now. Understand?"

"I'm sorry," Berry said, with his head down and his voice low. It wasn't much of an apology, but it satisfied everyone. At least, Berry acknowledged he did something wrong.

As Carry remembered the incident, it occurred to her, That is the only secret I ever kept from Abigail. But, I did warn her not to trust Berry and never be alone with him. Goodness. I'm sure nothing like that is going on. Carry's imagination ran wild. I wish I knew what Steven wanted to tell me. Why isn't Abigail picking up her phone? Why hasn't she called me back? I have all these questions and no answers. I'll just have to wait until someone calls.

Chapter Ten

"Lisa, you look tired," Abigail said. "It's been a long day, let's head for bed." Without waiting for Matt's response, she took Lisa's hand and said to Danny, "Let's go, young man."

Danny looked at Matt. After patting the boy's head, he said, "You heard your aunt, let's go."

After giving the man an angry glare, he still followed them to the cabin.

Good grief! He's going to observe us sleeping, she mused. It feels like a week since we slept. How can I clear my head with him watching my every move?

Once in the cabin, she shooed Lisa toward the head to clean up. She found PJs and placed them on the bed next to her. Danny lay with his legs dangling off and with his hands under his head. "Don't get too comfortable! You clean up next."

"I'm too tired. Do I have to?"

She took a deep breath and slowly released it. She found a washcloth, wet it and stepped toward the boy. "At least wash your face and hands."

Matt leaned against the hatch. I guess this is the most privacy I'm going to get. Wouldn't a hot shower be grand?

To stay alert, she examined their cabin more closely. A vivid painting hung on the wall. The vanity held a silver brush and comb set. Next to it was a tray with miscellaneous toiletries for both men and women.

Before the children were ready for bed, Matt sauntered over to the antique dresser and opened each drawer and moved his fingers as if trying to find a hidden compartment. He then reached for the jeweled egg Danny discovered, wrapped it in a T-shirt and placed it into the middle drawer. After it was closed, he turned and faced her without saying a word.

Lisa sat next to her aunt.

"Are you ready for prayers?" Abigail said as if not paying attention to her captor. The children and she knelt with eyes closed.

Quickly, Matt moved toward the hatch and leaned against the frame with his arms crossed.

They prayed for their mommy and daddy, Abigail's students and friends. They ended with, "Dear God, please protect and guide each man on this yacht. Let them know how much you love them. Help them to someday accept your son, Jesus."

"Okay, you two," she said. "Get under those covers." Then she listened to them giggle as they squirmed into bed. She kissed each child's cheek and said, "I love you." After the children became quiet, she, too, freshened up and put on her sleepwear. When finished, she reached for her book and sat.

"Why did you pray for us?" he said, irritably.

"Because, my dear man, we were taught to pray for our enemies and for those who spitefully use us."

Her words lacked malice, yet they stung. "Do you actually read the Bible? And believe that stuff?" He felt lines on his forehead form, and his eyes couldn't make contact with her, so he paced. "Don't you know that religion is for the weak? You seem smarter than that." His words felt stupid.

"You could never understand unless you were raised with Christian principles. How could you?"

He paced faster, rubbing his hands together. "Don't you know the Bible was written thousands of years ago? Do you actually think there's some God up in the sky who gives a rat's ass?"

"What button did I push?" she said. "Sorry, you can't understand my faith. But, without God in my life, I don't know what I would do. It must be difficult for you."

After turning red, he lowered his head and he walked away. After a few minutes, he returned. "It's hard for me to believe that some Creator up in the sky is listening to children's prayers. I think your faith is a bunch of crap. Do you really think you will have eternal bliss, just because you believe in Jesus?" He stared at her and waited.

She glanced at the bed. "Where do you plan on sleeping?"

"I'll take the couch," he said, forcibly.

"Can't you sleep in another cabin? I need some privacy."

"No. My men are using them, and they don't want to go near the master suite."

"I'm sure they don't," she smirked.

As he strolled over to her, he seemed calmer. He sat. "How are you related to the children?"

"My, you sure changed subjects quickly. They are my sister's children. As Lisa mentioned, they are on their second honeymoon."

"That's nice," Matt said, without showing interest.

Abigail continued as if he did, "After being separated for a year, they decided not to raise the children alone, and as Christians, divorce isn't an option."

"Why did they separate?" Matt asked, with a speck of interest.

"Over finances, I gather." Her eyes stared at Matt until she got his attention. "Are your men professional thieves?"

"Guess you can say that," he said, as he squirmed.

"How can you justify stealing?" she asked. "Am I being too direct, again?"

"Look. We have never hurt anyone; have we harmed you?"

It surprised her when her eyes teared up. "What do you think you're doing to us now? We can't even have our privacy."

"I'll make sure you get home safe."

"Don't you realize our family will be worried sick? You and your men have frightened us. Someone murdered our friends, and you won't let us go. What if the murderer is on board? That would mean we're still in danger. Have you even thought about that?"

He breathed deeply. His eyes examined hers. "Do you think we planned this? Do you think we're happy about the murders? None of us are thrilled about any of this." Sweat pooled on his brow. "I wish I knew who murdered them." His voice was low and uneasy. "Look, I'm as concerned as you, but for a different reason."

"What do you mean?"

"You're afraid for the children and your safety, and that I understand. And you're grieving the loss of your friends. Our fear is becoming murder suspects, or being jailed for years for something we didn't do. It might sound strange, but we have a reputation. Among thieves, we're known for our ethics. Once implicated in murder, that will end. It won't matter that we're innocent."

"You and your men placed yourselves in that position. You came to steal from our hosts. You could have stayed home."

Neither spoke for a few minutes. She studied his face carefully and said, "If Jack didn't do it, then who?"

"None of us, we're friends. It's the first time we've questioned each other. Jack thinks it was Robert and Brent, they think it was

Jack or me, and we all think it was Forelli. Once we found those bodies, everything changed. We have to find the killer. Understand? The money means nothing if we rot in some federal penitentiary for something we didn't do." With his head and shoulders in a slump, his eyes focused on the rug. "How well did you know the Kilgores?"

"They were family friends, why do you ask?"

"In some way, they were connected with the men who arranged for us to be here. Have you known the couple long?"

"Yes. My parents met them many years ago at the yacht club. They sometimes dined together. At times, they came to family parties."

"How did they make their living?"

"They never said, and we never pried."

Silently, he turned and stared at the bulkhead. Then, he abruptly turned. "Maybe someone set us up."

"Why? And who?" she asked.

"I think the same people who sent Forelli. Tell me what you know about them?"

"My parents and they were casual friends. We didn't know them intimately. I only saw them a few times a year. None of us knew much about them. We were curious about how they made a living. My mother joked and said they were smugglers, while my dad thought they inherited or retired young."

"From what Robert said, your mother might be right."

"What do you mean? Smugglers?"

"I don't know all the details, but it seems so."

"If that's true, it would explain things, but it doesn't eliminate your friends as murder suspects."

"You don't get it. We would never hurt anyone. It's against everything we stand for."

"So, you don't see yourselves as criminals?"

"We don't go around killing people."

"But, what about kidnapping?"

"What? Because we aren't letting you go? That doesn't qualify us as kidnappers. We don't plan on asking for money for your safe return, and we don't want to hurt you. Have you seen any of us with a weapon?"

"Does that mean you'll let us go? Can I call the Coast Guard?"

"No, we can't let you do that. Not until we find the murderer." Cold silence then filled the cabin. Matt leaned his elbows on his knees. He rested his chin on his folded hands.

"You said you suspect Forelli. If he did it, why would he stay on the yacht? And, what would he gain by murdering?"

"Money!"

Matt stood and moved away, then turned to face her. "Let's say the Kilgores were smugglers. That would definitely place the couple in harm's way. It would also explain why we were set up to look for something mysterious and valuable. The thing must have been smuggled. What if Larry tried to sell the object and things went badly? Perhaps the prospective buyer killed them and stole the treasure."

"But, why not kill us, as well?" Her eyes watched him.

"The person might not have seen you."

"Do you think the killer is still on board?" she said.

"We would have found someone hiding by now. The shore boat is gone. Maybe he took it."

"This far out at sea?"

They both sat back on the sofa. Matt said, "What if our theories are wrong? What if the Kilgores were killed for some personal justification, perhaps a jealous rage? There are endless possibilities."

"My brain's too full to think." Abigail sighed. "It's two in the morning. Let's get some sleep. Perhaps something will come to us in the morning."

After reaching for her hand, he held it warmly. His eyes were kind. "I'm sorry about my attitude and being critical about your faith. I had no right to do that. I don't know why I said those things."

Genuinely, she smiled and squeezed his hand before standing and walking to the bed. She moved Lisa over and crawled under the sheets. Within minutes, she was asleep. She dreamed of Matt. First, they were standing on the upper deck searching the evening stars, as he tossed her golden hair. Gently, he touched her face with the back of his hand. Her body wanted him, and she gave into his embrace.

Suddenly, they were lying together on a white sandy beach -- silently watching the playful waves splash. His passion stayed controlled as their bodies touched. Tenderly, he pulled her close with his hand, caressing her breast, her body wanting more. Slowly, he removed her pants and rubbed the inside of her thigh. As their bodies came together as one, her body exploded with pleasure.

After their passion, they laid on their backs, looking at the stars. Openly, they told each other their feelings. His tone was a hum in her ears, and contentment filled her soul. She didn't want her dream to end.

The first to awaken was Matt. After taking his shower, he felt refreshed. As he walked near the bed, he watched her sleep. *What a beauty,* he thought, with his heart beating rapidly.

When her eyes opened, they met his. Quickly she turned and covered her head.

Hurriedly, he backed away and turned to leave the cabin.

My God! He knows about my dream. No. That's not possible. Get ahold of yourself. The children need you. She panicked as she nudged Danny. "Get up. Lisa. Wake up, let's get going."

After Lisa's eyes opened, she was excited. "We found the treasure in my dream. It was a painting."

I found a treasure in my dream, too, Abigail wanted to yell, but instead she busied herself by helping Lisa get dressed for the day.

When Matt reentered the cabin, he looked at Danny. "Ready to go treasure-hunting, young man?"

"But, I already found it. Remember? The egg. The one with jewels."

"Yes. It could be. But, until we're certain, we'll continue our search. Who knows, we might find something even more valuable."

"Okay," the boy said, in a small voice.

Lisa blurted out, "Matt, I found the treasure. It was a painting."

"I already found the egg!" Danny yelled. "Don't you remember?"

"Okay, you two. Stop arguing and brush your teeth." While Lisa got ready for the day, Abigail couldn't get her dream out of her thoughts. *What kind of a person am I? Goodness. Each time I see him, am I going to lose my footing and turn pink? Abigail Wilson, you must get ahold of yourself!*

Chapter Eleven

While preparing toast, she asked her nephew, "Want peanut butter?" He grinned and nodded. She handed it to him and watched him gobble it down.

"Will you see who's in the main salon?" she asked Danny.

As he walked toward the hatch, he heard Lisa say, "Do you think Matt's cute?" He turned and gawked at his sister, and Lisa glared back.

"Do you like him?" the girl asked.

"Yes. He was kind to you and playful to your brother." They turned when they heard loud footsteps and saw Matt enter the galley.

Lisa said, "I'll watch the toast."

"I trust you'll do a good job." Abigail tried to ignore him as he stood and watched. She was embarrassed when she felt her face become flushed.

"Just checking the coffee," he said.

"It's still dripping."

When the coffee machine buzzed, he strolled over and placed cups on a tray. He left with the tray in one hand and the pot in the other.

As she watched him leave, she felt angry with herself for allowing him to stir such emotion in her. She decided to focus on escaping. *What are my options?* she questioned. *I have to find a cellphone to call for help. What if I pretend to look for female protection,* she chuckled. *No man would question a woman looking for that. Good idea, girl.*

As Danny returned to the galley, his face was beaming. "Everyone accounted for, Miss Head Chef."

Although she was glad he was cheerful, she hoped he wasn't too comfortable with the thieves -- one might be the killer. Although the thieves didn't intend on kidnapping, people can do strange things when faced with prison. The men, she worried, might come to view the children, and her, as a major threat.

The eggs were scrambled, and the toast was ready, but she hated to leave the galley. It was the only place she had some level of control. Lisa carried the toast on a platter and left. "Danny, will you bring the butter, salt and pepper?"

"I can't wait to eat," the boy said, with peanut butter still stuck on a corner of his mouth.

After Abigail put the serving bowl with eggs on the table, she stepped back and watched the men fill their plates. Danny sat with Robert and Brent, Lisa was next to Jack, laughing. The only place left to sit was next to Matt, unless she wanted to feel conspicuous.

His eyes were full of anticipation as she sat. He said, "Thanks. Breakfast looks great. You're some kind of woman." As he gazed at her, she glanced away. "This must be awful for you. Yet, you're willing to make us a meal."

Her fingers touched her face. "Good grief, it's hot."

He reached for her arm. "Is everything okay? Are you feeling ill?"

"It's that time of the month, that's all." She pulled away. She took a bite of her eggs, but could barely swallow. "If we were home, we would be at church right now."

"Did you attend church as a child?"

"Yes. My dad would drop us off and buy a newspaper to read while waiting." She was pleased with herself. Talking about her family diffused the awkward feeling she felt around him.

"Why didn't your dad go?"

"What?"

"You said he stayed in the car."

"Oh. Yes." She smiled. "I don't know, but I wished many times that I could have stayed with him."

"Why?"

"We couldn't eat because of communion, and sometimes I felt lightheaded. While waiting for the sacraments, we had to kneel, stand, and find our place in the monthly booklets. I seldom found the right page in time for the readings. I often wondered if those were reasons Dad didn't attend."

Matt put his hand over his mouth. "Excuse me."

"Once, when I was twelve, I remember going to confession. When I told the priest about having sexual fantasies, he actually came out of the confessional and accused me of trying to shock him. That was my last confession to a priest. After that, I went directly to God. He knew my sins already, so I couldn't shock Him."

"You bad little girl -- having sexual fantasies. I'll listen to them anytime."

She grinned. "Gee, thanks, but I don't think so."

"You can't blame a guy for trying."

Matt took his last mouthful of eggs, pushed his plate away, and patted his stomach. "Why did you go to church if you felt so uncomfortable?"

"It never occurred to me not to go. Besides, I don't regret it. I just found it exasperating at times. I should have gone to Sunday school."

"Years later, we changed churches, and Dad started going. Our new church was much better."

"What made you think about church?" Matt asked.

"Today's Sunday." She smiled. "Thanks for listening without being cynical." She saw Danny from the corner of her eye and adjusted to face him.

When he reached them, he asked Matt, "Why don't you think the jeweled egg is real?"

Matt whispered, "It might be genuine. We're not sure yet. I hope you didn't say anything about the egg to Robert or Brent."

"No."

"Please keep it that way, okay?" The boy nodded.

"Well. Let's get back to work." Matt stood and stepped toward the ladder.

Abigail walked behind him and glanced out a porthole. "Why is that vessel following us? Does it have some connection to you and your men?"

Matt didn't respond. Instead he moved faster. When they reached the cabin, he flung open the hatch. He said nothing to the children or her.

"Did I offend you by asking about the touring vessel?" When he didn't respond, she said, "Well, it looks like the subject is off limits."

Danny moved toward the bed to look under it. "Go sit. Over there." Matt snapped, while pointing to a chair. "I'll take care of this cabin." He lifted the mattress and scanned the space underneath.

"Need help?" Abigail asked, grimly. She came to help hold the mattress.

He accepted her help, but didn't look in her direction. Next, he checked the box spring for any unusual lumps. When he finished, he motioned for her to let go. The mattress dropped.

"Make the bed," he ordered.

Abigail complied, and Lisa helped. Danny sat examining Matt's face with his head tilted. Everyone noticed Matt's mood change -- anyone would have.

"Why did your mood change so abruptly after I asked you a question?"

Instead of giving her a verbal response, he became more agitated and kicked at some items on the floor. Both children were silent.

Chapter Twelve

The wind kicked up, the yacht swayed and Matt tried to get his footing. As he leaned against the bulkhead, he started to question himself. *Why am I so upset? Why did I act so cold to her and the children? I need to leave.* Matt pivoted to leave, avoiding eye contact. Harshly, he said, "I'm leaving. You stay. Understand?"

Abigail stepped closer to him. "What's going on, Matt?"

"It's none of your concern."

"Are you okay?" she asked.

"No. I'm not okay. I screwed up my life. Can't you see that?" He marched out of the cabin.

Abigail's eyes were large, as she placed one hand on her chest. *What just happened? What does he regret? Did he have something to do with the murders?* She sat on the edge of the bed and covered her eyes with her hands. *My God, what was I thinking?* Any security she felt earlier left with Matt as he walked out of the cabin.

There has to be some logical explanation for his behavior. Perhaps he had wanted to consult with Jack about the Fabergé egg. No. That's not it. He didn't retrieve it from the drawer. If Matt wanted us dead, he would have taken care of that by now.

Danny stood in front of his aunt, "Why did he leave?"

Lisa stepped next to her brother. "Why is he so angry with us?"

After glancing back and forth at each child, she said, "He's upset about something. He'll be fine. Give him time."

She sat on the edge of the bed, and Danny sat next to her. The children and she were silent. Lisa leaned against her, and Abigail placed her arm around her.

Okay, what now? she asked herself. "I have to find a cellphone. Do you two want to help?"

Lisa jumped to her feet. "Sure."

Danny stood and walked over to the vanity, pulled out a drawer and started to search inside.

Abigail remembered something her mother often said, "Honey, when you expect the best out of people, they seldom disappoint you." But could that apply to a thief? She heard footsteps coming. She walked toward the hatch, but, to her disappointment, it was Robert.

His face was expressionless, "Come with me."

Abigail moved out of the hatch and waited for the children. The boy seemed cheerful, as if on some new adventure.

The boy chatted with Robert and seemed unaware that they might be headed for trouble. The boy glanced up. "Did you find anything?"

"Not yet," Robert said. He placed his hand on Lisa's shoulder, she pulled away.

"Did you see Matt?" Lisa asked.

"Sure did."

"Why did he leave us? Is he mad?"

"He needs a break, that's all." He smiled at the girl.

At that moment, Abigail tried to give the illusion that she had some level of control. She felt as if they were being led to walk the plank to their demise.

With Matt, I felt some level of security. But, now after my stupid dream, things have changed. Why didn't I keep my mouth shut? I always ask too many questions. My friends tell me I do. They stopped, just outside the engine room. Great! This is a good place to stuff our dead bodies.

Robert turned to them. "Stay in the passageway. We're almost finished in here." He watched her as if to make sure she understood. When she nodded, he returned to his search.

Soon, Brent arrived with two chairs.

She folded her arms and glared at him. "What's going on?"

"Nothing, he just needs a break -- that's all -- he needs time alone." He pivoted to leave, then reeled back. "Stay here. If you leave, it'll complicate things, understand?"

"Do I have any choice here?" she yelled.

Brent scowled at her before he walked toward the engine room.

She crossed her legs while standing. *If my mouth was any drier, it would be full of cotton.* Suddenly, she felt exhausted and sat.

Lisa jumped on her lap and gave her her best hug. "Don't worry, Auntie. Matt said he'll make sure we get home."

"Sure, I know, Honey." She didn't want to say their safety wasn't only up to Matt. Instead, she managed to give the girl a reassuring smile.

Danny came nearer. "Why is Matt angry with me?"

"You did nothing wrong. He's just upset about something and took a break."

"He acted mad at me."

Abigail's shoulders slumped. Her voice weakened. "Don't worry. Everything will be fine."

"You don't believe that, do you?" He turned and walked toward the engine room.

Lisa quickly stood and yelled, "They said to stay here, Danny."

The boy circled to leer at her and then walked into the engine room. "Can I help?"

Abigail quickly got to her feet and moved to the hatch. She saw Robert. He was smiling. "Sure."

The boy said, "If I find it, can I have five thousand dollars?"

She swallowed hard.

Robert grinned at Brent, and both their heads looked up as they let out a loud laugh. "So, you want to be our partner in crime, huh?" Robert bent down and stared at the boy. "Tell you what, if you find what we're looking for, you most certainly can have the money you bargained for." He rubbed the boy's buzz haircut.

Abigail returned to her chair, glad the men were in a better mood than Matt.

Lisa was quiet. "Are you okay, Sweetie?"

"I miss Mommy," she said, with tears spilling softly onto her cheeks. She wrapped her arms around her aunt's neck and held on tightly.

"I know. Right now, I miss my mother, too."

Sitting in the passageway caused Abigail to feel closed in and prickly. Too much had happened in such a short period of time.

Lisa's expression changed. "Are you afraid?"

Abigail let out a deep lungful of air very slowly and thought, *I must hide my emotions better.* She said, "When Matt left, I was afraid, but not now. Do you think I am?"

The girl watched her aunt for a minute. "No. Not now."

Memories flooded Matt's mind so rapidly, he was unable to pin any one down long enough to examine it. Once one stayed, he wished it didn't. It was the day he received his letterman jacket. While his friends were getting hugs or a pat on the back from their parents, he stood alone. So many times during football season, he glanced up at the bleachers, but quickly looked away. Not once did he see his father.

Now as he sat thinking, he realized neither parent showed much interest in his life. Not even when he was in trouble. Like the time he gave a party that resulted in the police being called. Instead of being upset, they were indifferent. It angered him to think his parents didn't care.

It feels like a dagger in my gut to admit my parents never gave a rat's ass about me. Even as a young child, in vain I got A's on my report card, trying to get their approval.

Stop this! he told himself. Obsessing about my childhood isn't getting me anyplace. I'm a big boy. I have to stop blaming them. It's now up to me to forgive and accept them for who they are.

As he sat thinking, he wondered, Why was I so icy to the children and Abigail, and why did her question stir such anger? It hit him. I hate being connected to the Top Dogs. They are cold, ruthless men. Yes. That's it. And what did I do? I acted just like them. Once again, I'm blaming those men for who I am. It was my decision to become a thief. I'm responsible for my choices. It's my lifestyle that makes me unworthy of Abigail.

The only good that has come from knowing those men is working with Brent and Robert. We make a great team, manning those touring vessels. We're friendly, helpful and informative to our guests. That's why we have the most bookings and highest profit every month. But, have we ever been acknowledged for our efforts? No. Whatever we do is never good enough. He let out his breath and shook his head. Here I go, looking for approval from those men.

I have to grow up, and quickly, or it will be too late. What a joke! Wanting respect for being an ethical thief -- it sickens me. All these years, I could have been building a good life for myself. What a waste!

Abigail. All this is about her. What is it that draws me in? She's a religious fanatic, but I find it refreshing. My aunt Francis was like her. She once gave me a Bible, which I seldom read. Most women in my life were more like Mother -- stuffy, social-climbing women. Aunt Francis was the only genuine woman I knew -- until Abigail.

Suddenly Matt remembered making a vow never to trust women -- right after discovering Jack's mother having sex under that car. *No wonder I never wanted a serious relationship.*

But, why did I let my guard down with Abigail? Why did I let her steal my heart?

Chapter Thirteen

The passageway was gloomy as she and Lisa sat waiting.

Abigail resolved to find a cellphone. After walking to the engine room, she peeked in. "Hey, I'm leaving." "No, you're not!" Robert yelled.

"But, yes I am, I have to find female protection."

"What?" Robert said. "It's that time of the month. I need protection." He stared at her, and waved for her to leave. Lisa and she walked away without an escort for the first time since the ordeal began. "Finally, some freedom," she said, as they climbed the ladder.

After reaching the main salon, she started pulling the padded seats around the portholes, but found nothing of interest. She stepped toward a cabinet, opened it and looked in, no phone.

Lisa blinked, "What's wrong, Aunt Abigail?"

"Just feeling discouraged, that's all."

"Why?"

"I can't find a phone, so I can't call the Coast Guard."

Lisa's face tilted. "Where do people hide them?"

"Good question. In plain view, unless disguised. Your grandmother had one like that given to her." While looking around, Abigail spotted a wooden container, stepped toward it and picked it up. After opening it, she found a stack of ashtrays and coasters.

Her discouragement became heavier. "I must find a way to get us out of this mess. The only place to signal for help is at the wheelhouse. Going there might be fruitless, but definitely worth a try." She and Lisa climbed the ladder and saw Forelli at the wheel. Perhaps the fact he didn't like the other men might work in her favor. Who knows, he might be receptive to a friendly face.

As they walked toward the helm, Lisa's eyes were wide. "Do you want me to act sick?" she whispered.

"Shush. No. You don't have to do that, only with Matt." The closer they came, the more apprehensive she felt. Not knowing what to expect from the man, she couldn't give her intent away.

Forelli jumped back a step and stared at them. In a gruff tone, he said, "What're you doing out here?"

"Thought you might want a break to get something to eat or drink."

No response.

She decided not to let him intimidate her. "My dad owned a smaller yacht." She took a few steps closer. "I helped Mr. Kilgore and Matt at the wheel. If you want a break, I can take over."

As he stared and smirked, he said, "Do you think I'm an idiot?" He turned to face the water.

Lisa piped in, "I'll be with her."

Forelli glanced at Lisa with his dull eyes.

Well, great! This is going nowhere. Perhaps I can wear him down.

"How long have you known Matt and the other men?"

"A while." He continued to fix his gaze at the sea.

"How do you know each other?"

"Work."

Cheerfully, Abigail said, "Oh, where?"

"What's this, a hundred questions? I should be asking you the questions: Where's Matt? And, why are you unescorted?"

"We're getting drinks for Brent and Robert, and we thought you might need a break. Besides, we needed fresh air."

"Well, you've had your fresh air, so get back to what you were doing."

Abigail's face dropped, her eyes were low. *If only I got my hands on that two-way radio.* As they walked down the ladder toward the galley, she said, "Well, at least we tried. Let's grab some drinks and head back to the engine room."

Lisa said, "Why is it taking them so long to search one place? You'd think they would have finished by now."

After smiling at the girl, she said, "I thought the same thing."

While in the galley, Abigail turned to her niece, "Decide what drink you want and grab it."

Lisa put her hand on her hip. "We didn't see Matt."

"I know, Honey. I think that's strange, too."

Abigail genuinely liked and missed Matt. She was worried about his mental state. In the past, she often was too optimistic about men. Sometimes, she stayed in flawed relationships long after they should have ended. Once a therapist told her, "Insanity is doing the same thing over and over and expecting a different result." Often she anticipated a different behavior from a man, yet he consistently had the same behavior. It had taken years, but she realized she must accept a man for who he is and stop projecting her values onto them.

What is it about me that I want to depend on a thief, for our safety? she questioned. When I get home, I'll call my therapist. But, for now, I must find a new plan of escape. The shore boat is gone, no access to the wheelhouse, what's left? We can jump off the vessel with life preservers. But, then we would be like ducks in a pond.

Lisa touched Abigail's hand. "Can we get some snacks?"

"No. Later, Sweetie, it'll give us an excuse to leave again."

Suddenly, Lisa's eyes teared, "Can we go home soon?"

"I sure hope so, Honey."

"Do you think Matt's gone? Maybe he won't come back for us."

The thought never occurred to Abigail. She felt stupid for relying on him at all.

As they entered the main salon, they both stopped abruptly. They saw Matt. Abigail took in some air. Her shoulders relaxed, and her head was high. "You look awful. Did you lose in a boxing match? Are you okay?"

He nodded and managed a smile for Lisa, he glanced back at Abigail. "We need to talk. Go give the drinks to Robert, and tell him you ran into me. Say I need to speak with you alone. He'll understand."

She stood and looked at him for a moment, then turned and walked toward the ladder.

As they left, Lisa spun around. "Goodbye Matt." She continued looking at him until they reached the first step on the ladder.

Once they neared the poorly lit engine room, they heard Danny say, "Is this it?"

"No. Be patient. We think it's hidden here someplace."

"But, why?"

"Because only the captain or owners come in here, making it a logical place to hide something of value."

When Danny saw his sister and aunt with drinks, he quickly took his favorite refreshment from the tray. "Where have you been? I waited for you."

The girl placed her hand on her hip with attitude. "Getting drinks, silly."

"Who wants the root beer?" Brent took the Coke, held it in Abigail's direction and nodded.

"I hope you don't mind, we visited the wheelhouse to get fresh air, and Forelli was there."

Robert and Brent looked at each other -- both seemed annoyed. She was unsure if they were upset with her or the mention of Forelli.

"We saw Matt in the main salon. He wants to talk to me alone; he said you'd understand."

After grunting something, he pointed to a chair for Lisa. "You can sit there." He then motioned for Abigail to leave.

Lisa asked, "Can I help, too?"

Robert pointed to the left corner. "You can recheck those things. See if you can find something we missed."

While walking toward the ladder, Abigail's heart beat faster. She climbed up the ladder and went into the main salon. *Perhaps he feels remorse, and wants to let us go. Or, is that my sanguinity showing?* As she took her last step, she saw Matt watching her. After moving to the table, she stood for a few seconds and pulled up a chair opposite his.

She noticed his slumped shoulders and dim eyes as he silently sat. He lifted his head. "I'm sorry you and the kids had to go through all of this."

"Then, let us go home. Lisa and Danny need to feel safe again. You know darn good and well that the murderer might still be on board. Don't say you don't."

"Look, Abigail. That might be true, but we'll not leave until we find the murderer. We must clear our names."

"You said you want to speak to me, what about? Or, was that it?"

His head slowly moved back and forth while saying, "I'm sorry for acting so weird earlier. When you asked about my connection to the touring ship, it triggered something."

"What?" "The men on that vessel arranged for me to become a thief. If I had never met them, my life would be significantly different."

"How?"

"For one, I wouldn't be a thief. Look, I haven't stopped examining my life since the moment I found your friends' bodies. And, being around you and the kids makes me realize how much I'm missing."

His eyes were brighter and his voice firmer. "I'm also painfully aware of my life decisions. Right now, my only close friends are thieves. I have no strong family ties, and no one to share my life with. What you stand for is appealing to me, but I can't kid myself. A guy like me could never be worthy of a woman like you, and that hurts." His eyes glanced down, and his worry lines deepened.

After reaching over the table, she touched his hand. Without looking up, he put his other hand over hers as they contemplated their predicament.

As he lifted his head, he passionately looked into her eyes. "To be worthy of you, I would have to start over. But, I can't. My past would be chasing me for the rest of my life. What kind of life would that be for us?"

Warmth filled her, "If you truly want to, you can ask God to forgive you and ask Him to help you change."

Her words seemed to have fallen on deaf ears or a hard heart.

"You made me realize what I'm missing." He gazed at her. "Do you have any idea what I'm even trying to say here? I want you, Abigail. But, I know I can't have you."

After squeezing his hand, she said, "But, you *can* start over. And, without the past haunting you."

"How?"

"Turn yourself in to the authorities. Tell them everything. And, be willing to pay your debt to society." She tightened her grip, and focused on his eyes. "Do you have money for a good attorney?"

Matt nodded.

"Let your attorney fight for your rights and help you get out of this legal mess. And, spiritually, accept what Jesus did for you and ask for forgiveness. You can start a new life with a clean slate."

"Abigail, please. I just can't do the religious thing. I don't want to be a hypocrite. Being a religious person just isn't me. Please understand that I could never believe like you. It isn't within me. Don't embarrass yourself to think otherwise."

His words stabbed at her heart, the pain was deep. She could have easily fallen for him. If only he would take responsibility for his mistakes. But, his words slammed the door on that. Years ago, she decided never to compromise her faith. After listening to what he had to say, she decided to guard her heart.

"My dear man, I can hear the pain in your words, and I know things are difficult for you." Her tone was sweet and her words were controlled. She carefully hid her disillusionment. "Thank you for being so frank with me. Please know, I'll continue praying for you long after this ordeal is over. But, always remember, Matt, there's always hope."

Chapter Fourteen

When Jack entered the main salon grinning, Abigail concluded that the Fabergé egg must have been authentic.

While staring at her, Jack said, "Does she know?"

"Of course, Danny found it."

After placing her weight on one foot, she yelled, "You must think I'm invisible!"

While ignoring her, he turned to Matt. "It's real, all right."

"That's great," Matt said, with a huge smile.

"Where did the boy find it?"

"The library, in plain view."

After belly laughing, Jack said, "That couple sure had a sense of humor."

"At first, I thought it was fake, them leaving it out like that."

"Do you know what this means?" Jack said, glancing over his right and left shoulders. "We're rich!"

"What is it worth?"

"Half mil.," he said, "More, with an intriguing history."

"How can we find out?"

"We need a computer."

As Matt altered his position to face her, he asked, "Seen a computer around?"

After responding by shaking her head, she turned to the children. "Have either of you seen a computer?" They looked at each other and said no.

Jack came closer. "No matter what the history, the egg isn't worth the ten million the Top Dogs are offering. At best, it might be valued at a million." After pausing, he said, "Now that we have this, isn't it enough? Can we leave?"

"You can, if you want," Matt said, glancing at him and then at Abigail. "But, I'm going to clear my name and figure out who murdered the Kilgores."

"How do you expect to find the killer?" Jack glared at him.

After standing erect, Matt paused while touching his chin. "I don't know, but it's something I have to do."

"Okay, once again, we'll do it your way," Jack said.

It's the first time she witnessed the depth of their friendship.

No wonder Matt doesn't consider him a murderer -- they're best friends.

Matt faced Abigail. "You're close to going home, young lady, be happy. We'll concentrate on finding your friends' killer and then leave. So, can you tell us anything you might remember before their deaths?"

"We already went through this."

"Enlighten me, again. We may have missed something."

"Like I said, the children and I were at the wheel. We wanted a break. When we looked for the Kilgores, we couldn't find them. Around that time, I heard a boat coming or leaving, but didn't see anything. I thought it might be the new captain. As we continued looking for Larry and Sandra, we heard your voices saying you were looking for something. Neither voice was Larry's, so I feared the worst, and we hid. You know the rest. The next time I saw them, they were dead." She cringed. Abigail stepped closer. "Is Forelli capable of murder?"

"Yes. But, they were already dead when he arrived."

Abigail looked at Jack. "You had time."

"When?"

"While Matt was questioning us, you could have done it. Do you have a gun?"

It surprised her when he started laughing. Within a minute, he looked at her with an intolerable expression. "Smell my hands and shirt. Can you smell gunpowder?"

"It might be washed away, by now."

"I guess you don't know much about gunpowder. You can't get rid of it that quick, especially on clothes."

"Do you own a gun?" she asked, again.

"Yes. It's in my store -- never been removed from there. Furthermore, I've never found reason to use it until right now!" He stared her down. When he moved closer, she backed away.

"Okay. Stop this!" Matt screamed. "Right now, both of you. This is ridiculous!" Matt grabbed his friend's shoulder and glared at Abigail. "He didn't even want to come; he is doing me a favor. Besides, he didn't know the Kilgores, so he had no motive. As far as I'm concerned, the only person capable of murder is Forelli, and he is ruled out. So, the only other explanation is the killer is hiding, or came and left."

"Did you check Forelli for gunpowder?" Jack asked. "What if he came, murdered, left and then returned?"

"You're making me dizzy with all the coming and going. But, let's go question him, anyway." He turned to Abigail. "Stay with the children. Hopefully, this whole thing will be over soon."

As Jack and Matt approached the helm, the radio was blaring. The moment Forelli spotted them coming, his body jerked. "What's going on?"

"We need to talk. When did you arrive?"

"Why are you questioning me? What are you two trying to pull?" His face reddened. "What kind of crap is this, anyway? You know I came after you."

"The reason we're asking is we need to find out who murdered the Kilgores. So, we need to smell your hands and shirt for gunpowder."

"Forget it. I don't need to prove myself to either of you."

"Not even to clear yourself as a suspect?" Jack said, gruffly.

"My only task is to man this vessel. So, that's my only concern. You four are the thieves, remember?"

"True. But, you and Luke are as cozy as bedbugs. If he wanted them dead, wouldn't he ask you?"

"He didn't ask; I didn't do it, so you're grabbing at straws here."

"Look, Forelli. We know Luke and his men, and wouldn't put it past them."

Forelli's eyes flickered. "Why don't you question Robert and Brent? Now, let's see, could ten million dollars be motive enough?"

"It's not worth my effort to respond." Matt turned to Jack. "We're not getting anywhere."

After Jack jabbed him, he said, in a low tone, "He's hiding something."

"You think?"

After reaching the main salon, Matt leaned back while sitting. "If Forelli didn't do it, what are some other possibilities? Who might want them dead?"

"Since we didn't know them personally, it's hard to know. It could be a bad business deal, a love triangle or some old enemy. Anything's possible."

Leaning back, Matt ran his fingers through his hair. "What if the Kilgores cheated some drug lord? That could result in murder."

"We can speculate all day, and it wouldn't help. Let's talk to Robert and Brent. They might know something."

"Perhaps one of them found a computer."

"Good thinking."

On their way, Matt thought about the Fabergé egg and its benefits. Jack could retire from his jewelry business and get a condo on a golf course. Who knows, he might find some young thing to have babies with. He grinned at the thought. At the moment, he was weary of his merry-go-round lifestyle.

Starting over is appealing. But, the last thing I want is to have my past chasing me, he decided. But, to turn myself in and ask God for forgiveness makes me laugh. With a few hundred thousand in the bank, I can regroup and find a legitimate job. Without thinking, he started humming "Money Can't Buy Me Love."

When he reached the engine room, Abigail and the children were in the passageway. She sat in a chair, and the children were on the floor.

"Hi kids," he said, smiling.

The children returned his smile, but Abigail kept her head and eyes low. After turning away from them, he walked into the engine room. "Hey, have either of you seen a computer?"

"No. Why?" Robert asked.

"Does it matter why?" he said. "Have either of you seen one?"

Brent came closer, and shook his head.

Soon Robert came and stood next to Matt. "It looks like we're finally finished in here. What's up?"

"We're thinking about abandoning the search and going home, boys."

"Okay with me," Brent responded.

While leaning on the hatch, Matt said, "Before we leave, I want to figure out who murdered the Kilgores. I don't want any of us to be a suspect."

The two men were silent while looking at each other, as if the thought had never entered their mind.

"I need to ask you both some questions about the murders," Matt said.

Instantly, Robert stood erect and slammed his fist. "Don't even think about it. My God, how long have we known each other? Our friendship is built on trust. Do you really think we murdered those people?"

"Robert. You're taking this too personally. We have already questioned each other and Forelli. Besides, once the authorities get ahold of us, we will be questioned. So, let's figure out what we plan on saying. What do you know? Can you tell me anything? What are your thoughts?"

"Besides Forelli, I have no idea," Brent said.

Robert turned to Matt. "How about you? Isn't the person finding the body the prime suspect?"

After pausing for a moment, he said, "Do you think I did it? Any of you, do you think that?"

The expression on Robert's face softened. He shook his head and said, "Of course not. But, how does it feel? Being questioned by a friend?"

"I get it," Matt said. "But, do any of you have any tangible evidence that points to Forelli?"

Robert sat on his heels, "No, but who else?"

"I agree. He's the only one of us capable, unless the killer is hiding someplace." Matt scowled. "Let's stop everything and poke around."

"It's unlikely the person is hiding," Brent said. "We would have found him by now. The yacht isn't that big."

"Let's look around, anyway." He walked down the passageway with Matt. Jack said, "Robert's right about one thing. The last one to see a person alive or to find a dead body is suspect. So, it might be the woman."

"Forget it, Jack. She didn't do it."

He pivoted. "How do you know that?"

"The same way I know you didn't," he said, while glaring.

After Jack finished staring at Matt, he calmed down and said, "Any other ideas?"

Robert spoke up, "Luke or one of the Top Dogs could have sent the killer to do the deed in their shore boat and returned. So, the killer might be on their vessel, making us waste time searching."

"Okay." Jack said. "We know the Kilgores smuggled for them, and there was bad blood between them. But, why would they risk being out at sea next to us. One would think they would remove themselves from the murder scene."

"That's true. If Luke and the hit man were the only two involved, that would explain why they are still nearby."

Matt scratched his head. "Forelli may not even know about Luke hiring someone to kill them. I'm getting a headache thinking about it."

"I'll check the shore boat to see if I can find any blood," Jack said. Robert responded, "I'll search the outer decks."

Chapter Fifteen

Steven's shoulders slumped as they headed to his parents' to check messages. Carry touched his arm. "Are you okay?"

"No. Not really. I'm very discouraged right now."

"Have you called Larry Kilgore?"

"No. I don't have the number. I'll call Mr. Jester. He must have it on file." After reaching into his pocket, he took out the man's business card and handed it to her. "Would you call?"

After she picked up his cellphone from the ashtray, she dialed his number. There was no answer, so she left a message. As they continued driving, he felt mentally fatigued. To soothe himself, he pushed the CD button and let classical piano music fill the car. When he glanced at Carry, she was in her own little world. *The ordeal is starting to take its toll.*

After she glanced his way, she said, "Talk to me, Steven."

"Right now, I feel numb," he said. "My next move is to call the police or someone, if we don't find out something soon. The only feasible explanation is they must be at sea."

While he stared ahead, he said, "Those children need to know about their parents. My God, if she doesn't come out of her coma, those kids are orphans."

"I'm sure she'll pull through, she has to." Carry lightly touched his arm. "Many people are praying for her. It's possible she'll wake up at any moment."

When they reached his parents' home, he parked and gave her a smile. "Wouldn't it be a great if Abigail left a message?"

"Your parents must be beside themselves with worry."

"Actually, they don't even know I'm having trouble finding Abigail and the children. They have too much on their plate with David's death and Alisa's coma."

After getting out of the car, he opened the side gate, and they walked to the back door. He reached into a pot and grabbed a hideaway key box, took out the key and unlocked the kitchen door; they entered.

"Hungry?"

"Remember? I just ate."

"Sorry, I'm not thinking." He grabbed two Oreo cookies and popped one into his mouth. "Mom buys them just for me, so I might as well eat them, right?" After a few minutes, he turned and walked into the living room to check the messages. There were calls of concern from the pastor, his aunt, and a few neighbors, but none from Abigail.

"Great! Now what?"

In frustration, after jotting down the other messages, he angrily deleted them. "Well, that didn't help us."

"You must not forget, your sister's cellphone is in her car, she might not have access to a phone. However, in case she does, I still want to check messages at my place and go back to her house."

"That's okay with me. But, right now, I need to regroup. I'm exhausted. Today has been a series of disappointments."

He sat on the floor and laid back using his arms as a pillow. Carry decided to relax in the easy chair with her feet up. Within minutes, she noticed he was out like a log.

After twenty minutes, he awoke. While stretching, he said, "Sorry. I guess I fell asleep." He sat up, and got up to go to the bathroom. He splashed water on his face, when what he really needed was a long, hot shower.

After returning to the living room, Carry stood holding a photo of his and her family together. "It brings back old memories," she said. Grinning, she returned the photo to the table.

"Are you ready to hit the road?" Steven asked.

"Sure."

Carefully, he placed the key back into the hideaway box, and they headed for the car.

With a smile, Carry said, "Do you remember that stream a few miles from our house?"

"Sure do, why?"

"Looking at that photo reminded me of an adventure Stan and I had as small children. We wanted to get wet in the stream. But, first, we stopped by Old Farley's Market to buy some balloons to use as floaters."

Steven nodded. He opened the car door for her, and then walked around to the driver's side. After sitting, he quickly lowered the windows and turned on the air. Soon, he pulled away.

"So, you were saying ..."

"After buying the balloons, we still had some change, so we headed for the candy." Carry glanced at him. "We put only one coin in the machine, but, each time we turned the knob, candy kept coming. It must have been broken. After stuffing our mouths and pockets, we hurriedly left so as not to get caught. We ran to the corner and crossed the street."

"That had to be exciting for you two kids," Steven said, with a smile.

"It actually was."

"So, go on with your story," he said.

"On our way to the stream, we ran barefoot on the hot cement and tried to find shade. But, the trees were few and far between, so, we were hoping to hitch a ride, but had no luck. And, boy did our feet suffer," she grinned. "We were both let down when we saw that the stream was dried up. We couldn't believe we walked on hot cement for nothing. We ended up sitting in the shade, blowing up balloons and eating our free candy," she chuckled. "We tried sitting on the balloons, but they popped from the heat. When Stan and I get together, we still laugh about that day."

"Days like that are unforgettable," Steven said. "Your story reminds me of an outing with Abigail. Remember that trail behind our houses?"

"Yes. It goes to the top of the hill."

"Remember the green water tank? One day we walked to it, but we took only one child-sized canteen of water. While hiking, I thought it was too hot to be walking up a hill. I wanted to go back, but Abigail insisted we continue. She said, 'We're not turning back, we're almost there.' While she was speaking, we heard what sounded like a rattler, so we slowly walked and listened. Suddenly, a snake snapped its head in our direction. Abigail screamed, and we both ran farther up the trail. Before we knew it, we were at the water tank with perspiration pouring down and laughing hysterically. We couldn't figure out where our energy came from as we gasped for air."

"After that ordeal, we were in no hurry to return down the path. So we sat, drank water and splashed some on our faces. Adventurous I started climbing the ladder to the top of the water tank, but Abigail didn't want to go. But, after thinking about the snake, she didn't want to be alone."

"So, what happened when you returned? Did you see the snake?"

"No. It was starting to get dark. I was concerned about finding our way back, but, like most boys, I called her sissy for being afraid. So, together, we ran so fast the snake didn't have time to coil or snap.

"You boys, you're all alike, aren't you?" She laughed.

Steven pulled up in front of Carry's place. They got out, went to her front door, and entered. He followed her into the living room.

After walking to the phone, she pushed the message button, listened, but none were from Abigail. "Can I get you a drink? I have iced tea and soda."

"Iced tea, thank you," he said.

While Steven waited, he grabbed a handful of nuts from a glass dish, picked up the phone, walked to the couch and sat. Then, he yelled, "Can I use your phone?"

"Of course you can."

After retrieving a business card from his wallet, he dialed Mr. Jester.

When Carry handed him his drink, he mouthed the words *thank you.*

This time, Mr. Jester was in, so Steven was relieved. "Hi, this is Steven Wilson. Did you get our message? We tried reaching you earlier."

"Yes. I was about to return your call. What can I help you with?"

"We need to reach Larry. Can you please give me his home phone number?"

"Those numbers are confidential, Steven." "Yes. I figured that. But, they are the last people to see Abigail and the kids. And, as you know, we must reach them. I don't think they would mind if you gave their number out under the circumstances, do you?"

"My heart goes out to your family. Because you're friends with Larry and Sandra, I don't think they'll mind. I'll get their number, hold on."

After a short wait, he said, "Ready?"

"Sure."

Steven jotted down the number and said, "Thanks, I owe you."

"That information is private. Remember that."

"I know."

As soon as Steven ended the call, he dialed Larry's home. A woman answered. "May I speak with either Mr. or Mrs. Kilgore?" He repeated it twice.

"No, señor."

"Habla English, señorita?" Steven asked.

"No. No, señor. No estan en la casa."

"Do you know when they'll return, señorita?"

"No estan en la casa, señor."

"Gracias, señorita." While ending the call, he was aggravated. "One more wall."

"What happened? I gather the Kilgores weren't home."

"You're right, so I still don't know if she is with them. I'll have to try later."

"I gather the person didn't speak English."

"The only thing I could get out of her was they're not home. But I have no idea if that means now, for the day or several days."

While trying to be cheerful, she said, "Well, I found Abigail's keys."

"Let's go," he said. He stood, walked to the door and waited for Carry.

On their way to Abigail's, little was said. She broke the silence with, "It's okay to be yourself with me. It's only natural you're feeling frustrated."

After giving her a grateful smile, he said, "Honestly. I don't know what I would have done without you today. I'm glad you're here. It's nice having a close family friend by my side. I'm sure it's painful for you to see us suffer."

"It is. And, I do care about all of you. You're family to me."

As they pulled up to Abigail's home, they hoped they might find something to lead them to her and the children. Carry took the key and opened the door. When they entered, the place smelled musty. She quickly opened the windows to freshen up the room with air.

Steven went to retrieve the messages and wrote down each person who called. "At least, we know she didn't make it home from Santa Barbara. Some messages were five days old." He silently tried to figure out what to do next. "They must be at sea. That's the only explanation for taking bags from the trunk. I'm calling the harbor patrol or the Coast Guard."

Chapter Sixteen

Elizabeth Wilson gazed out the window while the flight attendant announced to fasten seat belts and close tray tables.

After taking off, she turned to her husband, John. "It's the first time I've been afraid. What if Alisa dies, what will we do? I never thought one of our children might leave before us."

He reached for her hand and continued to listen.

"What will Danny and Lisa do? Losing both parents, it's unbelievable. This whole thing doesn't seem real. How can everything be great one moment and change so drastically a few minutes later? It's bad enough about David -- the children without a father -- but what if Alisa doesn't come out of her coma? What if she dies, too?"

While listening, John felt tears well and slowly creep down his cheeks. He quickly turned away and wiped them with his arm.

She pulled on his sleeve. "Honey, I'm so glad I have you to talk to, but I know I'm making things worse for you."

"For God's sake, Elizabeth, don't you start worrying about me, too, okay?"

The rain continued after the aircraft landed -- fitting for their moods. They sat, stood and waited around in the luggage claim. When their luggage arrived, they left and hailed a taxi. During their drive to the hospital, Elizabeth noticed their young driver. He reminded her to pray for the recovery of Alisa's young taxi driver.

While John peered out the window, he reached for his wife's hand. Soon, they arrived at the hospital, paid the driver and marched directly to the information table.

The clerk had a warm smile and said, "The intensive care unit is on the fourth floor, and her room is number 404."

After thanking her, they headed toward the elevator. They rode up, while staring at the button lighting up at each floor they passed. Once they arrived, they quickly walked out and went down the fourth-floor corridor, which was painted a cheerful yellow on one side and orange on the other.

Immediately, they found the nurses' station to inquire as to their daughter's medical status, and hoped for some good news. There were three people sitting and a few were standing and checking charts. Some flowers were on the counter and looked as if they would soon be tossed. There were many family photos on the office counters.

John found a middle-aged woman with dirty ash hair that was starting to gray. "Excuse me, miss," John said. The nurse looked up from her work. "We need to talk to you about our daughter, Alisa."

"Yes. What is it you need?"

"Can we get an update on how our daughter, Alisa, is doing? She's in room 404."

"I'll check with her nurse." The woman walked toward a young woman, possibly from the Philippine Islands. After conversing, the nurse left her station and walked out the door and then toward them.

"Hi. I understand you are Alisa's parents. I heard you might arrive today. I'm Sharon, your daughter's nurse."

"This is her mother, Elizabeth, and I'm her father, John."

"It's nice to meet you both," she said. "I'm sure you're quite concerned about your daughter."

"Can you give us an update on her condition?"

"The good news is she's stable and has a normal heart rate. Unfortunately, she is still in a coma."

"Do you think she might come out of it soon?"

"It's anyone's guess. It could be today or in a few months. We have no way to predict when she might wake up."

After thanking the nurse, they walked into room 404. Neither of them was emotionally prepared to see her hooked up to medical equipment, an I.V. and the sound of some device beeping to alert her caregivers. Above her, a screen flashed symbols with various vital signs. The room was warm, but the blanket was tucked up to her neck.

John held Elizabeth's arm tightly. She covered her mouth with her hand as she walked toward her daughter. After their initial shock, they went next to the bed and gazed at her. After Elizabeth bent closer, she kissed her daughter's forehead.

John pulled two chairs and placed them next to each other. The one closest to their daughter was for Elizabeth. When she sat, she held Alisa's hand and softly wept.

Slowly, John walked toward the window with tears welling up in his eyes. He looked out the glass and bent forward, holding his stomach. Within minutes, he walked toward the door and started to leave. "I'll be back in a few."

After nodding, her attention was drawn back to her daughter.

While trying to discover where the chapel might be, John avoided eye contact with each person he passed. After walking around for ten minutes, he found it and reached for the chapel door. When he opened it, it was unoccupied. He took in a deep breath and slowly released it. The small room was softly lit from the sun coming through the three stained-glass windows. On the podium was a Bible, and next to it, two chairs. The chapel pews could easily seat twenty. After sitting in the back row, he knelt with his head lowered.

At that moment, he didn't know if he felt angry or confused, so he prayed. "Haven't I done everything you've wanted? Why are you allowing my family to suffer like this? Please. I beg you. Don't take our daughter from us. Danny and Lisa need their mother. And, we need our daughter. So, please, I'll do anything, but don't let her die." While praying, he could no longer hold back his tears. He grabbed a tissue box and wept.

As he sat thinking about various Bible verses, he remembered, "God will never give us more than we can bear." So, he reminded God. "I can't bear to lose Alisa. She's my first-born, I love her. You know how close we are. I beg you. Don't take her from me." Crying, he said, "Please give me direction. I need to get the best possible care for her."

Exhausted, John slumped over the pew. His face started to relax, and his mind had some level of peace. "At least, I know she is in your hands, and you already know the outcome. I do trust you with our daughter."

When he opened his eyes, everything in the room looked brighter, and his mind felt as if it had been cleansed. Okay. I need to be prepared. What questions do I need to ask her doctor? Can she be transferred to San Diego, and, if yes, when? But, first, I should call Scripps or Scripps Green Hospital and find out what options we have once she is transported.

Quickly, he marched back to the nursing staff on the fourth floor. "Is Doctor Nelson here?"

"No. We're sorry, and we don't have an exact time to expect him. Most likely he'll be here after six."

"Can you page him?"

"I can, but it won't do much good, He's in surgeries all day."

"Thank you. I'll check back later."

As he was walking to his daughter's room, a male nurse tapped his shoulder. "Hi, my name's Ian," he said. "I was working when your daughter was brought here. She almost didn't make it; her vital signs were alarmingly low. The doctor gave her a shot to bring her back."

John looked at the young man without a word.

"But, your girl's a fighter, that daughter of yours. I hope you don't feel discouraged because she's in a coma. It's a miracle she made it this far."

John touched the man's shoulder. "Thanks for putting things in perspective. I guess we should be grateful she is alive."

"Your daughter has a will to live, that's for sure. Otherwise, I think we could have lost her."

John's eyes become moist, "It's comforting to know someone like you is looking out for her. I'm glad you reminded me of her inner strength. Those words are precious."

When John walked back into the room, he saw his wife holding their daughter's hand, and her head lowered while praying.

He walked to the other side of the bed and stopped next to Alisa. As he glanced at her, he placed his hand on her face. "So, how's my beautiful girl? We love you, Honey. You're going to get better. We'll make sure you go home as soon as possible. Can you hear me, Sweetie? If you can, squeeze Mom's hand." He looked over at Elizabeth and waited. After she shook her head, he said, "It's okay if you can't react right now. You need your rest."

When he saw the exhaustion on Elizabeth's face, he was surprised when she offered him a smile. She stood and moved into the hall and motioned for him. When he joined her, she asked, "Did you find out anything?"

"The doctor won't be here until later, around six tonight. He's in surgery all day. I met the nurse who was on duty when she was admitted."

"What did he have to say?"

"That we should be glad she's alive. She almost didn't make it. He said it's a miracle she's with us."

"I'm worn out. I have no energy," she said.

John lifted her chin with his hand and said, "Look. We both need rest. We must be at our best when we speak to her physician. Let's go get something to eat."

"I can't leave her alone. Don't ask me to. You go if you want."

"But, we both need to be alert. Please understand, dear. Our minds must be clear when we speak to her doctor. We want to ask intelligent questions."

She shook her head. "I won't leave her alone."

"Be reasonable," he said, "for her sake."

Elizabeth softened. "Alright. I'll go, but only if you stay with her."

"Of course, I'll stay. You go now. Get something to drink and eat. Relax for a few minutes."

Reluctantly, she walked toward the elevator, got in and pushed the button to the basement. After getting off, she went directly to the cafeteria. While standing in line, a woman started up a friendly conversation, but she had difficulty listening. Her mind was preoccupied with her daughter.

After placing her food on the tray, she paid. The woman said, "Would you join me? I hate eating alone. My name is Nicole Wright."

"Hi Nicole, I'm Elizabeth Wilson. And, yes. I will join you."

The women selected a booth to sit at, but first they removed their food and drinks and returned the trays. After sitting, Nicole said, "My sister is in this hospital. I'm here to be with her."

"I hope she will be okay."

"A few days ago, I received a call. When I found out she was in the hospital, I took the next flight out of New York. I found out she needed a stent, but her blocked artery is next to a vital one, so they couldn't do the procedure."

"Oh my, what will happen to her?"

"I was told with medication and diet, she can get her strength back. When she is strong enough for open heart surgery, they will perform a bypass." Nicole took a sip of her coffee, put it down and added two more creamers. "So Elizabeth, do you live in town?"

"No. My husband and I are from San Diego. Our daughter came here for a vacation with her husband. But, they were in a car accident. I gather you live in New York, but you have another accent. Where are you from, originally?"

"Russia."

Elizabeth grinned, "Oh. I was raised in Croatia. My friend and I left as teenagers."

"Two girls, leaving that young. You must have been pretty brave."

"We were talking one day. Without giving it much thought, we went home, packed some things and walked across the border. We went to a small town in Italy, Trieste."

Nicole glanced up. "I know the town, I've been there."

Elizabeth sipped her coffee. "Some man noticed us, asked if we were from Croatia. When we said yes, he said the police department could assist us. He also told us about a camp, not too far away, for refugees. The police department arranged for us to stay at the camp until we got on our feet."

"That must have been quite an experience for two young women."

"You're right. Within a year we lived in three different camps. Mostly we worked in cafeterias or did housekeeping. Many of the men worked in a local sawmill. Eventually my friend and I saved enough money to leave Italy."

"Where did you go?"

"A farm in Washington state, where we culled sugar beets and picked corn."

"How did you get to San Diego?"

Elizabeth smiled. "My aunt lived in Escondido, the north side of San Diego. My uncle needed some workers, so we went. That's where I met John, my husband. Eventually my friend moved back to Washington. Some guy she met asked her to return, so she did."

"How long have you and John been married?"

"Thirty-five years."

"Is your daughter your only child?"

"No. We have two daughters, a son and two grandchildren." Elizabeth studied the woman. "How about you, are you married?"

"No. Not that fortunate. Never married or had kids. Once I was engaged, but he died in Vietnam, never got over him. No one could ever measure up."

"That's too bad. I'm sorry he didn't make it home for you. That had to be difficult."

"It was. But that's life. We all have our stories, don't we?"

Elizabeth stood. "I need to get back, but I enjoyed meeting you. I'm glad you invited me. I needed to get my mind off things. So, thank you."

The woman smiled, nodded and picked up her coffee to take a sip.

While walking back to her daughter's room, she was glad she listened to her husband. She did feel lighter. When she returned, she noticed the smallness of Alisa's space. The two green chairs barely fit. She walked toward the window and looked though the blinds at the ocean. The rain was subsiding. As she turned, she reached for the door to the small restroom with a toilet and sink. She glanced at John; he was stroking their daughter's arm.

Within a few minutes Elizabeth walked toward the bed and stood while going through her purse. She pulled out a brush. After running it through Alisa's hair, she kissed her forehead and cheek and hummed "Amazing Grace," her daughter's favorite worship song.

A skinny, dark-haired nurse abruptly came into the room and started checking Alisa's vital signs. She replaced the I.V. bag, but didn't show signs of social grace. She moved quickly to complete her tasks, and walked to the door to leave.

"Been on duty long?" Elizabeth asked.

"Since eight o'clock." She, then, quickly spun around. "Any changes or concerns, please notify me." She pointed to a board that had her name and phone extension, and left.

Chapter Seventeen

With Carry's stomach in knots, she heard the phone ring and hoped it was Steven with some news. But, instead, it was her brother saying, "Hello."

"Oh. It's you. Hi Stan, what's up?"

"I'm calling to invite you, Abigail and the children over for dinner. Can you find out what day works best for you and her?"

"Stan. You need to be sitting."

"What's wrong? Are you okay, Sis?"

"I'm fine. But, something awful has happened. Alisa and David were in a car accident."

"What? Are they okay?

"They were in Hawaii at the time. Their taxi rolled down an embankment and David didn't make it. He died."

Silence was on the other end of the phone. When he caught his breath, he said, "My God, how's Alisa holding up? Do the kids know? I can't believe he's dead."

"Stan, Alisa's in a coma; she's still in Hawaii."

As she listened to him take another deep breath, she said, "Are you okay?"

"I'm in shock. I can't believe this."

While they talked, she paced. "To make matters worse, we can't reach Abigail to tell her and the children."

"So, they don't know what's going on? What do you mean you can't find them? Why?" Stan asked.

"She isn't answering her home phone, and her car is parked at the yacht club with her cellphone. She might not be able to call." Carry exhaled. "All we can do for now is pray for them."

"So, where do you think she is?"

"She must be on someone's yacht. Steven and I have been searching and asking questions, but so far, no one knows anything."

"Great!"

"At this point, we're very concerned." Carry stopped pacing. "If Alisa doesn't make it, those poor kids will become orphans."

"I know. I hope and pray Alisa will come out of it."

When the doorbell rang, she said, "Hold on. I need to get the door." She placed the phone down, and tried to regroup from her feelings of sorrow. *If it's Steven, I don't want him to see me this gloomy.*

After opening the door, Steven greeted her with a warm hug.

"Thanks. I needed that. Come in. I'm on the phone with Stan. I told him about the accident. Give me a minute. I need to say goodbye."

When she returned to the phone, she felt a little better. "It's Steven. We're trying to figure out what to do next." After a short conversation, she handed the phone to Steven. "He wants to talk to you."

After he took hold of it, he said, "Hi Stan, it's been a long time."

Once the men started talking, she left to gather her things in the bedroom. After picking out a lightweight jacket, she sat on the bed. David's death, Alisa's coma, not being able to talk with Abigail -- it was all taking its toll.

When she heard Steven laugh, she looked up, stood and walked into the living room. When she entered, he was saying goodbye. He placed the phone in its cradle.

"What was so funny?"

"You know your brother. He has a story or joke for every occasion." Carry realized how different men are from women. *They know how to keep things on the surface.* At that moment, she liked the masculine ritual and decided to control her emotions, as well.

As they left, Steven checked the front door lock. When he escorted her to his car, she realized it was a BMW. Earlier, she hadn't paid much attention. While turning on the engine, he offered her a warm smile.

How can he possibly be cheerful with a dead brother-in-law, a sister in a coma and Abigail and the kids missing? On their way to lunch, their conversation lacked depth. After Steven pulled into a parking space, he stopped, got out and came to open her door. When he saw the sadness in her eyes, he said, "You look awful. Are you okay?"

"I'm sorry, Steven. After telling Stan the news, I started feeling incredibly sad. I'm worried about Abigail. She's my best friend. It doesn't seem possible to have this many bad things happen at once. I just feel overwhelmed right now."

Steven took her hand until she stood up and wrapped his arms around her. While her head rested on his shoulder, she wept. "That's okay, let it out," he said. Once she was composed, he moved his thumbs under her eyes and wiped her tears.

"I'm so sorry, Steven. I should be comforting you. They're your sisters."

"Don't worry. I already had a good cry today. I even had to call Mom to cheer me up. As always, she did. I'll tell you all about it later. But first, let me work on soothing you, okay? Are you up for lunch?"

While nodding, she tried to put on a happier face and offered a smile.

"I'm glad you had a good cry," he said. "When we hold things in, the burden gets too heavy."

When they reached the restaurant, a male host greeted them. Within minutes, they were seated in front of a window looking out at the bay. After reading through the menu, he glanced at her. "So, what's going on with Stan? I haven't seen him for a long while."

"He recently celebrated his thirteenth wedding anniversary. He has two sons Lisa and Danny's age. He and his wife both work. Together, they were able to buy their first home, so I would say they're doing well. But, like all of us, they have their moments."

"I'm glad for him. He's a nice guy."

"When did you buy your car?" she asked. "It smells new."

"Four months ago."

"BMW, can you afford it? Your job must pay well."

"I sold my company a little bit ago."

"So, you no longer have a job?"

"Actually I do, I'm a consultant for the investors who bought my company. I specialize in connecting Internet sites.

"Why did you sell your business?"

"I didn't have a life. I worked seven days a week. I'm in my thirties and not married. I didn't have time to meet a woman, let alone start a family."

"Any regrets selling your company?"

"No. It was a good decision, and I got what I wanted -- my life back."

When the waitress arrived, he ordered a bottle of Chardonnay and water with lemon.

"Thanks for taking me here. Anthony's is one of my favorite places because it's near the water, and I like eating fish."

She grinned after he said, "You're welcome; I remembered you like this place."

"You said you talked to your mom -- how's Alisa?"

"No changes. She's still in a coma, but her vitals are good. The doctor said no one knows when or if she might wake up. He said, 'Everything medically is being done, so now it's in God's hands.' Mother was relieved when he included God in the equation. Just hearing her voice lifted my spirits. She's always so hopeful."

After ordering and receiving their food, Carry picked at her meal. "So, what do we do next?"

After he took a few bites and swallowed, he said, "I'll call the Kilgores again after lunch. If I can't reach them, I'm thinking about reporting them missing to the authorities."

"Do you think something bad happened?"

"I'm not sure. But, I don't want to take any chances."

The conversation slowed down while they digested their meals and enjoyed their wine. When the waitress came with the bill, he asked if she would cork the bottle.

Carry reached for her jacket, but then remembered leaving it in the car. Steven paid the bill. As they walked outside, a young man pulling a two-seated pull cart greeted them. "Would you like a ride?" he asked.

Steven took her elbow and said, "No, thank you, my car's not far."

While they strolled down the sidewalk, they enjoyed the bay view and seeing Coronado Island to the left. As they watched small boats sail in front of the USS Ronald Reagan, he said, "When you see small boats next to a naval carrier, you see its largeness."

After glancing at him, she said, "I enjoyed lunch. Thanks."

"You're welcome, Carry. It means a lot to me having you by my side. This situation would be unbearable without you. This crisis makes me appreciate the importance of family and friends."

After Carry abruptly stopped, she said, "As far as I'm concerned, you're doing me a favor. I can't imagine sitting around waiting for news."

They continued walking and soon reached his car. He used his cellphone to call the Kilgores. After a minute, he said, "This time there's no answer, not even a voicemail message. Let's check the yacht club and see if Abigail's car is still there. I need to talk with Mr. Jester one last time."

During their ride, they had little to say. Once they arrived, they saw that her car was still in the same spot, so he pulled up and parked. They silently headed toward Mr. Jester's office. When they reached his door, he knocked, causing the door to open enough to see him sitting with his arms behind his head and eyes closed. After he knocked again, the man quickly sat upright.

"Excuse us. Sorry to disturb you," Steven said.

"Oh, hi. It's you. Find your sister yet?"

"No. That's why we're here." He introduced Carry. The man nodded. "Did you learn anything new?"

"No. But I've been thinking, if her car is in the lot, she must be at sea with someone."

"At this time, we're very concerned," Steven said. "I have to take some action soon. Can you think of anyone they might be with?"

"Only Larry and Sandra, they were last seen with her."

"We called, but they weren't home. Have either Sandra or Larry come in since they were with Abigail and the kids?"

"No, I haven't seen them, which is unusual. They eat here daily when in town."

"Let's try again." Mr. Jester grabbed his phone, dialed and let it ring. "It's ringing." He glanced up. "But, no one's answering."

"I'm going to call the authorities," Steven said.

"You might be overreacting, Steven. If Alisa wasn't in a coma, would you still be this concerned over Abigail?"

He had to think for a minute. "Yes. Actually I would be. Abigail is the type of person who calls several times a day. She keeps Mom posted on what she's doing and where she's going. And, no one has heard from her in two days. Besides that, something caused her to leave so quickly she didn't grab her cellphone. So, yes, I'm very concerned."

Carry said, "Do you think we need to call the police, harbor patrol or the Coast Guard? What do you think?"

"That's your decision, not mine." Mr. Jester had a degree of annoyance in his tone.

"Will it be a problem for you? Having an investigation at the yacht club -- I guess it would -- sorry, but we have no other options here."

As they walked toward the car, they decided to speak with other yacht owners. Perhaps someone saw something. While walking on the dock, they saw a gray-haired man in his sixties wearing blue shorts and a white t-shirt.

After Steven introduced himself and Carry, he said, "I'm looking for my sister. She was traveling with two school-aged children, a boy and girl. The three of them were here a few days ago."

"Why are you looking for them?"

"We're having a family crisis, and we need to let them know. Have you seen them?"

"It's not often I see children around, so I would have noticed. But, to answer your question, no, I haven't seen them. Would you like for me to check around for you?"

"Yes. Thank you," Steven said, while shaking his hand. "I'm very grateful that you want to help, that's wonderful. Here's my card. If you can't reach me, you can call Mr. Jester."

"Have you called the Coast Guard?" the man asked.

"No. We didn't know who to call, the police, harbor patrol or the Coast Guard. What's your opinion?

"If it was my family, I'd call the Coast Guard. Their authority extends beyond the harbor. And, the police can't help if they're out at sea."

"I see. That makes sense," Steven said. "I'm glad we talked with you. Again, thank you."

They walked back to the car and discussed if they should go directly to the Coast Guard office or phone.

"Let's go back to my place," Carry said. "We'll call and make an appointment." At home, we can relax for a few minutes."

"That sounds like a plan."

As they drove, Steven's mind was preoccupied with the thoughts of the day. When he glanced at Carry, her eyes were closed, her seat was pushed back and her head was resting.

After turning on the CD player, he chose a song with piano music. It soothed him and let her rest. While in deep thought, he almost ran a red light, so he quickly stopped. He was glad it didn't disturb Carry's rest. When he reached her house, he pulled up and turned off the engine. He decided to sit in the car while she slept. He, too, was weary, so he closed his eyes.

After Carry awoke, she opened the door to let in fresh air. When she looked over at him, he was shaking his head. He said, "I must have fallen asleep."

"I think I'm a hopeless optimist," Carry said. "I can't wait to go inside to see if she called, yet, deep inside, I know better. I'm starting to worry that she's in some kind of trouble. Oh, Steven, what will we do if she isn't okay?"

Chapter Eighteen

When Carry walked through her front door, immediately she moved toward the answering machine. But, to her disappointment, the few messages she retrieved were not from her friend. After motioning for Steven to be seated, she went into the kitchen, and poured two glasses of iced tea. When she brought them into the living room, she handed one to him.

"I need a city phonebook; do you have one?" he asked.

"Yes. It's in the other room, I'll get it."

When she returned, she gave it to him. "Do you need a pen and paper?"

He nodded. While she was walking away, he called out, "Just paper, I have a pen."

Steven called Mr. Kilgore's number and was disappointed when no one answered.

Carry returned with paper, and he wrote down the number of the Coast Guard.

While smiling at her, he said, "The air conditioning sure feels good, it's nice in here. I thought I would die of heat in the car."

"Tell me about it!" she said, while grinning.

Once she settled down on the couch, he dialed the Coast Guard's phone number. The operator transferred him to a man named Mark Lane. Steven introduced himself, explained the situation, and expressed his concern.

"Do you suspect foul play?" Lane asked.

"I'm not really sure what to think, but it's possible. We haven't heard from her in days, which is out of character for her. She contacts us several times a day, no matter where she might be."

"I see."

"We must let the children know about their parents."

"It must be difficult for you. I'm sure you're very concerned. Can you tell me why you think your sister and the children are at sea?"

"Because her car is still at the yacht club, and she was seen dining with family friends who are yacht owners. When we first started looking for them, we questioned some people. We spoke with a Mrs. Harding, another yacht owner. She saw a woman with a boy and girl taking bags or luggage from her trunk. Later, she identified the car as Abigail's. From what I gathered, she was the last person to see them. We're not sure what happened after that. But, things don't feel right. She would have called us by now, that we're sure of. But, wherever they are, we must find them."

"What vessel might they be on?"

"Likely, they're with Mr. and Mrs. Larry Kilgore, on their vessel. Someone overheard them talking. Larry wanted to show them his new yacht. We phoned their residence three times, but they haven't been home, and they don't have an answering machine. When we spoke with Mr. Jester, the dock master, he said the Kilgores had been planning on staying ashore. But, who knows, they may have changed their minds."

"What's the name of their vessel?"

Steven put the phone on speaker. "I don't know. But, I'm sure Mr. Jester would know."

"I need the names of each person missing."

"Abigail Wilson is my sister. Danny Glover is my nephew and Lisa Glover is my niece."

"I need the children's ages."

"Danny's twelve. Lisa's ten."

After his call, Mark Lane started an official report. He grabbed the phonebook and searched for the yacht club's number and called. He asked to speak with Mr. Jester and was soon connected. He stated the reason for the call.

Defensively, Mr. Jester said, "I was going to call you."

"About three missing people?"

"Yep. What can I do for you?" Jester asked.

"Can you give me the name of the Kilgores' vessel?"

"Of course, it's called the *Great Discoverer*. Do you need the length and color?"

"Sure."

After he had given the information, Jester asked, "Is there anything else you need?"

"Is the vessel in its slot?

"No. But, I'm not sure if the captain took it out by himself or if the Kilgores were with him."

"Was a float plan filed?"

"You mean by Larry? If he's on the yacht, I'm sure he did."

"What's their captain's name?"

"Don't know. Their regular guy's on vacation. They hired someone to help temporarily, but I haven't met the man."

After the conversation ended, Mark hung up and quickly grabbed the VHF radio, turned it to channel sixteen, and hailed the yacht. "Calling the *Great Discoverer*, this is the Coast Guard, come in please. Calling the *Great Discoverer*, this is the Coast Guard, come in please. Switch to channel sixty-eight, if you read me." No response.

After waiting for a few minutes, he tried to hail the vessel again, but still no answer. After phoning his department head, he requested permission to get a search team together.

*   *   *

When Matt heard a motorboat, he peered out the porthole in time to see Forelli leave in a rush. "Great! What now?" He turned to Robert. "You need to take over. Our captain just abandoned ship."

Jack turned to the others, and said, "If Forelli left, something's up. We need to leave, too. Now!"

While Matt continued to look out the porthole, Forelli and the boat got smaller until it was next to the touring vessel. Then, the touring vessel changed course.

"For God's sake, let's get out of here." Jack paced, the lines on his forehead deepened.

After Matt stepped closer, he said, "Hey, for us to panic now is the worst thing we can do. We need to stay calm and decide what to say when the authorities get involved."

"Let's say that the Kilgores invited us. They're dead, so they can't dispute it. Or, we could say Forelli invited us." Jack continued to pace with his hands folded behind his back. "If we stay, we will be murder suspects, guaranteed."

"But think for a minute! Wouldn't it look more suspicious if we ran off? Believe me, it's going to seem bad for Forelli, especially with his federal criminal record."

"What will the woman say?"

"What do you mean?"

"Whatever story we give, she can dispute it," Jack said.

"We already told her Forelli invited us, so let's stick to that," Matt responded.

Jack abruptly stopped. "She knows we're looking for something valuable. That alone would be a motive for murder."

"You're right, she does know. But, I would rather take my chances with a good attorney than run away. If we leave, it will give the authorities something to sink their teeth into. Let's decide what to say and stick to it. Okay? So, if anyone wants to leave, do it now."

Brent stood and stared without any verbal response.

"Okay. We're in this together, right?" No response. "None of us are murderers, right? It was Forelli and the Top Dogs who fled, correct? So, pointing the finger at them will be easy, agreed?"

"But, what will the woman say?" Jack asked. "Once she tells her story, we might be in big trouble. She might even accuse us of kidnapping. That means that the FBI will get involved."

"The FBI? They'll be called, anyway."

"Why?"

"Because the murders took place at sea, that's why," Matt said.

"Hey, let's not sweat it too much. It's our word against hers," Brent said, calmly.

"Hopefully, when she tells her side, it won't sound like a kidnapping," Matt said. "I'm sure we'll be questioned on why we didn't return, once the bodies were found."

"Tell the truth. We were trying to find the murderer."

"I'm not sure if anyone will buy that," Jack said, while crossing his arms. "We should have notified the authorities the moment the bodies were found."

"Don't forget, those bodies were dead when we arrived. We'll say the woman may have done it."

"The woman's name is Abigail. Besides, what would be her motive?"

"That's for the authorities to discover," Brent said.

"If we say we suspect her, it might protect us from being accused of kidnapping."

"Okay, let's stay on the yacht and head back to the dock, all in agreement?" Everyone stayed silent, so Matt pivoted. "I'm going to the helm. I need to tell Robert what's going on."

After he reached the wheelhouse, he gave Robert the rundown, and he agreed to stay on the yacht and take his chances. Quickly he, too, altered his course toward the dock.

"It will look bad for Forelli, him running off," Matt said.

"The same holds true for the Top Dogs," Robert said, with alert eyes.

"Matt, will you convince the woman to say we were invited?"

"No, I don't want to involve her. I don't think she'll hurt us too badly, anyway."

"Hope you're right, Matt."

"Besides, if I ask her to lie and she tells them that, it'll make us look worse, as if we're hiding something."

"When we're questioned, what should I say?"

"That Forelli asked us to help out, and to have some pleasurable sea time. Saying we're deck hands might work. We all work together, and our jobs are on a vessel. The Top Dogs have no choice, but to back up our story."

"Okay, that sounds good."

Abigail and the children sensed something was going on, but had no idea what, except that the vessel had changed course, and, earlier, they heard a motorboat leave. She hoped that the ordeal would soon be over. *Okay, stay calm and keep the children safe,* she told herself. *Your only task right now is to stay out of the men's way.*

While trying to decide what to do, she heard Matt calling her from the main salon. While climbing the ladder, she decided to keep her distance from Jack. She still had no use for him and would never trust the man. When she stepped into the main salon, she saw Brent. He said, "We're heading back."

As she listened to those words, she felt both joy and fear. She was glad they were returning, yet feared they may not make it back alive.

The children ran to the porthole while pushing each other, trying to peer through the glass.

"Look." Danny pointed. "That big boat's leaving."

Soon, Matt came up behind Abigail, grabbed her shoulders and spun her around. "We're heading back. Forelli jumped ship. We think he knows something."

"Are we safe? Will we get home okay?" She told herself, *I'm actually expecting an honest answer from him.*

"As long as I'm alive, you and the children are safe. I promise you that."

"Matt, I'm sure you're sincere, but I'm not convinced our safety is completely in your hands. There are four of you. And, we know everything."

"You are right," he said. "I think we'll kill the three of you and dump your bodies overboard. That will solve our problems permanently."

"Funny."

"Well, that's exactly what you were insinuating," he said.

"You make me feel like an idiot."

"That isn't my intent. I only want you and the children to know you're safe. We are not going to harm any of you. Far from it; I want to protect you." Slowly, he sat.

Her face turned red once she realized he cared about her. It was the first time she allowed herself to believe him.

"I'm sorry, Matt. I've treated you with such disdain while you have done nothing to deserve that attitude. Right now, I don't know who the good guys are or the bad. I thought the Kilgores were nice people, but found out they were smugglers who had cheated other criminals. So, right now, my perspective is a little warped."

"You're so cute," he said. "I love your openness, it's so refreshing. Someday I would love for us to reevaluate the events of the past two days -- see what insight we might have."

Soon, Jack came in and sat next to Matt. "Has anyone touched the bodies or the bed area?"

"No, why?"

"I want to make sure no one left any evidence pointing to any of us."

"No. But, that might be true of the assassin, too. If the person wore gloves, and disposed of the weapon at sea, it'll be difficult, at best, to find the real killer."

"If there's no evidence pointing to any of us, they can't very well bring criminal charges, right?" Jack asked. He turned to

Abigail. "If you point to us, we'll do the same to you. We know the murders took place before we arrived. So, you, young lady, like it or not, are the main suspect."

She grinned at him. "Right now, Jack, I don't care who did it. I just want to get the children home safely. That's my only concern. After that, I might start being concerned about who the murderer might be, okay?"

Matt stood, placed his hands on her shoulders and stared at his best friend. "You heard the lady. Enough talk already. Let's chill out for a while. We'll be needing our strength soon enough."

Chapter Nineteen

After Wayne Dryer ended his phone call with his wife, he became weary. Once again, she was blaming him for their son's school suspension for fighting. When he heard the door open, he glanced up.

When Officer Joe Martin entered the room, he was wearing his hat and uniform, and as always, was clean shaven. His left eyebrow was raised, which was a dead giveaway something important had come up.

While Dryer sat at his desk, his chin was high to better see around his droopy eyelids, half-covering his eyes, which gave him a sleepy look. Some accused him of being arrogant because it seemed as if he was always looking down at people. "What's up?" he asked.

After Martin came closer, he leaned forward and placed both hands on the desk saying, "I need you to head a mission. A woman and two children are missing, and presumed to be on a ninety-foot yacht called the *Great Discoverer*."

"Who reported them missing?"

"The brother of the missing woman called saying he thinks there's a chance of foul play. But, in any case, he needs to find them." "Why? What's the urgency?"

"A family crisis -- two family members were in a car accident, which resulted in the death of a man and put a woman in a coma. The two accident victims are the parents of the missing children."

"Wow, how sad for the family."

"You'll need to get a move on it."

"Who's on my team?"

"You decide."

"How many?"

"Four."

"Has the helicopter gone out?"

"No. They won't be used this time."

"Why?"

"I'm not sure, didn't ask."

Dryer waved for him to sit and walked from behind his desk with a tablet and pen in hand. While resting his body on the desk, he asked, "What else can you tell me about the case?"

"The missing woman had a parked car at the yacht club with her cellphone in sight. She must have left in a hurry. Earlier today, we hailed the vessel, but no one responded. To me, that's suspicious."

"Did they file a float plan?"

"Matter of fact, they did. If you'll excuse me, I'll get it."

Officer Martin stood and walked until he was out of sight.

Thirty minutes later, Dryer had his team in place and they were moving northeast on a Coast Guard cutter. He figured the missing yacht was someplace between San Diego and San Clemente Island, it was the most likely location for an overnight stay.

Once on their way, Dryer asked his captain to hail the *Great Discoverer*. To his surprise, this time, someone quickly responded.

"Switch to channel sixty-eight," Dryer said. "What's your longitude and latitude?"

Robert gave their precise location.

"After hailing your vessel earlier, no one responded, why was that?"

"We have a situation," Robert said. "The yacht owners were murdered, and our captain abandoned ship."

"Murdered?"

"Yes. And, our captain took off on a smaller boat, so we're heading back to the harbor."

Quickly, Dryer's expression changed. His jaw and lips tightened while he stiffly stood. "We're on our way, over." Immediately, he contacted the FBI and spoke with Special Agent Roger Weatherman.

Once Weatherman understood the situation, he said, "Bring the yacht to the FBI docking area. We'll notify you later as to which slot. I'll have a team ready to conduct interviews. Don't let anyone off the vessel, including the woman and kids! Everyone must be questioned before disembarking, understand?"

"Yes. I know the routine."

The Coast Guard Cutter was on its way. Once it reaches the *Great Discoverer*, the men can easily gain access to the vessel. Matt was the first to greet them and offered his hand. "We're glad you found us so soon."

Dryer glanced around. "Where are the woman and kids?

"They're waiting inside."

After he and his men took a quick scan of the exterior, Dryer asked Matt, "Where's a good place to talk with Miss Wilson?"

"Follow me." Everyone quietly walked into the main salon. When he saw her with the children, he walked over, extended his hand and said, "You must be Abigail Wilson."

"Yes. But, how did you know my name?"

"Steven Wilson, your brother, called to report you missing."

"He phoned you? But, how did he know we were in trouble?"

"When no one heard from you for several days, he became concerned. Normally, he said, you communicate with family and friends several times a day."

"How did you know where we were?"

"From what I understand, he found your car at the yacht club, and a woman said she saw you and the children getting things out of your trunk."

"I see. He's right, I do call Mom several times a day."

"Are you and the children okay?"

"Yes. We're okay. But I'm sickened about what happened to Sandra and Larry."

"I can understand why." He turned to face Matt. "Where's Robert? Was that him at the wheel?"

"Yes. Do you want him?"

"No. Not now. When I'm finished speaking with Miss Wilson, I'll find him. But, first I need to instruct my men." After turning his back to her, he said, "Please give me the names of each man on the vessel. She pointed to each man as she said his name.

Once Dryer knew the name of each man, he walked over to Officer Clint Hale. "Stay with Matt and search the lower deck." As he looked over his shoulder to Matt, Hale nodded.

As the man moved toward him, Matt noticed his bright red hair against his light skin. Even with his tan, he was pale.

After Officer Hale extended his hand and introduced himself, he asked. "Are the bodies on the lower level?"

Matt nodded.

"I'll need for you to take me there." When Matt didn't quickly respond, he said, "Let's go now."

"Sure," Matt said. "Follow me." They headed toward the ladder and went down to the lower level.

Abigail and the children silently listened to Dryer give instructions to Officer Butch Smith, telling him to bring two chairs into the galley, and interview Jack. When he finished, he was told to interview Brent. "And, for God's sake, Smith, take good notes."

While Officer Smith and Jack were on their way to the galley, Dryer told Brent, "Go join Robert. When Officer Smith is finished, he'll come for you."

From a distance Abigail could hear Jack's abrasively loud voice responding to his interrogation. Then, Smith quickly closed the hatch.

When Danny turned to his aunt, he asked, "What's going on?"

"Don't worry. They need to talk to everyone separately, that's all."

"Can we go home now?"

"Soon we'll all be heading home."

Lisa tugged on Abigail's arm. "Will you stay, if they talk to me?"

"Sure, if it's allowed."

"When can we call Mommy?"

Abigail took Lisa's chin in her hand. "You can call her as soon as we get to a phone. Perhaps one of the men can loan us theirs."

While looking down, Danny said, "I miss her and Dad."

"I know."

Lisa blinked while inspecting the tabletop, and then stared up at her aunt. "What questions will they ask?"

"I'm not sure. But, please, only tell the truth."

After Agent Butch Smith completed his interview with Jack, he told him to wait outside and not to talk to anyone.

After finding Brent, Officer Smith and he went directly into the galley. While asking some basic questions, he neglected to record his answers. Smith noticed the similarities between him and Brent. They were both stocky, had sandy blond hair and were in their mid-thirties. Something about Brent reminded him of his kid brother.

Little time was wasted on small talk. Instead, he started with some direct questions.

"What do you know about the murders?"

"Not much. I know they were shot, and the bodies were found on their bed. That's pretty much it."

"Who found them?" he asked.

"Matt."

"Do you know who killed them?"

"No."

"Any suspect?"

"Not sure."

"Come on; now, don't tell me you have no suspicion."

"No one on the vessel right now," he said, while adjusting his legs.

"What do you mean by, right now?"

"Our captain jumped ship, so that makes me wonder -- why?"

"I see."

"What's the name of your captain?"

"Forelli, Anthony Forelli."

"How long had he worked for the Kilgores?"

"A few days."

"Why such a short time?"

"He's just filling in a while."

"How can we find this Forelli guy?"

"Contact the T.D. Harbor Cruise Ship's administration. He is one of their captains. Their company gives harbor tours."

"How do you know Forelli?"

"We work for the same company."

"How did you end up on this yacht?"

"He invited us, in case he needed help."

"What kind of help?"

"Deck hands, cooks, whatever was needed. We agreed, so we could spend time on this beautiful yacht."

After Officer Smith ended his interview, reviewed his notes and asked, "Can I get your last name?"

"I already told you," Brent said, and then spelled it.

"Where can we reach you?"

After Brent stated his home and work addresses and phone numbers, he stood and turned. "Can I leave now?"

"Yes. But, you'll be questioned again by the FBI."

"I understand."

Abigail and the children held hands and listened to Officer Dryer.

"They'll be okay," Dryer said. "This interview won't take long."

He asked for general information, wrote it down and asked, "Did the three of you come on this yacht on your own accord?"

"Yes. The Kilgores were family friends. We had a meal with them at the yacht club. They showed us their new vessel. Lisa asked to go out sometime, and they insisted we stay and go on an overnight venture."

Abigail was uncomfortable when Dryer glared at her through his half-covered eyelids.

"What happened to the Kilgores?"

"I think you know what happened. It's not something I'm willing to talk about in front of the children. Can't it wait?"

"What else would you like to say about your experience, Miss Wilson?"

After pulling away from the children slightly, she said, "Everything was fine until we were at the wheelhouse. Larry wanted to talk to his wife, so he left me in charge of the wheelhouse. The children and I were at the helm for a few hours and needed to leave."

"I'm sorry, miss, but did you say you were at the helm for several hours?"

"Yes, until we needed a break. So, I shut down the engine, and the three of us used the head and found some refreshments. When we searched for Larry, we couldn't find him anywhere."

"When did you discover what happened to them?"

"Please. Not now."

"Sorry, it can wait," he said and turned his attention to his paperwork. He reviewed a few things and asked, "Is there anything you would like to add?"

"The men were looking for something valuable. Matt offered us five thousand dollars if we found the thing and said we could then go home. We wanted to leave so we decided to help. However, the item was never found. Danny discovered a jeweled egg, but the men determined it didn't have the value of what they were seeking.

"What were you told to find?"

"That was vague. All we knew was that it was smaller than a breadbox and worth a fortune."

"Thank you, Miss Wilson, that information might shed some light on things." He stood. "That will be all for now." He walked away in the direction of the wheelhouse.

After her interview, she entered the galley for water and to get something for the children. When she returned, Agent Smith was talking to Danny and Lisa. Nearby Jack stared out the porthole.

It didn't take too long before Dryer returned and waved for Officer Smith to come to him. Dryer walked over to the children and smiled. "Okay, you two. I'll need to talk to you next."

"Can my aunt stay?" Lisa asked.

"She certainly can, young lady."

After reviewing his earlier notes from Abigail, he said, "Danny, do you know what happened to Mr. and Mrs. Kilgore?"

"Something bad, but I don't know what."

Lisa piped in, "They went home in a small boat and didn't tell us." Her chin was low and her eyes were tearing. After Abigail placed her arm around her, she became calm.

Dryer thanked the children. He said to Abigail, "When we return, each of you will be questioned by the FBI."

When the interview was over, Dryer decided to have Steven tell his family the bad news.

Chapter Twenty

Officer Dryer smiled, while glancing at Danny. "You're going home with us on our Coast Guard cutter."

The boy grinned. "Can I visit the wheelhouse?"

After nodding, he said, "Sure, let's go." When they stepped onto the cutter they went directly to the helm. Once they arrived, he said, "Danny, this is Captain Larkin."

With a wide grin, the boy said, "Hi."

"Is this your first visit to a wheelhouse?"

"No. For several hours, we were at the yacht's helm, and I helped at the wheel, too."

The captain chuckled. "So, you're experienced; I could use an extra crew member." While motioning for him to come closer, he said, "If you want to help out, you'll need to come place both hands on the wheel." After Danny complied, the captain stood behind the boy.

When the men heard voices, they turned to see Lisa and Abigail standing near the hatch. Danny glanced over his shoulder, saw Lisa and snickered. Soon, Abigail came closer and touched his arm. "We're going to the lower level -- are you okay?" After he nodded, she said, "Come find us when you're finished, agreed?"

With a cheerful voice, Danny said, "Yes, but I like it here."

When she and the girl turned to leave, Dryer said, "Would you like me to escort you two ladies?"

"That'd be nice, thank you."

While leading them to the main deck, he put his hand behind Lisa's head. "What do you think of our vessel, little lady?"

"It's nice," she said, sweetly.

"Do you have a place for us to rest?" Abigail asked. "Is it possible to have some privacy?"

"Sure. The lounge is small, but you won't be disturbed."

Shortly, they reached their destination. Although the lounge was small, it had a certain charm. There was a sofa and end tables with lamps. To the right, there was a chair with a magazine holder nearby. The decorative round rug and throw pillows on the couch brightened the cabin. Abigail took in a deep breath and reached for a magazine. Once seated, Lisa came and sat next to her and leaned in closer.

Dryer decided to talk to his men. "Before I leave, is everything satisfactory?"

"Yes. Thank you, this is perfect."

After he was gone, Lisa glanced up. "Is Matt in trouble?"

"Why? Are you worried about him?"

"Yes, he isn't with us. He is on the yacht."

"I know, Honey. But, don't worry, he is a big boy -- he can take care of himself. He'll be just fine." But, her thoughts were similar to Lisa's. She, too, worried about him getting caught up in a murder investigation, even though her gut said he didn't murder anyone.

Before speaking to his men, Dryer reviewed the paperwork from the interrogations. It seemed that Captain Forelli was the one person each man thought capable of murder. Yet, the timeline indicated he arrived after the bodies were discovered.

When the last member of his team arrived, he asked, "What's your opinion of Robert or Brent? Do any of you see them as suspects?"

"No. Not of murder."

"Do you think Matt or Jack could be the killer?"

Smith said, "I think Matt's the ringleader, and Jack's his close friend, while Brent and Robert are followers. As far as Forelli goes, he works with them, but there's no closeness."

"Thank you, Smith," he said and then turned to address his team. "Each of you did a great job taking notes, even you, Smith. But, as of now, the investigation is over, and the FBI has taken over the case. Because of our team, however, the woman and children are safe. So, thank you. You may end your day and go home."

After they were gone, Dryer went into his office. His cabin had a desk, a phone, a chair and a lamp, and little else. While working on his report, he included all the facts and details. So far, there was no direct evidence linking anyone to the murders. If Forelli was ruled out, it was possible for someone else to have come, murdered the couple and fled, unless the murderer was still hiding.

As the Coast Guard cutter pulled up to its designated slot, Dryer noticed three FBI special agents standing in wait. Special Agent Ned Parker came on board the Coast Guard cutter with his tan face and white forehead. The man was five feet, eight inches, and weighed around a hundred and seventy pounds.

After Dryer greeted him and had a proper introduction, Dryer asked, "Do you play golf?"

"Yes. Why? It's my favorite pastime since my family moved up north."

"Do you have a handicap?

"Yes, but nothing to brag about," said Parker. "Enough about me, we're told two dead bodies are on the yacht."

"That's right, the owners, Larry and Sandra Kilgore. Both were shot and killed."

"Have any suspects?"

"Yes. Three men need further investigation. Two are on the yacht."

"Do you have names and phone numbers?"

"Yes. The men on the yacht are Matthew Willingham and Jack Oliver."

"What makes them suspects?"

"Matt's the ringleader of three men, and Jack is a close friend. Captain Anthony Forelli fled after he heard us hailing them -- making him also a suspect. In addition, Miss Wilson indicated that Matt and his cronies were searching for some valuable object. Also, we discovered that four of the men work for the same company, with the exception of Jack Oliver, who is a business owner."

"What company do the men work for?"

"Let's see." Dryer opened his folder. "It's in here," he said. "Yes, it's the T.D. Corporation." He handed a copy of the report to the special agent. "This is for your records."

"Good. That's helpful, it'll save time." While thumbing through it, he pivoted when he saw Special Agent Mitch Vorty. After greeting him, he introduced Dryer.

Parker said, "Vorty, you'll be questioning the woman and children on this vessel while I'll be on the yacht."

Turning to Dryer, he said, "Thanks again, your men were quite helpful. Can you do something else for me? Will you introduce Special Agent Vorty to Miss Wilson?"

"Consider it done." The men shook hands, and Parker was on his way.

While walking toward the lounge, they saw the yacht pulling into the FBI slot. Dryer said, "That didn't take long." When they reached the lounge, he opened the hatch and saw Abigail and Lisa asleep. He said, "I'll go get the boy."

Instantly, Lisa and Abigail opened their eyes and became aware of their surroundings. Once they seemed alert, Dryer introduced them and said, "Special Agent Vorty needs to talk to you alone. Can I take Lisa with me?"

She nodded.

Dryer turned and said, "Young lady, want some hot chocolate?"

"Sure." When the girl came closer, he reached for her hand.

"Miss Wilson, once again, my name's Special Agent Vorty. I'm with the FBI. I need to get an official statement from you."

She glanced at him. "First, I prefer being called Abigail, and second, I need a drink and to use the ladies' room, is that all right?"

"I understand." He stood, while she left the cabin. While alone, Vorty opened the report Dryer gave him. Abigail returned with a bottle of water. She handed one to him.

He remained standing until she was seated and thanked her. "Can I get the correct spelling of your full name?"

She reached for her purse, thumbed through her wallet, pulled out a card and handed it to him.

After examining it, he placed it in his pocket.

"Please tell me everything you can remember and let me decide what's important and what's not, understand?"

She nodded and leaned forward. Her elbows rested on her knees with her fingers intertwined. She recounted the events, starting with running into the Kilgores at the restaurant and ending with being on the Coast Guard cutter. Vorty stopped her a few times to review his notes. Once the interview was completed, she stood, looked out the porthole and sat again with both hands on the seat as she stretched.

"Who murdered them?" he asked.

After crossing her legs and looking down, she said, "I told Officer Dryer. I don't know."

"Miss Wilson, I'm here to help you remember. Each time you repeat your story, you'll recall more details. So, please, don't get annoyed with the same questions by different investigators. It's done intentionally, and it's difficult, we know that, but we need to ask."

"I see. Maybe Jack did it, but I don't have evidence, I don't like or trust the man, that's all. Or, it could be Captain Forelli; he was very secretive."

"Abigail. Did you murder them?"

Instantly, her cheeks flushed, and she turned away while tears fell.

"I need an answer. Did you kill them, Miss Wilson?"

Tearfully, she glanced at him. She slowly said, "I do feel responsible. They would be alive, if it wasn't for us."

"What do you mean?"

"They planned on staying ashore, until we ran into them. But, because they were kind enough to ask us to stay overnight at sea, they're dead. If I had said no, they would still be alive right now."

"Did you murder the Kilgores, Miss Wilson?"

Slowly, she shook her head. "But, I feel indirectly responsible." Once she sat straight, she became more focused. She stared into his eyes. "No. I did not kill them. They were family friends."

Special Agent Vorty reached over and patted her hand. "We'll find their killer, okay?"

She nodded. "I hope so, will you notify us?"

"Yes. I'll phone you. That's a promise." They sat in silence for some time. Then, he said, "That's all for now. Can you please arrange for the lad to come?"

"Yes. Of course." When she stood, so did he. She smiled and touched his arm as she passed him to fetch Danny.

Special Agents Parker and Morris quickly gained access to the yacht. Morris tapped his fingernails on his teeth while Parker grimaced at his gross nervous habit. After entering the main level, Parker thanked the Coast Guard officers and asked them to return to the cutter.

While interviewing Matt and the others, he asked, "Have any of you been to the crime scene?"

Matt stepped forward. "Yes. I found their bodies."

Parker instructed Morris to interview Jack, Robert and Brent separately. He turned to Matt. "Where's a good place for privacy?"

"Maybe the library. Come, I'll show you." Once they arrived, Parker leaned his backside on the desk.

"Please be seated, Mr. Willingham."

"Call me Matt."

"Matt. Why is it you and your men were on this yacht?"

"Captain Forelli asked us. He said it was a new yacht, and he wanted help."

"Miss Wilson said you and your men were searching for something, what might that be?"

"What?"

"You heard me."

"Oh. You mean some mysterious object?"

"Yes."

As he sat, Matt's shoulders slumped and his chin lowered. "There were rumors that the Kilgores smuggled some valuable object, and it was hidden on the yacht. We were curious, so we decided to search."

"Did you find it?"

"No. It must have been just a rumor."

"Why didn't you report the murders immediately?"

"I wanted to find the killer. I didn't want to be accused."

"But, was it you?"

"I'm no killer! I don't believe in, or own, guns…they're too dangerous."

"It was you who found them dead, right?"

"Yes. That's true. The only person capable of murder is Captain Forelli, but he came after I found their bodies."

"Are you sure Forelli arrived later?"

"Yes. Robert and Brent went directly to the wheelhouse, he wasn't there."

"Tell me the relationship between you and the captain?"

"We worked for the same firm."

"What's your relationship with Jack Oliver?"

"We're childhood friends. I asked him to join me. I wanted him to be on the water on a beautiful yacht. But, look how that turned out."

"Did the Kilgores invite you to board their vessel?"

"No. I told you, Forelli did."

"Who do you think is the killer?"

"None of us had a motive. We didn't even know they were going to be on the yacht."

"You had motive. The valuable object is the motive."

"We didn't know what it was and still don't. So, why would we kill for some unknown object? In addition, Forelli said they were staying ashore. And, he neglected to inform us of the plan change. But, he had to know; Mr. Kilgore must have given him the course chart. We were shocked to see a woman and kids, let alone two dead people."

"Where did you find their bodies?"

"On the lower level, in the master suite, do you want me to show you?"

"Yes." Parker and Matt headed for the ladder. Once on the lower level, they walked toward the master suite. Parker was literally breathing down his neck. Matt started to open the hatch, but hesitated and left it partially open.

"Is something wrong?"

"I can't go in there. It's too creepy." He backed up into the passageway.

"Stay there," Parker said, as he proceeded. When he saw the bodies, he was taken aback. He took his camera and photographed the crime scene from all angles. "Where are the damn crime-scene investigators when you need them?" he muttered. "Has anyone touched the bodies?" he asked Matt.

"No, absolutely not. Even when Abigail and I were in here, we didn't enter much past the hatch, and the men wouldn't come near here."

"Thank you, Matt; please return to the others, I'll be up shortly." Parker pulled out a small pad and wrote, "Future investigation is needed: Matt seemed to feel too guilty to return to the crime scene. Also, speak with Forelli and the owners of T.D. Corporation."

Chapter Twenty-one

Once Abigail and the children were told by the FBI agent that they were free to go, they headed for the gate. She was concerned about Matt and his men, but, at that moment, she was too exhausted to care.

After picking up their personal belongings, they walked to the end of the federal property line. She saw Steven and Carry waiting for them. "How did you know we would be here?"

"The Coast Guard kept me posted," Steven said. "Come here." He extended his arms to give a big hug. Danny and Lisa joined in.

"What made you contact them?" she asked.

"Your cellphone, it was on your front seat overnight, so I knew something was up. You're never without it." Steven picked up her traveling bags.

"You never go off without telling us," Carry said.

While walking to the car, Steven said to the children, "I bet you're hungry."

Danny grinned and nodded enthusiastically.

Lisa grabbed her uncle's arm. "Can we go to McDonald's?"

"No way," Danny yelled. "Any place but there, let's go to Rubio's." The adults expressed amusement at their negotiating skills.

They reached the car. Steven knelt down to Lisa. "I was thinking about the Harbor House, at Seaport Village." He stood and turned to his sister. "How does that sound?"

"Sounds good to me, isn't that nice of your uncle?"

When they reached his car, Steven drove them to the parking lot at the yacht club. Once they arrived, they got out and headed for Abigail's car. After placing the luggage in her truck, the adults discussed who would ride in which car. The children made the choice for them. Lisa asked, "Can we ride in your new car, Uncle Steven?"

"Sure. That's fine." After saying goodbye to the women, they returned to his car.

Once alone, Abigail and Carry hugged. "I'm glad we're together. Boy, do I need a friend."

"I'll drive," Carry said.

"That would be great."

Once Carry was behind the wheel, she pulled away and started questioning Abigail. "Were you forced to leave?"

"No. Nothing like that."

"What happened? Why no calls? Do you know how concerned we were?"

"Everything happened too fast, so I forgot my stupid phone, and we couldn't find one on the yacht."

"Are you okay?"

"No, Carry, I'm not. I just went though the most horrific ordeal of my life. Someone murdered the Kilgores."

"I know. We heard. Who did it?"

"We don't know yet. They're still investigating."

"It had to be one of those men."

"It's possible, but not likely."

"Well, it had to be one of them, who else?" Carry's tone was spiced with sarcasm.

"Frankly, I don't know. It's also possible someone came, murdered them and left."

Carry reached over to touch Abigail's arm. "You're right about the FBI agents. They're trained professionals. Let them figure things out."

"I'll tell you one thing. Not knowing was nerve-racking."

"Steven and I were so worried about you guys."

"I'm concerned about him, Carry, he looks exhausted. Is he okay?"

"Yes, now that you're safely home, he'll be fine." She looked ahead. "Stan called. He wants you and the kids to come for dinner."

"That sounds wonderful, perhaps next weekend, when we get back to a routine. Tell him thanks for the invite."

"Sure."

Abigail spotted a space not far from the restaurant. After parking, they held hands, while strolling toward the entrance. They said, "What a beautiful day," in unison and chuckled at the coincidence. Hugging each other, Abigail said, "It looks like we still think alike."

"Hi Steven, did Danny and Lisa behave themselves?" she said, lightheartedly.

"Those two, they're a handful," he said, while winking at his sister.

"Ask for a window seat, will you?"

The hostess greeted them and showed them to a booth by a window.

"This is pleasant, thank you, Steven," Abigail said, with a warm smile.

Once seated, Lisa and Danny stared out the window at a mime doing his routine.

The waiter approached the table and silently waited until Steven looked up. He then handed each of them two menus, one for specials and one with daily offerings.

"I'm Vince. I'll be your waiter."

When he said, "I'm Steven, I'll be your customer," Vince wasn't amused.

"I'll return to take your orders."

When he came back, he said, "Is your party ready to order, sir?"

The women ordered wine, the children asked for chocolate malts, and Steven ordered iced tea.

"Give us a few more minutes for our food orders." The man backed away, circled and headed to leave.

Steven asked the children what looked good to them. They both asked for hamburgers and fries.

Once again, Vince returned. "Ready, sir?"

Steven placed the order for the children and himself, the women requested specialty salads.

Vince backed up and turned to leave. Steven whispered, "He walks as if he has a stick up his ass."

When Danny laughed, Lisa elbowed her brother. Steven said, "I wonder if he's trained to be like that or if it comes naturally?"

"What do you mean?" Danny asked.

"That waiter, he's so formal. This is a nice restaurant, but that guy needs to relax a little."

"Guess what, Uncle Steve? I found an egg; it was worth lots of money."

"Where?"

"In the library, on the yacht."

"So, it belongs to the Kilgores, right?" Steven's cellphone rang. When he answered, it was FBI Special Agent Parker wanting to speak with Abigail. "I tried your sister's cellphone, but no one answered."

"She's with me, we're having lunch. I'll put her on."

After speaking to the agent, she handed the phone back to Steven. "I need to check with them before leaving town. They might have questions."

"Haven't you been through enough?"

"But, Steven, you don't understand. I want to help. I need to know who did it."

The waiter reached over Abigail's shoulder to place food in front of Lisa and Danny. He left and then returned with salads for the women. "I'll be back with your meal, sir."

Abigail picked at her salad. She was thinking about Larry and Sandra's dead bodies lying on their bed. And, about Matt and how he did when he was interrogated.

During the meal, the conversation was light. When they finished eating, Steven paid the bill, and they walked out to Abigail's car. "I'll take the kids," he said. "I'll follow you home."

"Can we go on the merry-go-round?" Lisa asked.

"No, not today, Honey, I need to take you back to your aunt's." The child didn't argue or pout. After the women were in their car and drove off, he walked the children to his car.

During the drive home, Abigail and Carry kept the conversation light. "The first thing I want when I get home is…"

Carry grinned. "I know, you want a nice long bath, with lit candles all around, and a glass of wine."

Abigail laughed. "You know me too well." She turned down the volume on the radio. "I can't express how exhausted I feel."

"You three have been through a lot."

"Yep, but they're more resilient."

"They're children. They depend on you. But, you have all the responsibility, so, of course, it was mentally and emotionally harder on you."

"Remember the last time we spoke?" Abigail asked.

"Yes."

"I often wished we had made dinner plans for that night. I would have said no to their invitation, and they would still be alive."

"My dear friend, there's nothing you can do to turn back the clock. And, I know you. You're blaming yourself, aren't you?"

"I hate you," Abigail said, while giving her friend a push and a smile.

The minute they reached the house, they went inside and opened the windows. The breeze was warm, but the fresh air was pleasant as it flowed through the house. Abigail opened a bottle of wine, poured a glass and told Carry to help herself. Then she excused herself and went to draw a bath.

She filled the tub, lit candles and stepped into the water. It felt heavenly. She pushed the jet button and leaned back while sipping on wine. As she tried to relax, the past few days flooded her thoughts, and she worried about Matt.

A knock at the door surprised her, Lisa asked, "Can I use your tub?"

"In a few minutes, when I'm finished, then you can." She smiled, while thinking about how Lisa, at such a young age, cherished bathing. It must be a girl thing.

After her bath, Abigail got out, emptied the tub and draped herself in a robe. With the door open, she yelled, "Lisa, are you ready?" Within seconds she came in, and they filled the tub. After she was in the water, Abigail asked, "Want jets?" "Yes. Can I have bubbles, too?"

"Sure."

When she returned, she poured the bath oil, turned off the water and activated the jets. "I'll be able to hear, so yell if you need me, okay?"

Once she was dressed and returned to the living room, she saw Danny talking to Steven about being at the wheel while on the yacht.

"Want a shower, Danny? You can use the other bathroom."

As he shook his head, he stood and marched into the spare room. Within minutes, he came out with a ball and headed outside.

This was the first opportunity the adults had to talk, so Abigail gave the details of her ordeal. "At times, I actually feared for our lives, especially after seeing Larry and Sandra's dead bodies with bullet holes. To make matters worse, four men took over the yacht and were searching for some mysterious treasure. Then, next to us was a touring ship. I tried to signal but failed. Later, I realized it had some connection to the men on the yacht. The whole thing was nerve-racking. While all this was going on, I had no idea you two were looking for us."

Steven grabbed her arm. "Did they hurt you?"

"No, not at all, but I worried about who might be the killer and feared he might kill again."

Carry stood and said, "One of the men must have done it."

"If you're right," Abigail said, "I hope we'll find out soon."

After a period of silence, Steven scooted closer to his sister and took her hand. "You need to know why we searched for you. Something terrible happened, and we needed to tell you and the children."

Instantly, Abigail's eyes became alert. "What? Did something happen to Mom or Dad? You're scaring me. What is it?"

"David and Alisa -- they were in a car accident. It happened in Hawaii."

"Are they okay?"

"No. I'm so sorry, Sis, but David didn't make it -- he died."

"Oh my God." She said, with her hands covering her mouth. "Is Alisa all right?"

"No. She's in a coma."

"I can't believe this." She shook her head with her hands covering her face, then leaned forward with her elbows on her legs, crying. Soon, she glanced at her brother. "Will she come out of it?"

"The doctors think she might. There are no external injuries. She was smart enough to wear a seatbelt. Unfortunately, David didn't."

"This is more awful than what we went through. It affects all of us. Lisa and Danny, what will they do? When did it happen?"

"Two days ago. It doesn't seem possible. David and she just reunited, now this, those poor kids."

"Where's Alisa now? Does Mom know?" Abigail stood and paced. "My God, this can't be real."

"She's still in Hawaii, but Mom and Dad are there. You need to sit."

"No! I'm sorry. I'm having a hard time processing this."

"I know. It's hard for all of us."

Soon Abigail slowly came to a stop and sat next to her brother. "This feels like some bad dream. How on earth are we going to tell the children?"

"I don't know. That'll be tough. Want me to?"

"I'm not sure what to think or do right now." Silence filled the room. Quickly, Steven got up. "I'll go get Danny and bring him in."

Abigail grabbed his hand. "Let's wait. When Lisa finishes bathing, we can tell them together."

"Will you be okay to do that?" he asked.

"No. But, I'll find a way to pull myself together. The children need to know."

When Carry suggested they pray, they agreed and asked her to lead.

"Dear God, we give this situation to You. It's too much for us to handle alone. We need You to direct us on what to say. Please be with the children when they find out about what happened to their parents. We love You. Amen."

Just as they finished, Lisa yelled, "I need a towel!"

Abigail tried to get up.

"Are you sure you're up to this?" Carry asked, placing her hand on her shoulder. "I'm so very sorry that you have to go through this."

"How am I going to tell them? Those poor children, what will become of them? I just can't believe David's dead. Now, they're fatherless. What if Alisa doesn't make it? What then?"

"I have the same concerns."

Lisa yelled again, "Aunt Abigail, did you hear me? I need a towel."

While going to her niece, she wished it was all a bad dream that would end soon, but she knew it was the truth, because it felt all too real. While walking to the bathroom, she told herself, *I have to be strong. Lisa needs me.* As she choked back tears, she prayed, *Dear Heavenly Father, please help me, give me strength. Help the children understand.* Somberly, she walked toward the bathroom and glanced back at her friend with a heavy heart.

Chapter Twenty-two

After Matt and his men spent hours being questioned by the FBI, they were finally free to leave. Special Agent Parker scheduled for Matt and Jack to return the following day. The men were relieved that the worst was over.

After dropping his friends at their cars, Matt was fatigued beyond belief. While being interrogated, he told the truth about everything, but didn't offer anything. Tomorrow's interrogation he could do without, but had no choice in the matter.

Once home, he took a quick shower and headed for the pool.

After ten laps, he relaxed by floating on his back as he visualized her pale blue eyes and dazzling hair. *I never met a woman with such incredible inner strength*, he mused.

Although it was only hours since he saw her, he longed for her and hoped he found a place in her thoughts. It surprised him that he missed the children, Danny with his adventurous spirit and Lisa with her big brown eyes. It was useless to stop obsessing about her - - the more he tried to dismiss her from his thoughts, the more she occupied them.

After towel drying, he laid down on a lounge chair, near the pool. As he closed his eyes, he saw her alabaster skin and wanted to touch it. How hopelessly he wanted her. Yet, he didn't even know her last name. When he heard his cellphone ring, he answered. It was Jack wanting to meet up at Starbucks in an hour. After agreeing, he quickly went to his condo, took a shower and changed. Then, off he went to see his friend. Once he arrived, Jack stood waiting. After they entered, they ordered coffee and found a private table.

While Jack stirred his coffee, he asked, "What happened to the Fabergé egg?"

"The boy has it. I put it in his carry-on."

Jack's eyebrow lifted, "What? Why there?"

Matt sipped his coffee and wiped his mouth. "Did you actually think the FBI would let me take it home? I don't think so. So, I wrapped it in the leg of the boy's dirty jeans."

"What now?"

"Good question. I don't know where she lives. In fact, I don't even know her last name." Matt crossed his legs, and took another sip.

"But, I do."

"What do you mean?"

Jack grinned. "The Coast Guard agent asked how I knew Miss Wilson. How many Abigail Wilsons could there be? She should be easy to find."

"Boy, did the Coast Guard screw up, that's great." While shaking his head, he said, "You're the man. I'll find where she lives and go tonight."

"But, what about the FBI? Won't her place be under surveillance?"

"Why?"

"I don't know, but do you want to take that risk?"

"Yes! If I don't get it now, Abigail might find it and hand it over to the authorities."

"Okay, but make sure you park on the next street. Go in through her backyard."

"You're telling me how to break in?" Matt grinned.

Jack laughed out loud. "Sorry. I keep forgetting your line of work."

"Don't worry, I'll be careful."

After Matt returned home, he grabbed the phonebook, found her address and got directions. Quickly, he got in his car and drove by her place without stopping. There were no cars around. He drove on the street behind hers and discovered that he could gain access through the backyard. The only obstacle was a four-foot cement wall that stood between the two houses. Easy!

On his way home, he stopped by a deli near his home. While consuming his sandwich, he planned the break in. First, he'd check the boy's room, then the laundry area. When he remembered that the boy had wanted a telescope, he decided he'll mail him a gift certificate, but then decided against it. If Abigail discovered that he had her address, she'd freak out. If she calls the FBI, it will make things worse for him. So he decided to wait until after the murder investigation.

At three o'clock in the morning, Matt woke up. After getting dressed, he headed out the door. Not wanting it to appear like a break in, he took his locksmith keys. Once he drove near her home, he parked. As he walked into her neighbor's backyard, he reached the wall and a dog next door started barking. So he threw the meat he brought, and the dog quieted down.

When he reached Abigail's back door, he took off his shoes and reached in his pocket for the keys. Within five minutes, he opened the door. Then, he carefully tiptoed down the hall and listened for any movement. The first room he entered belonged to Abigail. The moonlight was shining brightly through her window.

My God, she looks like an angel, with that golden hair framing her face.

As he backed out, he stepped on something causing his shoulder to hit the wall. He stood perfectly still, and she didn't awaken, so he headed toward the next bedroom, which was Danny's room where he was sound asleep.

While vigilantly searching the room with his flashlight, he nearly tripped over a baseball on the floor near the closet. Danny's shoes and clothes lay in the middle of his room. In the left corner, next to the headboard, the flashlight exposed a bag. Quietly he tiptoed, so as not to disturb the boy's sleep. After snatching the bag, he traced each step back to the door. Danny turned and made some noises, so Matt again stood silently.

After Danny settled down, Matt stepped into the hall, placed his hand into the bag and felt around until he pulled out a tightly wrapped pair of jeans. Quickly, he placed it on the carpet, unrolled the jeans and grabbed the treasured egg.

After returning the bag to the boy's room, he tried to exit when Danny rolled over and kicked back his blankets. Soon, he returned to his slumber. As Matt passed Abigail's room, he glanced at her beauty again, smiled and left without a trace.

Once he returned home, he gave the Fabergé egg a thorough examination and sat the magnificent piece on the kitchen counter.

He'd have to wait until after the FBI interview to give it to Jack -- then he could determine its true value. But, for now, he must get some sleep. Soon, he'd awaken for his morning appointment. As he thought of Abigail, he relaxed.

When Matt arrived for his appointment, Jack was waiting and reading a magazine. They greeted each other.

Jack whispered, "What do you think she told them? Would she mention kidnapping?"

"We'll soon find out. What time's your appointment?"

"Eight thirty."

"Is yours with Agent Parker?"

"I'm not sure."

Within minutes, Special Agent Vorty walked into the waiting room, introduced himself to Matt, and, as they turned to leave, he glanced over his shoulder at Jack and shrugged. As the two men walked, he noticed that the hallway gave the allusion of going on forever, due to its gun-metal gray color with a black stripe.

As they walked past one door after another, they reached the end of the corridor, turned left down another hall and stopped at the third door on the right. Vorty stood at attention at the door, waiting for Matt to enter. The large room held a small desk, a phone and four chairs around the walls with a floor lamp in between. There were two chairs in front of his desk. Vorty motioned for him to sit. The unwelcoming walls held credentials, certificates and plaques.

Agent Vorty continued to stand until Matt was seated, then he proceeded to go behind his desk and sit. He took out papers from a leather folder and read. After a few minutes passed, he set them down, opened a drawer and pulled out a yellow pad. After grabbing a pen, he glanced up. "Would you like some water or coffee?"

"Yes, coffee, black please."

Soon, he pushed a button and said, "Linda, please bring two black coffees. That'll be all, thanks."

Matt swiveled around in his chair, crossed his legs and then uncrossed them while tapping his fingers on the armrest. "Why am I here?"

"I read the notes from your interview. Things don't add up." There was a soft knock, then the door opened and a short, auburn-haired woman with freckles entered.

"Coffee, gentlemen?" After placing the cups on the desk, she asked, "Anything else?" Vorty shook his head. The woman turned, walked out and closed the door.

"We're puzzled about a few things. What can you tell me about Mr. Forelli?"

"He works for the T.D. Harbor Cruise Ship Corporation as a captain and gave harbor tours. Besides that, he's pretty mysterious."

"What else does he do for them?"

"You'd have to ask him or the administrators at the corporation."

"Miss Wilson stated that there was a touring vessel out at sea next to the yacht. Do you know anything about that?"

"Yes, it belongs to the Top Dogs. They knew our course and came out near us. There's nothing sinister about that, is there?"

"Then, why did they depart when your captain fled?"

"You're asking the wrong person. I haven't communicated with them to ask."

"Who are the Top Dogs?"

"They're twenty men that own the touring vessel and T.D. Harbor Cruise Ship."

"How did Forelli end up on the yacht?"

"From what I understand, the Kilgores hired him to replace their captain for a few weeks. They got his name from one of the Top Dogs."

"Then tell me, how is it that you and your friends ended up on the yacht?"

"I told your other agent, didn't he write it down?"

"I'm asking you the questions, Mr. Willingham. Who gave you permission to board the yacht?"

"Forelli asked Robert and Brent, and Robert said he would if he could invite Jack and me -- we're all friends."

"Did the Kilgores know?"

"Forelli might have told them, but I don't know for certain."

"Why did you decide to go?"

"Because in return for our service, we had the pleasure of being out on a new, beautiful yacht, and we weren't expected to do much."

"What were you and your cohorts searching for?" Matt folded his arms and stared, while taking in a deep breath. "Please answer my questions. What were you looking for?"

"Something the Kilgores may have smuggled."

"I understand that your real motive was to steal something." he said, without taking his eyes off of Matt.

"Then, you understand incorrectly."

"What do you do for a living?"

"What does my employment have to do with a murder investigation?"

"Do I have to remind you, I'm conducting the interview?"

"The same company as Forelli."

"Did you murder Mr. and Mrs. Kilgore, Mr. Willingham?"

While glaring at the agent, he took another deep breath and slowly let it out. "No, I did not."

"Can you prove it?"

"I'm presumed innocent, remember? It's your job to prove differently. Isn't that true, Mr. Vorty?"

"If you're so innocent, who killed the couple?"

"Again, that's your job to find that out." They were staring each other down.

"Miss Wilson said you became upset when she asked about your connection to the touring vessel. Why?" Matt was stunned and unable to speak. He wondered why she told them as he squirmed in his seat. "You must answer my question."

"That's personal. It has nothing to do with the case."

"Let me decide that, Mr. Willingham."

"Why did you get so upset?"

"Look. Do I need to call my lawyer?"

Vorty tapped his pen on the paper nervously, then slowly stood and said, "No. This interview has ended, you're free to go. But, don't leave town. Do you understand?"

"Yes. That won't be a problem."

"Goodbye, Mr. Willingham. I'm sure we'll speak with you again, soon." His deadpan expression didn't give a clue as to his thoughts.

When Matt reached the parking lot, he didn't see Jack's car, so he pulled out his cellphone. It rang, but there was no answer, so he left a message: "Call Me."

Chapter Twenty-three

While Abigail tried to stay busy, she worried when she saw the children's grieving faces. They both seemed to be going through the motions of everyday life. Constantly, they asked to be with their mother, but were told not yet. They needed to wait until arrangements were made to bring her back to San Diego.

As she stood at the sink looking out the window, she turned when she heard footsteps and saw Lisa's sad brown eyes squinting.

"Can I call Mommy?"

"Come here." Abigail opened her arms to hug her. After giving her a love tap on her butt, she said, "Go get your brother, we'll call your mom." Lisa grinned as she ran to fetch her brother. When he came, his face was a little less gloomy. "Remember, you two. We may not get through. We'll need Grandma to place the phone to her ear. Understand?"

Lisa eyes widened. "Will she be awake?"

"No. Not enough to speak, but she'll hear you."

Abigail reached for the phone, dialed the hospital and asked for Alisa's room.

"She's in a coma, miss," the person said.

"Yes. I know." She tried not to be annoyed. "Can you see if Mrs. Wilson, her mother, is there?"

"Hold on."

After placing her hand over the mouthpiece, she said, "They're checking to see if Grandma's there."

"Why can't the nurse do it?" Lisa said, with a hand on her hip.

"Good idea, I'll ask the nurse if Grandma isn't there. But, don't worry, if we can't connect now, we'll try again later." Abigail touched the girl's chin.

"But, I want to talk right now!" Lisa said, with a tear in her eye.

"I know, Honey. But, please be patient."

After a while, Danny's smile dissipated. "Why's it taking so long?"

"It's only been five minutes," Abigail said.

Lisa pouted, "It seems like forever."

Soon, the nurse returned. "I'm sorry, miss. I can't find Mr. or Mrs. Wilson."

"Thanks for trying. Can you, or someone, put the phone to Alisa's ear? Her children need to talk to their mother."

"No, miss. I'm sorry, but I promise the minute Mr. or Mrs. Wilson return, I'll tell them to call. What number can they reach you at?"

"Ask them to call Abigail; they have my number." While hanging up, she saw the disappointment on their faces, but neither of them complained.

"You both need a change of scenery, how about visiting Carry? You can stay with her while I get some things done."

"No. I want to stay with you!" Lisa said with a pitiful expression on her face.

"Then, go get dressed. Put swimsuits on under your clothes. We might end up in La Jolla, so we can visit the sea lions."

Quickly, the children left to change, and Abigail placed water and sodas in a small ice chest and organized a bag with snacks. She grabbed three beach towels and a blanket and put them in the trunk. When she saw the children coming toward the car, she yelled, "Is the door locked?"

Quickly, Danny returned to check the door handle and nodded.

After they reached the car, Lisa jumped into the backseat and snapped on her seatbelt while Danny hopped in the front and turned on the radio. Abigail's neighbor, Mr. Gilder, slowly walked toward the driver's side. He pulled out a card from his pocket and handed it to her saying, "Hey, Miss Abigail. This man stopped and asked about you. He said he was your brother, and he needs you to call."

"Thank you. We already spoke. He knows I'm home."

"Is everything okay?" he asked. "He said it was a family emergency."

"Yes. Steven told me all about that. I appreciate you stopping by and for your all your concern."

The man stood with his arm on the top of the car while leaning.

"I'll tell you all about it sometime, okay?" Quickly, he stepped back and watched her pull out of her driveway.

While fiddling with the radio, Danny asked, "Where are we going now?"

"First, we're going to the harbor, then to La Jolla."

On their way, the children and she didn't seem to have the energy for small talk. When they arrived downtown, she quickly found a parking space and they headed toward the Harbor Cruise Line. The boy could see Robert and Brent. They were on the other side of the street having coffee in an open-air restaurant. After crossing, he ran to the men and said, "What're you doing down here?"

"Well, hi, Danny. What a surprise." Brent said.

When Robert saw Abigail, he stood. "What caused you to come our way?"

"Oh. Hi. I'm trying to put some pieces together." She pointed. "Is that the touring vessel that followed us?"

Robert turned his head to look, and then faced her. "No. Not that one. That's ours. We're heading out soon. Want to come? No charge."

"Can we?" Lisa asked.

"No, Honey, we've had enough sea for one week."

"Can we go some other time?"

"Perhaps."

After she swirled to face Robert, she said, "Thank you. Can we take a rain check?" He nodded.

"Do you know anything that might be helpful regarding the investigation?"

"Oh. So, that's why you came," Robert studied her. "We've been talking. It must have been hard for you, that ordeal. We're really sorry about your friends -- wish things could have been different."

"Thanks, Robert, that means a lot." Abigail stepped closer. "Have you heard anything at all?"

"Well, the FBI questioned our boss, and, after that, Forelli didn't return to work. What all that means, I can't tell for sure. Neither of us will ask our boss anything; he and the other men aren't very congenial."

"I see." She glanced away while thinking, and then faced him. "Thank you. I'm glad we ran into both of you."

As they returned to her car, Abigail was concerned. Although, she thought the men were harmless, she also felt guilty for bringing the children, because no one knows for certain who played a part in the murders. She couldn't stop feeling responsible for Larry and Sandra's death. She was determined to, at least, find out who killed them.

Each time Danny changed the radio station, Lisa objected. But, Abigail smiled. She never thought she would be glad to hear them arguing. When they reached La Jolla, she drove to the business district, looking for Jack's jewelry store. Each time, she passed one, she used her cellphone to call and asked for Jack. One store clerk said, "You mean Jack Oliver?"

"Yes. Does he work there?"

"Well, no, but he does own Real Deal Jewelers around the corner on Prospect."

"Thank you, that's helpful." She drove down Prospect looking for that name on a building. When she saw it, she drove past and around the block. She parked across the street. Her thoughts were reeling with unanswered questions.

Then, Danny asked, while gawking at her, "Why did you stop?"

She pointed. "That's Jack's jewelry store."

"Are we going in?" he asked.

"No. I just wanted to see his place."

While pulling away, she gave one last glance, wishing she were alone, because she felt brave enough to go in and ask the man some questions. But, instead, she drove on, heading for the ocean nearby.

"I need help finding a parking space," said Abigail.

After circling twice, Lisa yelled, "There!" She pointed to a spot near the cove.

"Good. We don't have to carry things too far."

Swiftly, she and the children gathered things from her trunk. Lisa had the blanket under her arm, Danny grabbed the ice chest and, she, the towels and snacks. They saw a large historical pine tree and decided to spread the blanket under it. From a distance, she could hear the sound of waves crashing and breathed in the ocean air.

After settling in, Danny and Lisa ran off holding a Frisbee. As she watched them, she heard a familiar voice. When she turned, it was Matt standing at the edge of the blanket.

"Hi," he said, "mind if I join you?"

"Where did you come from?"

"I was at Jack's store, you drove right past me. I couldn't miss that strawberry-blond hair of yours."

When the children saw him, they came running. Lisa said, "Hi. How did you find us?"

"I saw you drive by me."

Danny lifted the Frisbee. "Want to throw?"

"Later, right now, I need to talk with your aunt. You two go have fun."

After the children wandered off, Matt observed Abigail. "Do you mind if I sit?"

"If you want," she said, hoping he couldn't hear the thump in her heart from excitement.

After he removed his shoes and socks, he placed his jacket over them, and made himself comfortable. Once he faced her, he gazed curiously and said, "Are the kids okay?"

"Yes. Why?"

"They seem different, almost sad."

Not wanting to cry again, she reluctantly told him what happened to the children's parents. As she spoke, tears came and she quickly wiped them away.

"My God, Abigail, it's okay to cry. Just look at all you've been through."

"It's too painful still, can we change the subject? How did things go with the FBI?"

"Okay, I guess. We weren't too thrilled about having to return for questioning, but we survived."

"Are you worried?"

"About being a murder suspect? Of course I am! Who wouldn't be? Now, I want to change the subject." They chuckled.

"So, what brings you to La Jolla?" he asked.

When she turned, her eyes faced the grass. "I'm trying to figure out who murdered my friends." After she glanced at him, she noticed his erect back.

"Since you parked across from Jack's store, you must think he did it?"

She, too, stiffened. "He might have."

"You just don't understand. We didn't even know they were on the yacht. So it's close to impossible for any of us to have done it. None of us had a motive or the time to kill them."

"You would do anything to protect him, wouldn't you?" Without waiting for a response, she said, "Do they have any leads yet?"

"They certainly wouldn't tell me. I'm sure the Top Dogs were questioned."

"Who might be the Top Dogs?"

"They own the Harbor Cruise Line, the one traveling near the yacht, do you remember?"

"Sure. That's why you abandoned us."

"Sorry about that."

"You scared me, Matt. We didn't know if you were coming back or not." Abigail saw the children walking toward them, so she became silent.

Once Danny was standing over her, he said, "Where are the cookies?"

After standing, she opened a bag of cookies and gave two to each of them along with a bottle of water.

"Want something to drink?" she asked Matt.

"Sure. Water, please."

While she handed him water, the children sat on the blanket, leaving no room for her.

"Thanks a lot, you two."

Lisa giggled while Danny tried to push her off the blanket.

"Stop that, you two," she said, while taking a beach towel and placing it near the blanket.

When Lisa sat, she wiggled while talking to Matt. "We saw Robert and Brent today. They said we can take a harbor tour for free. Can you go?"

"That sounds nice. I'm flattered you want to include me." He took out a business card and handed it to her. "Call me when you go."

Lisa took a while to gawk at it and said, "This is my first card."

Not wanting to make a scene, Abigail decided to get the card from her later, but it was at that moment that she realized there was a bond between them and Matt.

As he watched Danny gobble down his two cookies, he said, "Are you starving? Haven't you eaten lunch yet?" After turning to Abigail, he said, "I would like to treat the three of you to lunch. I know a great restaurant nearby. You can follow, if you prefer."

The boy quickly jumped to his feet. "Yes. I'm hungry."

Lisa poked his leg. "You're always hungry."

"Do you like Mexican food?"

After she saw Danny's eyes light up with excitement, she was glad a little life had come back to him. So, she decided there wouldn't be any harm in sharing a meal. The children could use a break from grieving, and she needed a distraction. Spending time with Matt would be a good diversion for them. After gathering their things, they brought them to her truck, started the car and followed him.

While driving, she asked herself, Am I taking too many risks? First, seeing Brent and Robert, then going by Jack's place of business, and now having lunch with Matt. I think I lost both my alarm and commonsense button along the way.

Chapter Twenty-four

While sitting next to Matt, waiting for their waiter, Abigail questioned herself again. *Why did I accept his offer for lunch?* But, as she watched the children eating tortilla chips with salsa so contently, she decided she had made the right decision.

After ordering the combination plate, she later regretted her choice. *It's too much food.*

Once Matt stopped people watching, he swiveled to face her. He stared at her for a minute, "What's wrong?"

"What do you mean?"

"You look concerned about something."

"I'm mad at myself. I just ordered a big meal, but only want a salad."

"Good grief. Order one."

"It's too late."

"Then, add a salad to your order, silly. Why in the world are you making such a fuss over something so small?"

After thinking for a minute, she said, "I guess, ordering a meal gives me some level of control, unlike everything that has happened in recent days."

When he saw their waiter, Matt stopped him, "The lady would like to order a salad."

Their slender, sandy blond-haired waiter was tan and relaxed. He patiently waited for her to select a salad from the menu. She decided on a taco salad.

The children were still busy eating chips, and Matt was back to his people watching, which left her time to think about her sister, brother-in-law, and the Kilgores. She was also concerned about how the children might respond to seeing their father's dead body.

Matt nudged her, "You're in deep thought."

"Yes. That I am." She quickly changed the subject. "It's a beautiful day, why aren't you on your sailboat?"

"Who told you I had one?" She grinned and nodded toward Lisa. "Oh. The little one told you, huh? But, to answer your question, I have plenty of time for sailing." He waited until she made eye contact, "Frankly, there's no place I would rather be than sitting here with you three."

Although she felt self-conscious, she smiled and said, "Thank you, Matt. That's kind of you." At that moment, she realized how much she enjoyed his company and found it refreshing that he didn't probe.

When the waiter came with the food, Matt teased, "Now, who ordered the combination plate?" He grinned when the plate was set before her.

After receiving her salad, she smiled and said to the waiter, "Can you box up my food? I decided I only want the salad."

The young man nodded and came back later with more food items and her box. "Want me to do it?"

"Yes. Thank you. Looking at it makes me feel full."

While eating, she picked out the meat and beans and mostly ate only the lettuce. While relaxing, she listened to the children talk about wanting to see three different movies. They couldn't decide which one to see first.

When Lisa added another favorite movie, Danny glared. "That's old, it's already on DVD."

While leaning back in his seat, Matt looked at Abigail. "Do you have plans this afternoon?"

"No, we don't. Why?"

"How about the four of us go to movie?" he asked, while sitting upright. "Can I take you to a movie of your choice? Go write down what you want to see on a napkin, two out of three wins." The children were excited as they asked for a pen or pencil.

"What movie do you want to see?" Lisa asked her aunt.

While responding with a smile, she desperately wanted to get out of the situation gracefully. To say no would disappoint the children and make Matt feel bad. And, to say yes wouldn't hurt anyone. *How weird is this, going to a movie with him? Right up there with having lunch with him, I guess,* she mused, while smiling. She picked up her purse to search for a pen.

Soon, Matt got to his feet and left. He quickly returned with a newspaper in hand. "Have you decided on a movie?"

"Our aunt broke our tie."

After telling him their selection, he opened the newspaper to the movie section. It was scheduled to begin in an hour in Mission Valley. He signaled for the waiter.

When Abigail handed Matt two twenty-dollar bills for lunch, Matt's disgruntled expression caused her to quickly retrieve her money.

After paying, he walked them to her car. But, before she got in the driver's seat, she insisted on paying for the movie tickets.

"Look, young lady. You and the children have been though a lot. You deserve to be spoiled." Inwardly, she was grateful to have someone take care of her, even if for a few hours.

While driving to the theater, she started getting her senses back and considered driving home. She couldn't when she heard the children happily chatting about the movie they were about to see. She had to admit, having him fuss over them felt good. When she was with her friends, there were too many questions and emotions -- making the results of the car accident too real.

The suffering they experienced on the yacht paled in comparison to the anguish of losing David and knowing her sister's condition. At times, she was like the children and only went through the motions of life. Her thoughts almost caused her to miss the driveway into the underground parking near the theater. While sitting for a minute, she hoped she wasn't making another huge mistake.

After the boy unbuckled his seatbelt, he asked, "Are we here?"

"Yes."

Once the children opened the car doors, she slowly got out and put on her best happy face. While reaching for Lisa's hand, she said, "Let's go, love bug."

"I'm not a bug. People step on bugs. I want to be a sweetie pie."

"Okay, let's go, Sweetie Pie."

Once they reached the ticket booth, Matt was standing with tickets in hand, so he must have expected them to show. The children ran up asking how he got there so fast.

"I know a shortcut."

"Show me," Lisa said.

"Maybe later."

The man seemed jovial as they entered the lobby. Together, they went to the counter and ordered candy and drinks. Once they were seated, Danny and Lisa jumped up and decided to sit higher, but the adults stayed put. Although Matt had little interest in the movie choice, he was sitting as if he did. As Abigail tried to focus on the screen, her thoughts were flooded with the events of the past few days. Desperately, she wanted her sister to come out of her coma and come home. The more she tried to push those gloomy thoughts aside, the more they reentered her consciousness. As a Christian, she shouldn't have worried, so she decided to pray: *Let Alisa recover and come home. Please comfort David's family, and help the FBI find the murderer.*

After, Matt patted her hand, then he whispered, "In time, everything will be okay. You'll see." His words came at the close of her prayer, as if God Himself was reassuring her through him. Once again, he comforted without intrusion. She genuinely liked the man, even in spite of how they met. For a thief, he had some wonderful qualities. *I could easily fall for this guy.*

When he nudged her, he asked, "Need to talk?"

"No. I'm okay."

"If you change your mind, remember, Lisa has my card."

"By the way, Matt, I didn't appreciate you giving it to her.

"Does that mean you'll call me later?"

She pushed his shoulder. "Don't you wish?"

After grinning, he said, "Actually, yes I do."

Soon the children returned, saying they didn't like their seats. After the movie ended, they walked out of the theater. Lisa said, "Don't forget, you said you would show me your shortcut."

He pointed down the walkway. "I parked over there. It's closer to the theater."

"That doesn't look shorter to me."

After laughing, he said, "It is, if you drive fast."

Lisa pushed his leg. "Oh, you."

Abigail noticed Danny's mood change, "Are you okay? You seem quiet."

"Can we go now? I want to call Mom again."

"Of course we can." She gave a tender smile and placed her hand on his shoulder. "It'll be the first thing we do, okay?"

When she reached for Matt to say goodbye, he wrapped his arms around her and gave a warm hug. After she pulled away, he bent to give Lisa a hug and she returned it while saying, "Thank you."

After approaching Danny, he said, "Young man, take good care of your sister and aunt, okay?"

The boy's face was somber, but he still had a hug to give and said, "Today was fun."

After saying goodbye, they turned toward the stairs leading to the lower parking. Abigail was concerned about Danny and hoped he was not depressed. During the drive, the children promptly fell asleep. As they dozed, she wondered, *How can Matt detach so quickly, knowing we'll never meet again.* She wasn't so eager to let him go. They both shared the horror of finding her friends' bodies, and she genuinely liked him. He did seem to be fond of the kids and her.

Once home, she was grateful. Although she enjoyed their outing, she needed a mental break. But first, she needed to empty the trunk and get the children settled. While the trunk was open, Danny reached for the leftovers from lunch and the ice chest. Lisa held out her arms while Abigail gave her the towels and blankets. After she got her keys out, she opened the door, and they dropped everything in the foyer.

As she entered the living room, she saw the message light blinking and quickly checked the messages. Steven called and said the funeral arrangements were made for David. Also, he said that Alisa would soon be transferred to San Diego.

As the children listened to Steven's message, they became quiet. Suddenly, Lisa was inconsolable as tears rolled down her cheeks. So, Abigail knelt and wrapped her arms around her, allowing her to sob.

When Abigail saw that the boy was holding back his tears, she said, "It's okay to cry, Danny." After saying that, something broke in him, and he ran into his bedroom, bawling.

Between sobs, Lisa asked, "Can I see Daddy? I want to see him again."

"Sure, Honey."

"When?" she demanded.

"Soon. I promise."

"I don't want him dead; I want him alive."

"I know, Honey. We all do."

"God can bring him back. He did it before you know. He can make Daddy alive again."

"Is that what you want? For God to bring your daddy back to life?"

"Yes," she yelled. "Let's pray for that, okay?"

So, Abigail prayed, "Dear God. You heard Lisa. She wants her daddy. Will you please bring him back to life? Lisa needs him. We put his life into your hands, but Your will be done, not ours."

"Why did you say that?"

"What?"

"About His will, that means if God doesn't want my daddy to be alive again, then it's okay."

"There's a reason we pray like that. God knows everything and knows what is best. Your daddy might be happy being in heaven, he might have a special job like watching over you and Danny.

Maybe, he can do it better while in heaven. We don't know everything, but God does. So, if He thinks it is best for your daddy to stay with Him, we must accept that, Sweetie. But, remember, Lisa, when you are old and go to heaven, you will see him again. Then God and your dad can explain things to you better. Can you accept that?"

"Yes, but I don't like it -- I want my daddy here."

"Honey, I try to trust God with everything. I hope you can learn, too. Do you want to trust God?"

"Sure, if he brings Daddy back."

"But, that isn't trusting."

After being silent, something changed within her, as if some inner enlightenment took place. "I want to trust God, even for my daddy."

"Good. Let's thank Him for hearing us and answering our prayer." When she finished, Lisa said, "Amen."

"Now, go wash up, I need to check on Danny."

As the child walked away, her head was held high, and she was singing a song from Sunday school.

Quickly, Abigail went to see Danny. When she reached his room, she slowly opened the door, peeked in and saw him kneeling by his bed, while crying and praying at the same time. She was grateful that he knew what to do, so she tiptoed away, so as not to disturb him.

After entering the kitchen, she placed a pot of water on the stovetop and selected her favorite teabag. While waiting for it to boil, she vowed, *Once those kids are asleep, I'm going to open up to God and be as honest and real as they have been.*

Now that everything had settled down, she then decided to call Steven. When he answered, she asked, "Do you have the date and time for the viewing and funeral?" Without waiting for his response, she asked, "When's Alisa scheduled to come home?" Then, she asked, "Is Mother home yet?"

"Hey, Sis, what's going on? You're asking me questions without waiting for my answer -- that's not like you."

"I'm sorry. I guess I'm too exhausted to listen to the answers. Steven, it's so hard for me to watch Danny and Lisa deal with adult issues. I hate to see them suffer. But, I'll tell you, they're handling things better than most adults would be."

"Good for them. I'm glad. They need to grieve. But, how are you doing? I'm sorry I'm not more helpful."

"You are, believe me. I'm grateful you're handling the arrangements to get our sister home. That's significant. It'll be good for the children to see and feel her, even if she can't speak. Who knows, they might give her the will to pull through her coma."

Chapter Twenty-five

When Abigail phoned her sister's hospital room, her mother answered. After speaking to her for a few minutes, she asked her to place the phone to Alisa's ear. "We all miss you terribly, Sis. We hope you come home soon. Many people are praying for your recovery. I love you. Now, your son wants to talk with you."

After giving the boy the telephone, he said, "Hi, Mommy. This is Danny. How are you? I know you can't tell me because you're resting. Guess what? We went to a movie. I wish you were home, because then you could go, too. I love you and miss you. Bye, Mommy." He then handed his sister the handset.

"Hi, Mommy, I miss you sooo much. I want you to get better real soon. When you get home, I can give you a big hug. I love you, Mommy. Bye."

After Lisa handed the phone to her aunt, Abigail said, "Goodbye, Sis, we'll see you soon. We love you so much."

After the phone call, Abigail beamed at the children. "I'm sure she was so pleased to hear your voices." But, while she spoke, Danny's head and eyes were down. Abigail asked Danny, "What's wrong?"

"I didn't know what to say."

"What you did say was perfect."

"Really?"

"Yes. Really."

After sitting on the couch for a while, Abigail stood and headed for the kitchen. She heated her water and selected a tea bag. "I have herbal tea, do you want some?"

Lisa walked in and asked, "What kind?"

"Lemon's my favorite, try it."

After nodding, she waited while sitting on a kitchen chair.

While making the tea, Abigail wondered if the FBI had arrested anyone, yet. Perhaps, Brent or Robert would know. She decided to check with them, but, for tonight, she and the children would stay home and get mentally prepared for their father's funeral.

After having tea with Lisa, she called Ruth, David's mother, and asked if anyone wrote an obituary.

"Yes, I did, Honey. It was sent to the San Diego Union Tribune. You and the children were mentioned, hope you don't mind."

"Is there anything I can do for any of you?"

"Yes. Please keep us in prayer."

"We have and will continue to do so."

After their conversation, she sat down with the children and explained what to expect at their father's viewing, service and burial. Danny and Lisa had many questions, and she answered them as well as she could.

Within a few minutes, Carry phoned. "Hi, girlfriend, how are you holding up?"

"Not great, but okay."

"Can I help in any way?"

"No. Not really."

"I'm willing to do anything you ask."

"Well, that's tempting -- anything, huh?" The women laughed.

"There's one thing bothering me. Marcella and Diana have called several times, but I'm not ready to talk. Will you give them a phone call? Let them know what's going on. Tell them I'm with the children, and they need my full attention."

"Sure, anyone else?"

"Yes, there is, but you can just send emails. I'll forward you their addresses. They'll just need an update."

"No problem, I can do that."

"Tell them we need their prayers, okay?"

"Sure."

"After the kids are asleep, I'll call and tell you about my unbelievable day."

"Now, I'm curious, do I have to wait?

"Yes."

"You're mean."

"We'll talk later."

While warming some tomato soup for dinner, Abigail pulled out bread from the freezer and took out cheese from the cold-cut bin for grilled cheese sandwiches. Danny and Lisa came into the kitchen to check things out.

"Smells yummy," Lisa said. "Can I help? Mommy showed me how to turn them."

After placing a step stool in front of the frying pan, she gave the girl the spatula, then handed Danny three plates and silverware and asked him to set the table.

When he returned, he said, "Where are the napkins? Mommy puts them on the table." Abigail grinned and pointed. He grabbed them, folded each and placed them next to each plate. Once the food was prepared, they sat down at the table, said grace and eagerly devoured the food.

"Can Mommy hear us?" asked Danny.

"Some patients have reported that they remember what people said. But, in any case, I know, for sure, it was good for your mother to hear your voices."

With a worried face, Lisa said, "I didn't know what to say."

"You did just fine, Sweetie Pie," they both smiled. "But, if you want, you can write down what you want to say next time and read it to her. Tonight, I'll help you do that."

The girl smiled. "Okay."

After dinner, Danny jumped up. "I know what I forgot to tell her—about our yacht trip!"

While putting plates in the dishwasher, the children asked for some paper. Lisa wanted to tell her mother about going on the yacht and their lunch with Matt. Danny wanted to talk about finding the Fabergé egg and riding home with the Coast Guard.

After cringing, she said, "Your mom might be worried if you tell her certain things. She might have questions and feel frustrated she can't talk. So, we don't want her to worry, do we? You can tell her you had lunch at the Harbor House and watched the mime. She might like hearing about those things. Then, when she gets home, you can tell her about the other things, like finding the Fabergé egg, your ride home with the Coast Guard or being questioned by the FBI." To lighten up the conversation, she said, "Who wants ice cream and cookies?"

Danny said, "I'll get the ice cream and bowls, Lisa can put the spoons on the table. We like to help."

After eating their treat, they wrote their lists of what to say and placed them next to the phone. While playing games, Abigail observed that they were sleepy, so she ordered them to bed, and neither child resisted. Once sleeping, she found her sleepwear and called her friend.

When Carry heard Abigail's voice, she said, "I found Marcella's and Diana's phone numbers. It's a good thing you had me call. They were worried sick about you. Of course, they want to be of help in any way. Marcella said her church has you on their prayer line, for David's and your families. They were genuinely appreciative of being updated."

"Good. Thanks for doing that, it lightens me up."

"So, tell me about your day. I can't wait to hear this."

"Well, we started our day by going to the harbor to check out that touring-vessel company, the one I almost signaled for help. Remember? Anyway, we ran into Brent and Robert from our yacht ordeal."

"Why in the world would you risk getting those children or yourself into more danger?"

"Carry. You don't understand. I feel so powerless over everything, and I want to make some sense of what happened. I think someone must know something. And, you're right, it was foolish to bring the kids, but I did it, okay!"

"I'm already worried about you, so don't go getting into more trouble."

"If that's the case, you certainly don't want to hear about the rest of my day."

"You know I do. What happened? I'll forgive you, I promise, tell me."

"Well, for starters, Robert and Brent were very kind to the children and me. They offered a free harbor cruise with them."

"Please, whatever you do, don't go without an escort!"

"Okay, you can be my protector."

"Or, die trying."

"You're a good friend, Carry."

"I know there's more here, so give it up."

"Well, afterward, we drove to La Jolla. I wanted to find Jack's jewelry store."

"Now, who's Jack?"

"He's Matt's best friend since high school."

"And Matt is?"

"He's the one I told you about. We stayed with him while on the yacht."

"You mean, the person who kept you hostage?"

"Yes. That's right, Smarty Pants."

"You're scaring me, Abigail. Don't tell me you went into his jewelry store."

"No. But, I did find it. It's called Real Deal Jewelers."

"What kind of name is that?"

"It's peculiar, huh?"

"So, go on with your story. I'm all ears."

"Like I said, I didn't go into the store, but parked across the street. After a few minutes, I drove off, and we went to La Jolla cove. Once we were settled in, the kids went off with their Frisbee. And, guess who came up? I turned around, and there was Matt."

"Now, let me see this picture. Your captor comes and stands next to you, and you're alone?"

"Yes. Anyway, after talking for a while, the children came back and were hungry, so he insisted on taking us to lunch."

"Are you out of your mind? You didn't go with him. Please tell me you didn't."

"We did go, but in separate cars, we followed him to the restaurant."

"At least, you have a speck of sense left, so how did it go?"

"Amazingly comfortable, he was a perfect gentleman."

"Good grief, Abigail. You're falling for the guy."

"True, but nothing will ever come of it."

"Why?"

"Because he is a thief and an atheist, that's why."

"But, you're attracted to him, I can tell. So, don't be like Pattie Hurst, she also bonded with her captor -- look at what happened to her."

"Don't you think I haven't said that to myself a hundred times?"

"Then, you're not listening to yourself."

"Hey, do you want me to spill the beans or not?"

"So, what more could you possibly add?"

"While at lunch, the children were talking about movies they wanted to see, so Matt wanted to treat us to one."

"Oh my, you're captivated, aren't you?"

"So, let me tell you what happened. Again, we drove separately and met up in front of the theater, then sat and watched a movie. That's all. Frankly, mentally I was too preoccupied to get excited about him sitting next to me."

"So, what happened next?"

"He gave us a hug goodbye, and he left."

"I don't trust the guy, he must have followed you. How else would he know to find you at the La Jolla coves?"

"You're right. He did follow us, right after we passed him, when I pulled away from spying on his friend Jack."

"See what you're doing? Now, he has your license plate number."

"I never thought about that -- I wondered why he didn't ask for my phone number."

"So, you want him to call you. Oh my God. Abigail, you're a big girl, and I trust you as my friend, but I'm concerned that your strong will is overriding your good sense. So, I must warn you, you're playing with fire with that man."

*   *   *

When Matt arrived at his get-together with his friend, he spotted Jack feeding ground squirrels. He quickly found a place to park. The weather was perfect -- with a cool breeze. The beach, once a children's pool, was full of wild sea lions sunbathing on the sand. Many people watched the creatures from the pier. Before reaching his friend, he observed one that was swimming up to the sand and wobbling back and forth to get a spot on the shore.

When he walked up to Jack, he handed Matt a small bag of food for the ground squirrels, and gave another to a child standing nearby. Several other children watched as Matt held out his hand with food, and the creatures came and ate.

"So, tell me. What's the egg worth?"

"Good news and bad, my friend -- which do you want first?"

"What's the good news?"

"It's an authentic Fabergé egg from Russia."

"And, what might be the bad news?"

"Like I guessed, it's worth around eight hundred thousand, so it's not the mysterious treasure worth millions that the Top Dogs wanted us to find." "Great, the FBI impounded the yacht, now none of us can find it."

"That's okay with me. At least, we have something for our trouble."

"How will you fence it?"

"I have a list of collectors. I'll first contact them, if that doesn't work, a silent auction will be arranged, and it'll sell to the highest bidder."

"What if the highest bid is three hundred thousand?"

"If you want, we can start the proposal at five hundred thousand, the worst case is we'll split a quarter of a mil., not bad for a day's work."

The men were silent as they fed the squirrels and seagulls. Then, Jack said, "This was my last gig Matt. I had fun helping you, but I don't want to risk going to jail and losing my business. So, once the egg is sold, no longer ask me to help you, okay?" While glaring at Matt, he said, "Please respect what I'm saying. If you value our friendship, never ask again."

"I got it, Jack. You don't have to hit me over the head. And, don't worry. I won't get you involved again, okay?"

Jack became more relaxed, "Good. Then we understand each other." After facing Matt he said, "Why do you do it? What's your payoff, besides the money?"

"It's a question I've asked myself, without an answer. But, somewhere deep inside, I know I'm capable of earning more money legally than I have now. All I need to do is place the same diligence into some career. So, I don't know why I do it, but if I continue, I'll never end up with a woman like Abigail."

Chapter Twenty-six

Before seven, the children woke up and entered their aunt's room. "It's time to get up." Abigail pretended to sleep, and the more they yelled, the louder she snored. Suddenly she grabbed Lisa. "I got you." Lisa squealed.

"So, what's for breakfast?" the boy asked.

"Well, my dear lad, you have choices: pancakes at home or McDonald's? Or, if you prefer, a restaurant that brings food to the table?"

"McDonald's," yelled Lisa. "If that's okay with Danny." He nodded.

When Abigail wanted to get out of bed, the children left to watch cartoons. Once she was up and wearing a robe, she entered the living area. "Who wants to play on the Wii?"

Danny said, "Let's play baseball or soccer."

While they were busy with their games, she turned on water for tea and made hot chocolate. After giving Lisa and Danny their hot drinks, she sat on her favorite chair to work on her devotions. While reading the first chapter of James, she read, "If we want wisdom, we must ask for it with faith. Without faith we are double-minded, and shouldn't expect to receive anything." *That's me. Double-minded. I'm attracted to Matt, yet I want a man of faith. So I can either change my mind-set and accept him as he is -- a thief -- or avoid being near him.* She prayed.

Lord, Matt's the first man I truly desire to be with. Yet, I also want a man who shares my faith. So, what do I do? I need wisdom.

Do I accept him as he is or never see him again? Please help me. You know everything. What should I do? Amen.

Lisa came up, "Danny never lets me win."

"You'll win; it's just a matter of time. He's older, so he has more abilities than someone your age. Don't get discouraged, okay?" Lisa nodded and hugged her. "Go tell your brother to get dressed, so we can go eat." Lisa marched out of her sight.

While showering, Abigail wondered if the FBI had arrested anyone. Although everyone suspected Forelli, she wasn't so sure. He might be capable of it, but in her view, he was too obvious. She believed the killer was still out there.

After stepping out of the shower, she grabbed a towel. Her thoughts were of the Kilgores and how they planned on staying ashore, that is, until she came along. She was determined to see their killer in jail, even if it was the last thing she did. She decided to call Robert and ask if he had heard anything new.

Hurriedly, she dressed and walked into the living room, and was surprised when the children were taking longer than she to get ready. When Lisa entered the kitchen, she was frowning and looked away.

"Where's your brother?"

"I don't know."

Soon, the boy was in the living room dressed, but with uncombed hair.

"Can you do something with your hair?"

After looking at her for a minute, he spun around and went into his room. Within minutes, he returned with little changed.

She decided it was not worth making an issue of it, so she said nothing.

As they walked to the car, she said, "Danny, you can sit in front." But he didn't seem to care. After, he was seated, he turned on his favorite radio station, but this time Lisa wasn't arguing.

Soon, he glanced at his aunt. "Is Mommy awake yet?

"Do you mean from her coma?"

He nodded.

"No. Grandma would have called."

"When I phone her, I want her to talk, too. I miss her."

Lisa asked, "Is Daddy's funeral tomorrow?"

"Yes, Honey."

"What should I wear?"

"Anything you want, as long as you look nice for your dad. We'll stop by your house later and find something nice."

"Should I wear a dress?"

"Sure, if that's what you want."

When they arrived at McDonald's, Abigail asked the kids if they wanted to go through the drive-thru, or park and go in. Lisa chose to go inside and her brother didn't object. While standing in line to order, both children found it hard to decide. She ordered each of them a full meal, so they could eat from it want they wanted. While sitting and talking, Lisa asked to go on a harbor cruise.

"I'll give it some thought." Although, she remembered Carry's warning, she also recalled taking her class from school on a harbor cruise last year. So, if it was safe enough for her class, it would be fine. Plus, it would give her a chance to speak with Robert about the case.

"I'll call Robert to see if it's okay with him." She told Lisa.

"Can I call Matt? He said he wanted to come."

"No, he has better things to do. Let's not bother him." Then, she reached into her purse, pulled out Robert's business card and phoned him. When he answered, he said, "I can't talk now, but are the children with you?"

"Yes, why?"

"Matt told us what happened to their parents; we're so sorry."

"Thank you, Robert."

"Why don't you bring them here? They can have a harbor tour today. They'll be safe. It's not overly busy, and we can talk. If you hurry, perhaps you can make our ten o'clock tour."

After saying yes to his offer, they drove to the harbor. Although she knew Carry was right about Matt, she still wanted to see him again, but she thought, *I am proud of myself for saying no to Lisa. God must be helping me already.*

The children's moods were less somber after eating and planning a harbor cruise. They both liked being around Robert and Brent. Once they arrived at the ticket booth, she told the clerk, "We're Robert's guests." The pretty clerk stared at her for a moment, then picked up an envelope and handed it to her without saying one single word.

Before walking on the boarding plank, she noticed a photographer taking pictures. She and the children stood in line behind the others. When it was their turn, they stood in front of a life preserver and smiled. When finished, they walked to the side. The sign told them they could board fifteen minutes before departure, so that's what they planned to do.

As they entered the vessel, they went topside so they could watch as they pulled away from the dock. When they arrived, Abigail was taken aback when she noticed Matt speaking to Brent. With her heart fluttering and her feet unsettled, she thought, *I guess my willpower didn't help*. She was thankful she noticed him first. It gave her time to adjust to the situation.

It was another beautiful day. "I love summer," she said. As the vessel left the dock, the various contemporary and modern buildings started getting smaller.

Soon, Matt walked up and Lisa said, "Matt, it's you. How did you know to come? I wanted to call, but my aunt didn't want to bother you. She thought you might be too busy. Did you know we would be here?"

"Let's just say I have friends in high places." He winked at Abigail.

"So, Robert called you," Abigail said, with an edge. *It never occurred to me he would do that.*

"You sound disappointed." She didn't answer. "Robert said you wanted an update on the case, but he was afraid he might be too busy. Would you rather talk with him?"

"No. I'm sorry, seeing you just caught me off-guard. I didn't mean to be so rude. Please, let's talk."

When they walked toward the main cabin, he stood by the door. "Any preference on seating?"

"Someplace they can find me easily."

"No problem."

After selecting a table, she turned to Danny and said, "If you need me, I'll be at that table. Will you watch over your sister and not leave her alone?"

Lisa pushed her brother. "I can take care of myself."

"I know," Abigail said, "but I want you to stay together. If not, you have to come inside with me, okay?" The girl nodded.

"Coffee or some water?" Matt asked.

"We just ate. I don't want a thing. But, thanks."

While he was gone, she said a quick prayer. *I need wisdom, help me not be rude, or fall into his arms, he is so perfect for me.*

When he returned with a coffee, he sat across from her.

"I'm sorry for my attitude, Matt."

"Enough with 'I'm sorry.' I know what you thought." He gazed at her until her face was flushed, and she turned away.

While he sipped his coffee, she had a chance to regroup. "What do you know about the case, is there anything new? Has anyone been arrested?"

"After Forelli spoke with the FBI, he was told not to leave town. But, they kept him under surveillance. When he tried to split, they arrested him. Now, he's their official prime suspect for the murders."

"What evidence do they have?"

"I'm not sure. His bosses, the Top Dogs, aren't providing him with a good attorney. It would be a waste of money, with his federal criminal record to deal with."

"Do you think he did it?"

"He's maintaining his innocence, so who knows. It's possible someone else did it."

"I think so, too," she said.

"Why?"

"Probably from watching too many TV shows, oftentimes the obvious person is later eliminated as a suspect."

"But, if he is innocent, why would he jump ship?" Matt asked.

"Most likely because he didn't want to get caught with two dead bodies and four thieves. That would give a man a reason to flee. But, that's just one woman's opinion."

"And, I'm one of the thieves, I get your point."

"I wasn't intentionally trying to make a dig."

"Do you want to hear more or not?" he asked.

"There's more? What?"

"Someone else was arrested: Luke Percy, Forelli's direct boss."

"Why?"

"For many reasons, the FBI discovered he had a beef with Mr. Kilgore about some business deal gone wrong. Plus, Luke and Forelli were tight, so they concluded Luke might be behind the murders. They also heard that Luke's company had an audit. It resulted in evidence implicating Luke in embezzling several hundred thousand dollars from his partners. So, once the FBI discovered all that information, he became a suspect with a motive."

"What was the bad deal between Larry and this Luke fellow?"

"Robert said Larry smuggled something and used Luke's underground auction contact. When Larry received his money, he shortchanged Luke about a hundred thousand dollars."

She sat and stared, trying to digest everything. She said, "Based on what you're telling me, Forelli might be the murderer. That means my female instincts just left town."

"You're so cute. I love your humor."

When Abigail noticed the children walking toward their table, she gave a warm smile.

Danny postured himself by the table. "When can we visit Robert and Brent?"

"Right now," Matt said, while standing and waiting for Abigail. When she was ready, he said, "I'll show you the way."

While walking to the wheelhouse, Danny asked about the Fabergé egg.

"It's not what we were searching for, but it is valuable, so you'll get your telescope."

While grinning, the boy said, "Really, my own telescope?" He turned to his aunt. "Did you hear that? Matt's getting me a telescope." But, she didn't respond.

"Promise me something," Matt said. "You must let your sister look through it too, okay?"

Lisa gloated when Danny reluctantly had to agree.

"When can I get it?"

"That's up to your aunt -- today, if she agrees."

Suddenly, Danny stopped and spun around. "Can we get it today?"

Quickly, she said, "We'll discuss that later."

As they walked up the ladder to the wheelhouse, Abigail's face reddened. *How dare he use the children to get to me?* Once they entered the wheelhouse, the children ran up to Robert.

Suddenly, Matt pulled Abigail aside, "Look. I'm sorry if you're offended. But, I feel obligated to that boy. It was he who found the Fabergé egg. And, I did promise him a reward. Would you let me do this one thing for him?"

"You set me up. If I say no, I disappoint and hurt him. You seem to make a habit of placing me in awkward positions. That boy has gone through too much already, so you know I can't say no! In the future, please don't offer either child anything without speaking with me first in private!"

"Does that mean we have a future?"

"No. That's not what I'm implying. I'm saying you have invited them to lunch, to a movie and now offered to buy a telescope, each time putting me on the spot. I don't like it! Those children are in my care. I need to protect them."

"From a thief like me … is that what you're insinuating?"

"Okay, if you want honesty, then, yes!"

"But, you told me that all saints have a past and all sinners have a future. I guess that doesn't apply to me."

"It does, if you're a saint or a repentant sinner. So, let me ask you: Did you decide to no longer be a thief? Have you repented or paid restitution? Have you accepted God's grace and forgiveness? Frankly, I don't think so. Am I wrong here?"

Chapter Twenty-seven

As the Harbor Cruise came to an end, Abigail and the children thanked Robert for inviting them. "Let Brent know that we missed not visiting with him, will you?"

"Sure."

After a while, Matt said, "Can I walk you to your car?"

"Sure," Lisa said, while reaching for his hand.

As they headed for Abigail's car, they leisurely walked, and Abigail listened to him interact and laugh with the kids. She questioned why she was so judgmental and disapproving of him. *Is it to push him away? Was it right to assume he was being nice to them to get to me? That doesn't seem fair to him or the children.*

Deep inside, she knew he enjoyed them and wanted Danny to have a telescope. But, that meant Matt was in possession of the Fabergé egg. So, indirectly, the boy was being paid for helping a thief. *Talk about inner conflict: I have to decide what's more important, my high standard or Danny's dream coming true.*

When she thought about the recent days, and how they had been trying to survive their family crises, she decided, *I'll gladly exchange self-respect for Danny's happiness.* Her next decision was how to handle its purchase. Should Matt help select it, or should they choose, and he pays later? She decided to let him help select and buy it. They could take it home and be done with it. No further contact.

As they neared the car, she listened to them talking. Lisa asked, "Can I get a dollhouse?"

Matt said, "No." Abigail beamed and wanted to give the man five gold stars.

She swiftly turned to Danny. "Which stores sell telescopes?"

"There's one at the mall. A science store, I think it's on the same floor as the theater."

"I know the place," said Matt. "When do you want to go?"

"Today," Danny said, with his eyes bright, giving the situation his full attention.

"That's your aunt's decision," Matt said. "Would today work for you?" He searched her face, as he waited for her response.

First, she transferred her weight to one foot, placed her hand on her hip and took in a deep breath. She let out her breath and said, "Around three thirty."

"Call if plans change." He handed her his card.

"No, thanks. We have one, remember?" She then, softly, grabbed hold of his arm. "I truly appreciate the update. I find it interesting."

He grinned, "You're welcome." He turned to the children. "Goodbye, have a safe trip home."

As they drove off, they waved.

The first thing Danny did was tune the radio to his station, then glanced at his aunt. "I wish my parents had a safe trip home."

She reached for his hand. "I know, Honey, so do I."

"Where now?" he said.

"Your house, to get clothes for tomorrow."

"Can I pick my own outfit?" Lisa asked.

"Yes, you may, Sweetie Pie." She smiled.

While driving, she thought about the arrests, but questioned if Forelli was the murderer or an easy scapegoat. To her, she wanted justice to be brought to the right person, whoever that might be.

When they reached her sister's home, she searched for the right key. When she opened the door, it smelled stale, so, speedily, she opened the windows. The children headed for their rooms. Abigail yelled, "Don't forget. You need something for both the viewing and the service."

At once, Danny came and found her. "What's a viewing?"

"It's a place to visit your dad in his casket. It'll be open so you can see him."

"Why?" He asked.

"So, you and others can say goodbye, or remember him. Close friends and family will be at the viewing, but, at the service, there will be a much larger group."

"Why have both?"

"The viewing is for you, the service is for everyone who wants to pay their respects and say goodbye to your dad. It's like a church service, but people will come up and talk about your father."

"Do I have to say something?"

"No. Not unless you want to."

"I don't," he said, while quickly shaking his head. "Is there anything else?"

"Yes, after the service, the casket is closed and brought to the burial site. You and your sister will sit next to me in chairs. The minister will talk, say some prayers and then we leave. When everyone is gone, the casket will be placed underground."

"Do I need to say goodbye at each place?"

"Only, if you want. You can also look at him, touch him, talk to him or just recall things about him. The viewing helps you to accept his death."

Soon, his shoulders slumped and his eyes drooped. He silently returned to his room and sat on his bed in thought. When she checked on him, she sat and held his hand. "Danny, I'm so sorry you have to go through this at such a young age. Are you going to be okay?" After nodding, he stood and walked to his closet and selected some of his Sunday's best clothes, and some games.

"Can I bring these?"

After, Abigail nodded yes, Lisa called out. When she entered Lisa's room, she saw some dresses and pants outfits on her bed. With tears, she said, "I don't know what to wear."

"Pick your two favorite dresses and a pants outfit -- tomorrow you can decide."

"But, which shoes should I wear?" she asked, while sniffling.

"Show me what you have."

Lisa dragged out three pairs of shoes from her closet. Abigail pointed to the black patent leather. "These will work, they'll go with everything. Do you have a hanky and a purse?"

The girl found a small handbag, "I have this."

"That'll work."

The girl gathered some dolls and stuffed animals to sleep with. "Can I bring these?"

"Sure. That'll be nice."

Once they packed, locked up, and left, they headed for the grocery store. When they finished, they returned to Abigail's place and made sandwiches for lunch. Soon, Danny and Lisa retreated to their separate rooms with games and toys in hand. Abigail decided to lie down for a few minutes, but soon fell asleep. Once she woke up, she quickly checked on the children. They, too, were sleeping.

After walking into the kitchen, she took out a container of frozen apple juice. After putting it in a pitcher, she added water and ice. While stirring, her thoughts were of Matt. *What a mess. I need to nip this and tell him not to contact me again.* She laughed at herself. *I'm the one that visited his friend's workplace, and placed myself in a position to run into him. I feel like an idiot, thinking about pushing him away when he isn't pursuing me. The truth is, I'm desperately trying to avoid falling in love with the man.*

Soon, Danny came into the kitchen. "What's the time? Do we need to go? Should I get Lisa?"

"Not yet. Have some apple juice." She handed him a full glass. "When you finish, go get your sister." But, as he turned, Lisa was walking toward them.

While rubbing her sleepy eyes, she said, "I fell asleep."

"We all did, Honey. We needed it."

"Can we call Mommy?"

"Yes. Have Danny dial for you."

As she listened to them speak to their mother, they were much more talkative and didn't seem to mind that she couldn't respond. They avoided asking questions she couldn't answer. Instead, they eagerly told her about their day.

Quickly, Abigail grabbed the phone. "I need to talk." She said, "Hi Alisa, I want to tell you that you did a wonderful job raising your children, I'm proud of you. Lisa and Danny love you so much." After placing her hand over the speaker, she said, "Don't say anything about the funeral, she doesn't know Daddy died."

After grabbing the handset, Danny nodded.

When the call ended, they sat silently while sipping their beverages. Danny asked, "When's Mommy coming home?"

"This week, that's my understanding."

"Can she go to the funeral?"

"No, she needs to get better before going anywhere."

"But, she is coming home, to San Diego."

"I know. But, she'll have a team of medical professionals to keep her stable."

"What does stable mean?"

"To make sure she is okay. They'll check her blood pressure and vitals." As they listened, they also quietly tried to process.

"Now, go get dressed. We'll get to the mall early and look around.

Lisa looked at her feet. "I need socks."

"Anything else?"

"A hanky."

"You can use one that belonged to your great-grandmother."

After Abigail finished her shower and got dressed, she felt refreshed. She went to check on Lisa. "Need any help?"

"No. Come in."

When she entered, she saw Lisa's dolls and animals propped up on her pillows.

"Did they take a nap with you?"

She grinned and nodded.

"Ready to go?"

They got in the car and headed to the mall. When they arrived, Abigail decided to shop for socks first. After finding them, Danny asked to check out the boys' department. He found a shirt he liked that fit. "Can I wear this to the viewing?"

She nodded. "It looks nice on you. Your parents would be proud of your taste."

Abigail thought they were both dealing with their father's death as well as could be expected. But, she was somewhat concerned about the viewing the next day. "Okay, you two, we need to go. Danny, lead the way."

When they reached the store, Matt was leaning against the building with his arms crossed. He looked handsome with his green Tommy Bahama shirt and tan slacks. His shirt brought out the green in his hazel eyes.

Danny ran up and asked Matt, "Did you go inside?"

"No. But, look at this." He pointed to one in the store window.

"Wow! That's great."

"Let's see what else they have."

While shopping, they checked out every available telescope in the store, but none of them grabbed Danny. So, Matt asked the clerk, "Can you bring us the one on display in the window?" The tall, slender clerk delicately squeezed into the window and retrieved the item, and then placed it in front of the boy.

Danny checked out the eyepiece and asked, "What's the distance I can see with this one?"

"Farther than our other telescopes."

Meanwhile, Matt took Danny by his shoulder and turned to him. "Do you like it, or should we go check other stores?"

"I like this one. Can I get it?"

"Sure. If it's what you want."

"Is it in stock?"

"I'll check." As quickly as he pivoted and left, he returned. "Sorry. It needs to be ordered."

Danny cocked his head. "Can we take this one?"

"No. We can't sell displays, but once you place an order, it'll arrive in a few days."

"That's fine," Matt said. "Do I pay now?"

"No, when you come back."

"Can it be engraved?"

"Sure. It'll be around twenty dollars more."

After giving the clerk their cellphone numbers, Abigail also gave Danny's complete name for the engraving.

She mused, Well, I failed miserably. This is not a one-stop event.

As they left the store, Matt said, "Are you through shopping?"

"Yes, unless Danny wants to look elsewhere."

When he saw the kids checking out toys in a window, Matt said, "Can I ask you something?"

"Sure. What's up?"

"Want to go to the Cheesecake Factory?"

"Goodness, it's a miracle. You mean, you didn't ask the kids first?"

"No, Smarty Pants. So, what's your answer?"

"My answer is … let's see, yes!"

"That's great, thanks for saying yes."

"Tomorrow is the viewing, so having vanilla cheesecake with raspberries sounds pretty good. It beats sitting at home agonizing." They headed for their separate cars and drove to Fashion Valley. It was busier than usual, so parking was hard to find. Abigail decided to use the valet. When they reached the restaurant, Matt was outside. He said, "I gave my name, but it is a forty-five minute wait. Want to check the directory? There might be another telescope store."

They agreed and went to the directory. After checking it, there was no specialty store listed, so they decided to window shop. After going into a few stores and walking around, Matt checked his watch. "Hey, we need to get back."

Once they returned and were seated, Danny told Matt, "I like the telescope we ordered, I don't want to look anymore. Can't we just wait for it to come in?"

"You're the boss, it's yours. End of subject."

"Now, it's my turn," Abigail said to Matt. "I insist on paying for our meals, and don't argue, I already gave my credit card. We want to thank you for all of your kindness."

He counter-offered, "Can I get the drinks and tip?"

"Fair enough." She smiled, triumphantly.

After ordering beverages, they studied the menu. Abigail said to the kids, "Order your meal. After you eat, then select a dessert."

Then, Matt looked at her. "Does that go for me, too, Miss Wilson?" They both heard the children giggling.

"No. You're a big boy. Order any way you like."

While sitting with the menu, it hit her. *He knows my last name? I never gave it, so how did he get it? I'm playing with fire here; is he too clever for me? What should I do, confront him and make a big deal of it, or let it go?*

Chapter Twenty-eight

The children would need their grandparents by their sides, so Abigail was glad her parents came home in time. As she was getting ready for David's viewing, there was a knock on her bedroom door. "Is it time to go?"

After opening it, she said to Danny, "Soon. We're leaving early to eat at the Soup Plantation."

"But, I'm not hungry."

"That's a first, but, I do understand why. None of us are in the mood for food. But, at least, let's try to find something to eat, even if it's fruit or soup."

"Okay," he said, with his head hanging low.

Later, when she went into the living area, the children were quietly sitting on the couch. Lisa looked like a little lady in her pretty pink dress with white trim. Danny had on his new blue-plaid shirt and khaki slacks. "Well, look how nice you both look. I'm impressed. Are you ready to go? Do you have everything? Lisa, where's your purse?"

"In my room."

"Is your great-grandmother's hanky in it?"

Lisa nodded.

"Can you get it? We need to get going."

After locking up, they got in the car and drove, but the boy didn't turn on the radio. Danny and Lisa were both too quiet.

"So, Danny," Abigail asked, "Can I ask you something? Are you afraid?"

"Of what?"

"Seeing your daddy in a casket?"

"No. I'm afraid of not saying the right thing."

"There isn't any right or wrong here -- just be yourself. And, don't worry about others -- that goes for you, too, Lisa."

"I don't feel good," Lisa said. "My stomach hurts."

"None of us feel great. This is hard on all of us."

"But, I can't eat."

"That's fine. If you don't find something, you don't have to, okay?" When they arrived at the Soup Plantation, they went through the line with trays. Abigail selected a salad, wheat roll and some iced tea. Lisa had Jello with whipped cream and chicken noodle soup, while Danny's tray was full with an array of food items.

When they sat, they ate what they could and left the rest. When they were finished, Abigail said, "Ready?" Each of them slowly walked to the car without saying much. While she was driving to the viewing, Abigail was looking forward to seeing her parents, but was concerned about the children. "Are you two okay?"

"Can I touch him?" asked Danny.

"Yes, but his skin will be cold."

"But, why?" asked Lisa.

"Because, after people die, their blood stops flowing."

After parking and getting out of the car, Abigail suddenly was filled with dread. Nonetheless, she led them through the lobby and into the viewing room. Ruth, David's mother, and her family were standing and greeting visitors. Abigail gave the woman a long hug. "I'm so very sorry about your son." Soon, Ruth turned to her grandchildren. "You both look so nice for your daddy." Danny hugged her without letting go, and Lisa held onto her aunt's arm and cried. So, Abigail said, "Let's wait for Nana and Papa in the lobby. Okay, Honey?" Lisa grabbed her hand, and together they walked silently to the foyer and remained.

Within a short time, her parents pulled up and came though the entrance. They looked exhausted and seemed as if they had aged. After exchanging hugs with Abigail, Elizabeth wrapped her arms around Lisa. "I love you, Sweetie. You'll be okay. Your family loves you, and we'll take good care of you."

Sometimes, Abigail thought, a child needs the comfort that only a grandmother can give.

John, Abigail's father, was tearful, while asking, "Where's Danny?"

"With Ruth."

"Good. How's he doing?"

"We'll soon find out."

Together, they walked into the viewing room. As they entered, they saw Ruth next to the casket with Danny. When he reached into the casket to touch his father, he quickly pulled away. "He's cold."

Lisa came and stood next to her brother. "Aunt Abigail told you, Danny."

"I know."

While in front of the casket, the boy occasionally tried to touch his dad's face or hand, as if trying to comprehend the situation. On the other hand, when Lisa glanced at her daddy, she tightly hugged her Grandmother Ruth's arm and buried her face while whimpering. As Abigail and her parents looked on, tears filled their eyes. Everyone wanted to protect the kids from such pain, but they also knew that Lisa and Danny must grieve.

When Steven and Carry appeared, they hugged his parents. Steven stood behind them while touching his dad's shoulder. Occasionally, he glanced toward his sister. Suddenly, Lisa noticed them and ran into her uncle's arms. "Daddy's dead."

Soon, Danny noticed Grandpa John, so he quickly went over and said, "Did you see Daddy?" Without waiting for an answer, he pulled John's hand and led him to the coffin. While standing next to his grandson, he took a glimpse at David's lifeless body.

After Ruth left to greet new guests, the Wilson family quickly came to the casket. It was hard for John to watch his grandchildren try to make sense of things. But his real concern was the future -- when Danny wouldn't have his dad as a coach or when Lisa couldn't have her daddy walk her down the aisle someday. It was good they couldn't think ahead. They had enough to contend with right now.

When Grandma Elizabeth was seated, Lisa sat on her lap and buried her head while sobbing. The child was comforted by her grandmother stroking her hair. Her sobs turned quickly into whimpers. "It's good for you to have a good cry after losing your daddy."

At that moment, as Abigail watched on, she was very grateful for her parents. While John was standing next to Danny at the casket, the boy talked to his dad. "I'm going to miss you. I love you so much. I was glad you and Mommy were together, but now I have to say goodbye forever … and I don't want to." The boy was so choked up that, when he touched his daddy's hand, tears fell into the casket.

Although, she hated to see them suffer, it was better than them holding it in. Soon, Lisa went and stood next to her brother and held his hand. As they gazed at their father, both grandparents came and stood behind them -- touching their shoulders. As

Abigail watched, she sensed God's presence and knew many prayers had gone up for the families.

In the background, Steven and Carry stood watching. There was little they could do, but be supportive. When Abigail came up to them, she asked, "Want some coffee?" Carry gave her friend a hug. "How are you? This has to be hard on you, seeing those children grieving." She stepped back. "I've been so worried about you. It seems like I've been praying for you and the kids all day long."

Steven scanned her face. "Are you okay, Sis? With all you've been through, I'm concerned for you, too. Tell me you're okay."

With tears in her eyes, she motioned for them to leave the area. When they reached the hallway, Abigail broke down. Steven embraced her and let her sob. Once she was composed, she said, "This is the first time I've allowed myself to grieve. My focus has been on the little ones. I'm glad I have you to lean on. I guess that's what big brothers are for. It feels good to let it out." After pulling away, she said, "I'm concerned about Mom and Dad. I can see the effects. I sure hope this isn't too much for them."

"They're tough people. They'll be okay; just give them time."

"When will Alisa be home?"

"In two days."

"Good, by then the funeral will be over."

"We planned it that way, Sis. Once she's home, she'll need our full attention."

"You did good, Bro."

"Tomorrow, we'll come get you?" he asked.

"Can five fit in a BMW?"

"Sure, if Lisa sits in the back, middle seat."

While waiting for his friend to arrive, Matt sat drinking a cup of his favorite coffee. Before long, Jack showed up and said, "I'm glad you're sitting. You might fall over when I tell you the news."

"What? You sold the egg?"

"Yes, for nine hundred and fifty thousand dollars."

"Great, that's more than we thought. Do you have the money?"

"It's in a Swedish bank, as we speak." Jack handed him the wire transfer.

"Can we access it, yet?"

Before speaking, he was silent for a minute. "Let's wait a while, at least until after the murder investigation. I don't want the FBI to use it as a motive for murder."

"You're right about that."

"What's your guess about Forelli or Luke Percy? Do you think they did it?" Jack asked.

"I haven't seen the evidence, so I don't know." After Matt checked his watch, he said, "Hey, I need to go."

"What's up with the suit?" Jack asked him.

"I'm headed to a funeral."

"Whose?"

"I'm sorry to say, it's Lisa and Danny's father."

"Were you invited?"

"No. The obituary section had an article about David Glover."

"How do you know it's the right person?"

"It mentioned that he is survived by his wife and two children, Danny and Lisa. The deceased's last name was Glover, the same as Danny's. So, I know it's his funeral."

"Is this the right thing to do?"

"Those kids need all the support they can get. I don't care if it ticks off Abigail. I want to be there for the children -- I'm concerned."

"Boy, Matt. You're really attached to the family. I've never seen you so involved before. They're lucky to have you as a friend."

"Thanks."

As Matt left, he headed for his car and drove to the memorial service. Although he arrived fifteen minutes early, the chapel was packed. He quickly noticed the children sitting up front and to the side with family and also noticed that the casket was still open. Danny and Lisa walked up and placed a long-stemmed red rose inside with their aunt by their side. They whimpered as they returned to their seats.

It was heart-wrenching for him to watch, so he needed a hanky. He found a restroom near the front of the chapel. As he walked toward it, he noticed Abigail talking to a man a few years her senior. Although he tried to avoid her, her shocked expression gave it away that she had seen him. The man with her turned to see why her demeanor had changed.

When Matt approached, he reached out his hand. "Hello. I'm Matt Willingham. Abigail and I were on the Kilgores' yacht together." There was dead silence. "When I read about the service, I decided to pay my respects." He turned to Abigail. "I hope you don't mind. I wanted be here for the children. My heart goes out to them. They're good kids, those two." After excusing himself, he walked to the restroom.

Both she and Steven had dazed expressions as they watched him walk away.

"He was on the yacht with you and the children?" Steven asked. "He has some nerve coming here. I'll tell him to leave!"

"No. The children like him. They'll be happy he's here."

"You must be kidding. He kept you three hostage, and the kids will be glad to see him?"

"Yes. He watched over us and was very kind to the children. In fact, in some strange way, we all felt protected by him."

"You never cease to amaze me, Abigail Wilson. You're still picking up stray dogs, aren't you?" After turning pink, she walked into the chapel. When she sat, she whispered to the kids, "Matt's here." They both grinned. "He's really here?" Danny asked. Abigail nodded. They sat back with their hands in their laps.

The minister walked up to the podium, said a few words and introduced a woman who sang "Amazing Grace." When she was finished, the minister asked David's brother to come say a few words. After him, some close friends said heartfelt and loving comments. Those present could hear the love and devotion his friends and brother had for David.

After the minister gave the sermon, he recited "The Lord's Prayer," followed by, "Those of you who are believers will someday be reunited with David, and it'll be for eternity. Let that be our comfort. Please come and give your last respects, starting with the last row."

Each attendee, one by one, walked by the casket before exiting the church until it was time for those in the immediate family to say goodbye. As the children left with their family, they heard the casket close behind them. The kids abruptly stopped, turned and stood, while they watched the casket being carried out of the church. Tears filled the children's eyes, and Lisa said, "Goodbye, Daddy."

Once the casket was placed in the vehicle, it started to drive away. Lisa waved and yelled, "Goodbye!" Once the car was out of sight, she turned to her aunt. "Is Mommy going to die, too?"

"We're praying she'll be okay, Honey. She's doing well and is resting, so that's a good sign."

"But, what will happen to me and Danny if she dies?"

Elizabeth was listening and quickly approached them. "You'll stay with us, and visit Aunt Abigail on the weekends." Danny and she were silent as they headed for the car. They saw Matt in the parking lot walking in their direction. As they got closer, he bent and sat on his heels and opened his arms. Danny accepted his hug, but quickly pulled away. "Why are you here?"

"For you -- I care about both of you. I'm so very sorry about your dad. Will you be okay?"

"They just closed the casket, and it was loud," Lisa said, with a solitary tear creeping down her left cheek.

"I'm so sorry. It must be awful for you."

The children both nodded, and their faces were grim. "We can never see him again," Danny said.

"But, I heard the preacher man. Didn't he say you'll see him in heaven forever?" The kids were silent as they looked away. "I guess that doesn't help you right now, does it?"

"No. I want him with me now," Lisa said, while crying. "I want him to stay here."

"It's hard to say goodbye to your daddy … he was the only one you had."

It surprised Abigail to see Matt comforting the children and how he seemed to know exactly what they needed to hear. *The man just keeps on amazing me with his contradictions. How can a thief be a kind gentleman? How can that be?*

Chapter Twenty-nine

While glancing out the window, Abigail decided to water her roses. Although the yellow ones were plentiful, she wished the peach ones would have produced more. It was a lovely day. The blue sky was arrayed with feather-like clouds that helped cool the temperature. For her, being outdoors was always uplifting, so she took a lounge chair and placed it under the old sycamore tree, and brought a book to read.

Though she missed the children, she enjoyed having a day of leisure. While reading, she fell asleep. Once awake, she went inside for a cold drink. While pouring iced tea, she heard the phone ring. It was the store saying the telescope had arrived. She searched for and found Matt's business card and called, but he didn't seem surprised -- he must have received the same call. They agreed to meet.

After being out in the sun, her shower felt heavenly. Soon, she was dressed, had a bite to eat, and was on her way. When she arrived at the store, Matt was outside and greeted her with a hug.

She stepped back, while searching his eyes, and said, "Thank you."

He stared at her for a second. "For what?"

"The children needed all the support they could get, and you being there was helpful as they experienced the most difficult day of their lives."

"You don't get it, Abigail -- I care about them." He turned to go into the store.

At the counter was a young red-headed clerk with his paperwork. His pockmarked face gave him a rugged look. When he didn't notice them, Matt said, "Excuse me."

"Oh. Sorry. Can I help you?"

After Matt handed the young man his receipt, he examined it, pivoted and went into the storage room. While waiting, Abigail recognized Matt's cologne. It was *Passion for Men*. Before long, the clerk returned with a box and placed it on the counter.

Matt shifted his weight and asked, "Does it require much assembly?"

"Some. But, it should be easy. A Phillips-head screwdriver might be the only tool you'll need. But, I might be wrong. It's been a while since I put one together."

After paying and thanking the young man, they left. Matt insisted on carrying the box to her car. When they arrived, he placed it in her back seat. "I'll follow you home."

"Why?"

"To assemble it for Danny."

His innocent way of asking caught her off-guard and caused her to feel foolish to refuse. While driving home, she realized her address was in the local phone directory, so there was no reason to be concerned about him knowing where she lived. She checked the rear-view mirror; he was still following.

When she got home, she was pleased that her gardener was finished. The man did such a wonderful job on her front yard. The colorful flowers that hugged her house looked fresher, the bushes were manicured, and he even trimmed the tree. She also noticed new flowers in the circular planter around the tree trunk. The yard gave her place a homier look.

After he parked, she walked up to her front door expecting him to follow, but he didn't. When she turned, he was taking a toolbox from his trunk and laid it by the garage door. Then, he removed the telescope from her car. "Want this assembled in the garage?"

"No, it's too hot. Come in, I'll fix some iced tea."

After entering her home, he said, "I like your place, it's cheerful." He walked to the large window and pulled back the pale, green sheers to let in more light. "It seems we have the same taste, we both like contemporary."

She yelled from the kitchen, "Matt, can you come in here?"

When he entered the room, he said, "What's wrong?"

"Nothing, I wanted to see if you prefer soda."

After shaking his head no, "I thought you saw some creature you wanted killed." After having a laugh, he asked, "I need a few towels or a sheet, so I don't mess up your light-colored carpet."

"Oh, sure." When she walked past him, she took in the scent of his cologne. She had given that product to her brother a few times -- it was her favorite. After finding some towels, she returned.

When he took them from her, he laid them on the carpet. "I need a box opener."

After searching the kitchen drawers, she came back with a knife and a single-edged razor. "Can you use either of these?"

After he nodded his answer, she said, "Use lemon?"

"What?"

"Do you want lemon for your tea?"

"No. No sugar either."

After bringing his beverage, she placed it on a nearby table and watched him at work. In the past, she might have questioned herself as to why she let a man in her home while alone. But, instead she was amazingly comfortable and felt safe in his company.

Soon, he finished assembling the stand, then he placed the telescope in its slot and secured it. When finished, he placed it near the window. He returned, sat on the couch and felt the texture of its fabric.

After refilling his glass, she sat at the other end of the sofa and watched him admire his finished project.

"I'm glad he selected that one," he said. "It'll last a while. Danny's old enough to take good care of it." While looking at her, he said, "If you ever have a chance, take him away from the city lights. It'll help him to see the stars and planets more clearly."

While finishing his tea, he asked about the children. So, she told him they were with their grandmother overnight. When he left, he went to the front door and stopped. He circled around to face her. "Go to dinner with me tonight, will you? I know a great place in La Jolla. It overlooks the cove and shore. I hate going to nice places alone, would you come with me?"

She surprised herself when she said, "Yes, that sounds pleasant."

"Pick you up around seven?" he asked, as if not surprised by her response.

"That'll work." She followed him to his black Porsche. "So, can two people fit in that thing?" After chuckling, he said, "You'll fit just fine. See you at seven."

Later, while getting ready for her hot date, she searched her closet for the right outfit. She decided on a navy blue dress and a comfortable pair of shoes. While taking a quick shower, she told herself, *After all I've been through, I deserve one night of pleasure.*

While waiting for him, she heard a knock, so she grabbed her things. But, when she opened the door, it was Steven. "Hi, Sis," he said and walked in. "I'm going to see Mom and Dad, want to come?"

"No. I have plans."

He looked at her. "It looks like you have a date."

"Yes, I do, a dinner date," she said, hoping he'd stop asking questions.

"Good for you, Sis, I'm glad you're getting out. Is Carry going with you?"

"No. Perhaps tomorrow night we will."

His eyes widened. "Gee, Sis, where did you get that neat telescope?"

"Matt bought it." She thought, *Great! Now the questions.*

"Who's Matt?" he scowled. "He isn't the guy who showed up at the funeral, is he?"

"Yes, matter of fact, the very same guy."

With his mouth opened, he stared at her. "He's trying to buy his way into your life with expensive gifts."

"Actually, no, he isn't. That isn't for me, it's for Danny."

"What? Why would he do that?"

She started pacing. "It's Danny's reward for finding something for Matt." "You sound defensive, Sis."

While staring at the floor and still pacing, she said, "I don't mean to be."

After getting a closer look at the telescope, he said, "It must have cost the man a pretty penny."

"You're right, it did. Danny always wanted one, but couldn't bring himself to ask his dad, because of the cost."

Unexpectedly, he came and grabbed her to keep her from pacing. While holding her shoulders, Steven studied her face. "Be careful with this Matt person. He might seem nice, but I wouldn't trust him, okay?"

"Thanks. But, it's important I make my own decisions and mistakes."

"You really like this guy, don't you?"

"Yes, I do, on many levels."

After Steven left, her enthusiasm was depleted. Matt pulled up and parked. Before he reached her door, she got her purse and jacket and waited for his knock. When she got to his car, he opened her door for her. As they drove, she enjoyed his selection of classical music. Their conversation was light. They reached their destination. He had to circle the lot only once before finding a parking space.

The Brock House restaurant was one of her favorite lunch eateries, so she was looking forward to their dinner menu. Matt gave his name and soon they were seated outside at a balcony table. After ordering drinks, they relaxed and watched the waves crash on the shoreline.

As they studied the menu, he asked, "What kind of food do you like?"

Without looking up, she said, "Seafood, chicken or specialty salads."

"Well, that's unusual. A woman who actually knows what she wants."

"You're right." She grinned. "I also know what I want for breakfast and lunch."

"Okay, Smarty Pants," he said, with a chuckle.

They ordered their meals and watched the day come to an end, enjoying the sky's orange and red rays just before the sun set into the ocean. She reached for his hand. "This was lovely, Matt."

He took her hand, brought it to his mouth and kissed it, searching her pale blue eyes. Never had she felt so excited, yet relaxed at the same time. She wondered, *Why am I falling for an atheist and thief? That isn't fair!*

When they finished their meal, he paid and left a tip. They walked across the street and used the walkway that snuggled the shoreline. The night was magnificent. It was warm -- a rarity for San Diego. There was no haze or fog to prevent the stars from shining brilliantly. They held hands and watched the waves spray against the rocks.

Matt pulled her closer. She didn't resist.

"What made you become a teacher?"

"It's my calling."

"What's a calling?"

"I'm sorry. Let me rephrase. I enjoy being a teacher."

"Don't do that! You didn't answer me -- what's a calling?"

"I'm sorry. I didn't mean to offend you. But, to answer your question, it's my passion, it's what fulfills me. It's what I do to serve God and society. The Bible refers to it as a calling."

"What might be my calling?"

"For starters, working with children. You have a way of making them feel valued. Many adults lack that ability. Or, perhaps you would make a good leader or business owner. Your cohorts seem to respect you, and you're likable."

"That's interesting," he said. His eyes focused on her lips.

Although, she loved his romantic attention, she blurted out a question. "What made you become a thief?"

"It just happened, without much forethought. Years ago, a friend wanted me to steal some of his jewelry and make it look like a break-in. Afterward, he put in an insurance claim and used the money to pay off his back taxes. I told myself, 'He paid for his insurance, so why not use it?' To me, it didn't seem like a big deal at the time."

"So, from the beginning, you made light of being a thief?"

Those words hurt. He turned and watched the waves splash against the rocks. Without looking at her, he said, "I justify my actions by telling myself, 'No one gets hurt.'"

"Why did you continue after the first time?"

"My boss found out and wanted me to do the same for him. When I said no, he turned on me. So, later, I agreed. Then, the word got out and his friends wanted me to steal for them, as well. He looked at her. "But, my jobs were only by request."

"You mean, stealing jobs, don't you?

"Yes, stealing," He stood. "Hey, let's change the subject."

While walking, she asked, "So, what do you do for recreation?"

"I play golf and tennis, but I prefer tennis. It's faster and I'm good. And you?"

"I'm your opposite. I play tennis, but prefer golf. I love the outdoors. While golfing, I can listen to the birds and, on occasion, see various creatures." After bumping into him, intentionally, she said, "Where do you bring your dates, besides dinner?"

"The Civic Theater, but only if something worthwhile is playing."

They walked to the car; both were silent as he opened her door. While driving home, they talked about family, friends and the children.

When he stopped in front of her place, he quickly jumped out to assist her. They slowly walked to the front door. He spun her around on the porch. When she didn't resist, his lips touched hers. He found them warm and inviting. With her in his arms, he slowly caressed her curves and nuzzled her neck. As their lips met again, her body experienced new sensations. She trembled, her stomach tingled, and her heart raced. When their bodies came closer, she was defenseless.

He gazed at her. "Wow. You're amazing."

Although, she was smiling, she was shaking inside.

He said, "Aren't you going to ask me in?"

She shook her head and avoided his eyes because it would be too hard for her to say no.

"If I come in, we can watch a movie," he said. "I'm not overly tired, are you?"

"No, Matt, I'm not tired. But, if I invite you to come in, I would also insist you stay the night."

"That tells me a lot about your feelings. When can I see you again?"

"We won't be seeing each other again," she whispered.

As he looked at her, he was bewildered. "But why? We like each other, don't we?"

She nodded.

"We have chemistry. So, what's the problem?"

As she turned toward the door, her legs felt wobbly. "Good night, Matt. I genuinely had a wonderful time. I appreciate what you did for Danny. He'll love it. But, please, I can't see you again. Things would never work between us."

As he pleaded with her, he gave it his all. "But, why?"

Finally, she was able to face him. "We're heading in different directions. I love you, Matt. You're the love of my life, so to say no is devastating for me. But, we're going down two different paths -- spiritually and ethically -- and they're too extreme to overcome."

"We can make it work, I know we can."

"So, tell me, how? If I continue to see you, you know I'll be helplessly hooked."

"Can't you just give us a chance?"

She stood with her weight on one foot and her hand on her hip. "Why, Matt? So we can fall madly in love, just to end our relationship later? That would be harder on both of us."

"You're breaking my heart. I love you, Abigail." He grabbed her by the waist and held her in his arms. "I can't let you go. I've searched for you all my life."

"And, I love you, too. I like and admire you, but our lifestyles oppose each other. It couldn't work. So, we need to nip it in the bud, or it'll be impossible for us to end it later." While she tried to be composed, her body quivered.

At that moment, she wanted to say yes, but said, "I'm sorry, I truly am, but I can't." While opening the door, she glanced at him. His shoulders were slumped, his mouth was open, and his eyes revealed disbelief. She wanted to grab him and pull him inside. She hated leaving him there without hope.

Chapter Thirty

While walking around Mission Bay, Abigail stepped over a rock, picked it up, threw it and watched it skip on the water. As she walked around the inlet, she tried not to think about Matt, but couldn't help it because she was worried sick. The expression on his face was similar to Gary's after she broke it off with him.

Abruptly, she stopped and pulled out her cellphone to call Carry. After they arranged to meet, she pleaded with God. *Please. I couldn't bear it if anything happened to Matt. Please protect him.*

She got into her car and headed for Coronado Island. After finding a parking space, she got out and walked to the restaurant.

When she saw Carry waving from a table, she joined her. Before they were able to review the menus, their young waiter, who looked like a high school student, was standing at their table. He smiled with his order pad in hand, but he didn't say a word. Abigail ordered toast and coffee, and Carry requested poached eggs with an English muffin.

After he left, Carry asked, "What's going on with Alisa?"

"She's still in a coma, I'm sorry to say."

"Will she come out of it?"

"The doctors think she might. They've said coma survivors can wake up after a month and be perfectly normal. So, who knows?"

When the waiter returned with the coffee, Abigail asked, "Is this your first job?"

"No. I worked at Applebee's for three years."

"You look too young for that experience."

"I'm twenty-two … I know, I look younger. I get that all the time."

Once the young man was gone, Carry asked, "So what's wrong? You sounded upset."

Abigail looked at her folded hands on the table. "I'm concerned. What if Matt does something foolish, like Gary? I don't think I could take it."

"Matt doesn't seem like the suicidal type. From what you have said, he has strong friendships and was bold enough to crash the funeral. To me, he seems secure, whereas Gary had no close friends, and he struggled with depression. Remember, you said he was on depression and anxiety medication for years."

Abigail looked into her eyes. "I'm troubled, because twice I saw Matt suddenly shut down. Once on the yacht, after I asked about his connection to the touring vessel and, last night, after dinner when I challenged him about being a thief. Both times, he became very upset. Doesn't that seem like he is emotionally distressed?"

Carry reached over and touched her folded hands. "The question is, how long did it take for him to bounce back?"

"Let's see, at least a few hours on the yacht and an hour last night, why?"

"If my memory serves me, Gary was depressed for days, if not weeks at a time, so I don't think you can compare the two men."

"Perhaps, you're right," Abigail said, while looking at her friend.

After Carry leaned forward, she said, "You don't have control over what other people say or do. It's not your fault Gary tried to kill himself. You're not responsible for his choices."

"I know. But, I regret not offering him hope. Instead, I abruptly ended our relationship."

"Now, Abigail, how could you offer Gary hope when he wanted a life commitment? Would that be possible? And, with Matt, your differences are huge, so how could you have offered hope?"

Abigail grinned at her logic. "It's hard for me to be objective. I know Matt's nothing like Gary, but I can't get over his tormented expression."

Carry adjusted to sit straighter. "Look. Even if he does something rash, you're not responsible. You can't control another person's thoughts, emotions or actions. You know that!"

"Yes, you're right, but I still hate seeing him suffer." After she got Carry's full attention, she said, "Matt's the only man for me. If I thought we could make it work, I would run into his arms as fast as possible."

"This is the first time I have seen you stuck on a man. Your face lights up each time you mention him, even your eyes show how much you care."

"So, what do I do now?" Abigail asked.

"For starters, you need a reality check. Are you willing to live the rest of your life married to an atheist? Will you be happy knowing your husband is a thief? Are you prepared to tell your children their father's in prison? Of course not! So, what's the struggle here?"

Abigail looked down at her folded hands, and then at her friend. "If we were together, I would end up making his life miserable. I'd hound him to see the truth about God and what Jesus did for him. Plus, I would force him to promise to never steal again and insist he pay restitution."

"So, why don't you tell him what you just said? Perhaps, he might want to change his lifestyle and embrace your faith. In your mind, you're trying to adjust to his lifestyle. Instead, let him find a way to adapt to yours."

"Carry, what am I going to do?"

"Let's look at it from another angle. You're thirty, so your clock is ticking away. Maybe it's not just Matt, but that your hormones are raging."

Abigail leaned in closer. "I love everything about the man -- how he interacts with the children, how he keeps me in check, his humor and how he gets mine. We're so comfortable with each other. With him, I can feel excited and at ease at the same time."

There was a snicker on Carry's face. "Okay, enough already. You're making me fall in love with the guy." They laughed so long that tears came to their eyes.

"As your friend, it's my opinion that it's too late. You're already hooked on him. So, what's the bottom line here? What is preventing you from letting him know your feelings and concerns?"

"For starters, you're right, he's the love of my life, but I love God foremost. And, He doesn't want me to marry a non-believer, and I trust God with my life."

*   *   *

Matt tried to get some sleep, but he couldn't. Instead, he tossed and turned all night. He got out of bed to watch TV. There was nothing worthwhile on, so he found a DVD of *A Few Good Men* and pushed play. He tired of it quickly and turned it off. Desperately, he needed someone to talk to, but everyone was sleeping. After an hour passed, he decided he couldn't wait until morning. He called Jack and waited.

"Who's this, why are you calling so early? It's four in the morning."

"It's me Jack. I know it's late. Should I call back later?"

"Don't be absurd, you know I'm already awake."

"I need to talk. My mind's racing so much I can't sleep, focus or even watch the damn TV, for God's sake. What's wrong with me?"

"It's the woman," Jack said, while fluffing his bed pillows so he could sit propped up. Matt paced and ran his hand through his hair. "What do you mean?"

"I saw you walking with her by the La Jolla shores. She's a sophisticated woman; so face it, she won't settle for men like us."

"But, I can't stop thinking about her, I can't sleep. I want her, Jack."

"I'm telling you to forget her, why would she want to reconcile with a thief?" Soon, Jack got out of bed and sauntered into the kitchen. "How will you feel if someday she had to visit you behind bars? And, don't kid yourself, 'cause that's where you're headed, unless you stop this nonsense."

"I already made up my mind about that. I took my last job. But, what will I do? Go get a job someplace?"

"You make work sound appalling." He opened the refrigerator and grabbed the milk. "Hey. People go to work every day, and they endure adequately, so why can't you?"

"It's easy for you to say -- you own your own business."

"Then, go find a company to buy; you have the money and the ability. All you need to do is figure out what's appealing to you and do it."

"Funny," Matt said while pulling the blinds and looking out the window. "It's still dark."

"Suit yourself, but from my view, what you're doing isn't working. You just lost the love of your life, and you have no plans to change that. So, your task is to decide what you need to do differently to get her back. But, it has to be genuine or it won't work, Pal."

Once Matt stopped pacing, he said, "Okay. I have decided that, with or without her, there will be no more stealing jobs. I don't care who puts pressure on me, I'm done with them."

"Good. It's about time. I was beginning to think you were dense. What made you decide with such conviction?"

"I realized I'm a thief."

"How did you fool yourself to think otherwise?"

"Because the people I stole from asked me to, and they committed insurance fraud, not me. I considered myself ethical because no one got hurt, and I never brought a weapon. But, now I get it. I'm a thief."

"Good. At least you made one good decision."

"Jack, I'm sorry for putting you at risk to lose everything for me. And, I want to correct things, so what should I do next?"

"She's a Christian, right?"

Matt stopped pacing. "What does that have to do with anything?"

"You must figure out why you're an atheist and lack faith. Then, decide if you have room for God in your life -- you either do or don't. But, only you will know the answer to that question. Who knows? This might be your turning point."

Matt hung up and was more confused than ever. This time, when he thought about Abigail, he also thought of his Aunt

Francis, perhaps because both women knew God. "Where did I put that Bible she gave me?" Although he hadn't read it much, he found it inspiring.

He said out loud, "I must accept my past, so I can change my future." As he looked at himself more clearly, he saw the truth and could admit his flaws and wrongdoings. And, for some reason, he was actually considering paying for his mistakes. Although he wanted her more than life itself, he was willing to go to jail, even if it meant losing her. "Without self-respect and dignity, I have nothing to offer her."

His life flashed before him. He questioned how a child, raised in Bel Air, California, with a stay-at-home mom and a hardworking father, could become a thief? Although his mother never worked, she did lack motherly instincts. She was too busy with women's groups, golf and card clubs. One time, she brought his sister Karen and him golfing, only to leave them in the car for hours until she finished. After school, he often had to wait for a long time to be picked up, because she forgot.

The times his family was home together, she busied herself on the phone with various acquaintances. She showed little interest in Karen or him and seemed to go through the motions of motherhood without pleasure.

Although his dad was a good provider as an insurance executive, he bragged about cheating on his income taxes and refused to give to charities. The man would never be accused of trying to live his life through his kids. He was too busy living his own life with sports and social events.

Sometimes, Matt felt as if he and his sister were an inconvenience their parents had to endure for eighteen years. So, to cope, Matt learned to self-parent, but failed miserably, while Karen found nurturing from her teachers, and the parents of her friends.

Though his dad made his living in the insurance industry, he said, "People who spend money on insurance are stupid; they rarely reap the benefit." So, in some sick way, Matt thought his dad might approve of his scheme to scam insurance companies. It was ironic, his dad made his living in the insurance industry, while he stole money through insurance fraud. In some warped way, Matt thought he was doing society a service by equalizing things. At least, that's what he told himself to justify his actions.

His Aunt Francis was loving and nurturing and seemed to care about Karen and him. It was she who gave him his Bible. When she was upset with his parents, she would say, "Your parents are nice people on their way to hell." Or, if she was feeling more congenial, she would say, "They're going to spend eternity separated from God."

But, Matt found it difficult to believe that good people like his parents would go to hell, when a thief like he could go to heaven just by believing Jesus died for him. That just didn't make sense -- it was too simple.

"I think I have too many questions and too little faith." The regret he felt earlier was quickly becoming despair. It had been three days of him being barricaded at home with sorrow as his only companion.

While looking for his Bible, he recalled that his dad often said, "Religion is for the weak or those in need of a crutch." But, at that moment, Matt felt pathetically weak and desperately in need of that crutch. So, he frantically searched for the book and found it in his nightstand. *What a surprise,* he mocked himself.

After reading awhile, he put it down and later read a little more, then put it down once again. Suddenly, he took a closer look at his aunt's handwritten note. "To Matthew, from Aunt Francis, read John 3:16."

It took a while, but he found the book of John, then chapter 3 and verse 16. "God so loved the world that He gave His only begotten Son, that whosoever believes in Him shall not perish but will have everlasting life."

While pondering why she wanted him to read it, he sat in silence, asking himself, *How does that apply to my situation?* He quickly grabbed a pen and pad of paper and tried to crack the code.

First: God so loved the world -- I live in the world. So God loves me.

Second: He gave His only begotten Son -- God gave me Jesus.

Third: That whosoever believes in Him -- If I believe in Jesus...

Fourth: Shall not perish -- Does that mean I'll live on?

Fifth: But will have everlasting life: I guess that means someday I'll go to heaven and live there forever.

"I need to figure out how that can be helpful right now." He stared at his notes.

He jumped to his feet, yelling, "Eternity! It starts now. Not when I die. I have life now!" As he fell on his knees, his tears welled up, "I want to believe. Help me. I need forgiveness. I know I screwed up my life. I'm done trying to do things on my own, it doesn't work." While weeping, he asked, "What should I do with my life?"

Instantly, as if someone opened the window on a rainy day and the sun shined brightly, peace came over him and he felt instantly clean inside. His mind was unmistakably lucid. He grabbed the phone directory and searched for the District Attorney's office. After speaking to a secretary, he made an appointment for the next day.

Within minutes of hanging up, his phone rang. It was Abigail's voice. "Are you okay?"

"I never felt better in my life, why?"

"You've been on my mind for days. I've been praying for you." "Actually, something did happen. I decided to turn myself in. I have an appointment with the District Attorney tomorrow."

"You sound like you've been crying."

"Yes. I have. But, they're tears of relief and joy because, for the first time in years, I can see things clearly."

Chapter Thirty-one

When Abigail arrived at her home, she was concerned because her sister's condition hadn't changed. She was hoping for some good news. As she opened the drapes, the sunlight was bright and brought warmth. When she listened to her messages, one was from Matt. But she decided to fix tea before dialing his number. When he answered, she said, "Hi. It's me. How did things go?"

"I'm glad it's you, I called earlier, but I guess you know since you're returning mine," he said, with a light chuckle.

"Did you see the District Attorney?"

"Nope, I changed my mind."

"Oh," she said, as her heart sank and her future dissipated. "But why?" she said with a punch.

"Because this morning, my dear, I discovered something new regarding the murders."

"What! I thought Forelli ... wasn't he awaiting trial?"

"Yes. He still is, but he might be innocent."

"Who's the new suspect? Why didn't anyone tell us? How did you find out?"

"By listening to the morning news," he said, while still grinning. "The news reporter said the FBI found an Iraqi hiding on the yacht. His spokesman said he was trying to recover a stolen artifact that dated back to early A.D. It belonged to a Samarian Village."

"I can't believe this. The man was found on the yacht! Where was he hiding? We searched everywhere."

"They didn't report that, but if he's telling the truth, we were searching for the same artifact."

Her thoughts raced, as she sat. She was stunned by the new revelation. Suddenly she remembered, "The guy might be telling the truth. Guess what? Larry and Sandra had just returned from the Middle East!"

"Wow. That's an interesting thought."

"Where do you think he was hiding?" she asked.

"My guess is in the Master Suite."

"Why?"

"It's the only cabin we didn't search."

"Oh. That makes sense." She said while walking to the kitchen, holding the phone to her ear. "He has to be the murderer. Did the FBI find the vase?" She switched the phone to her other ear, while pouring water.

"No. But I did."

Abigail stopped in her tracks and put down the pot. "What! You found it -- when?"

"Late morning, right after I heard the news report. I figured the historical artifact must be in the Kilgore's house, since it wasn't on the yacht."

While trying to digest what he was saying, she was silent, *don't get too excited about your future.* After taking a deep breath, she said, "So, you broke into their home?"

"Yes. Matter of fact, I did. At first, I searched to see if it was lying out conspicuously, like the Faberge' Egg, but it wasn't. After probing around, I decided to search where they stored their vases. I found the relic hidden in a box way behind the others. I didn't even want to touch it, the thing looked so fragile."

"How can you be sure it's what the Iraqi searched for?"

"It was obvious. If it's dated back to Christ, a vase or pot could easily be what they were searching for. It also looks like one-of-a-kind, it's so fragile."

At this point, Abigail was confused. She wasn't sure if she should be pleased or angry. "Do you realize what you're saying? During our last phone conversation, you were going to turn yourself in, but, instead, you broke into their home? That doesn't make sense. Why would you risk getting into more trouble?"

"Because, it was my first glimpse of God's grace."

"What do you mean?"

"Right before I was going to turn myself in, I switched the TV channel to the news. That's when I heard about the Iraqi and the priceless vase. So, perhaps God wanted me to use it as a bargaining tool."

"But how?" she said while carefully sitting so not to spill her tea.

"By going to the FBI and asking for a deal."

Silently, she was thanking God. "Did you call them yet?"

"My appointment is at three-thirty."

"Today?"

"Yep."

"Good for you, Matt. Do you think they'll go for it?"

"That I don't know, it may not be their call."

"Then who?"

"If they can't make a deal, it might be up to the U.S. Attorney's Office. But, I'm hoping that the FBI will at least get the ball rolling."

"Where's the vase now?"

"Someplace safe, don't worry. No one will ever find it without my help."

*　　*　　*

When Matt arrived to the FBI Headquarters, he asked for Special Agent Ned Parker. A dark-haired woman behind the reception desk said, "I'm sorry, but something came up. It might be a while."

"I'll wait."

"Can I get something for you?" Her cheerful voice matched her smile. "We have coffee, tea and water."

"No, thanks." He turned and walked into the waiting area and sat. After a while, he checked his watch, thirty minutes had passed. Within another ten minutes or so, Special Agent Parker came to greet him. "Sorry to keep you waiting, an emergency came up."

"No problem."

"Please come with me."

He followed Parker into a conference room. The man seemed preoccupied. When they entered, there was a round table with chairs. Parker held out his arm indicating to sit. After getting comfortable, he asked, "What can I do for you?"

Because Matt observed that he wasn't fully present, he waited until he thought he was paying attention. "What I have to say needs to be off the record. Is that possible?"

After surveying Matt for a minute, he said, "Sure, as long as no one's in imminent danger."

"No. It's nothing like that."

After explaining the news regarding the Iraqi being found on the yacht, he asked, "Is closing the murder investigation important to you?"

Parker didn't answer.

"Do you have any interest in finding the two-thousand-year-old vase?"

Suddenly, there was alertness in Parker's eyes, as he sat upright.

"What if I can produce the vase -- would that help your investigation?"

"I'm not sure where you're going here."

Matt leaned forward. "I would like to propose an exchange, the return of the relic for my immunity. Are you in a position to do that?"

As Parker sat back in his chair, he said, "Immunity for what?"

"For my many past crimes that were never closed."

"What crimes are we talking about?"

After explaining in detail about his part in various fraudulent insurance claims, Matt stated that he never used weapons, never harmed anyone and had never been investigated or suspected of any of the crimes. "In short, I have a clean record, you can check it out."

"Then, why turn yourself in if the authorities aren't looking for you?"

"Because I want to turn my life around, but can't -- not with my past haunting me."

As Parker swayed in his chair, he carefully surveyed Matt. "Okay. First, convince me you and your cohorts are innocent of those murders."

Matt leaned forward. "For starters, I know the Kilgores were involved in smuggling stolen goods, and that they had just returned from the Middle East. So, what the Iraqi said adds up."

"Go on."

While watching his face, Matt said, "Did you find the Iraqi hiding in the Master Suite by any chance?"

No response.

"Look at your notes. Miss Wilson and the children searched for the Kilgore's. They went to their Master Suite and knocked on the hatch several times. And that was before we arrived. Do you think the reason they didn't respond might be because the couple was already dead?"

"Go on," Parker's eyes darted as he grabbed a pen and wrote on a yellow pad. He glanced up, while squirming in his chair. "What do you want from me, Mr. Willingham?"

"I want for you to arrange immunity for me and my men with the appropriate authorities. When that is done, I'll hand over the priceless relic."

"I'll give it some thought and consult with my associates."

"I'm convinced that the Iraqi murdered those people. The vase will validate his motive to kill. By the way, I bet he isn't denying he did it."

Special Agent Parker was silent with his eyes looking down and his forehead revealed deep lines.

"It's my guess that if you, an FBI agent, solved a double murder case and recovered a priceless artifact, it would enhance your career. Am I wrong here? Wouldn't that be a plus for you with International Affairs? We already know that it's an embarrassment for our country. The Iraqi's spokesman accused our military personnel of taking it when we invaded them after 9/11."

"Yes, go on."

"My theory is that the Kilgores refused to return it to the man, so he became angry and killed them."

"But, you have not finished connecting the dots. Where's the vase?"

"What if someone had it, would it be worth immunity for its return?" he said with piercing eyes and leaning forward.

Parker sat erect. "Where is it? Or do you even know?"

"Yes. I have access to it and can bring it to you."

"I don't get it. Why is immunity so important?"

"Someday I might marry. I don't want to be sitting at home with my family and be arrested for a crime I committed years earlier. Now do you get it?"

Silently, Parker stood and then paced with his hands behind his back. When he stopped he glared at Matt.

"I want the same deal for my associates, and I promise you, none of them have priors and they all have good careers. They only helped me as a favor. Those men trust me. So, everything I request must apply to them. Is that agreeable?"

"I hear you."

"Just think of how many unsolved cases you will close, including a double-murder, and help our country politically at the same time."

"You make it all sound so easy," Parker said, while sitting back in his chair, his eye cocked while studying Matt.

"Hey, I'm not a high-risk criminal, nor are my men. This shouldn't be a hard sell to your people or the State Attorney."

Soon, Parker's eyes became more alert and his head nodded.

"Are you in a position to start the negotiation for me?"

"You're a smart man. You wouldn't be here if you didn't know the answer." Suddenly he pushed himself up from his chair. "I'll speak to my people and get back to you. But, I'll warn you, the immunity does not apply to future crimes. And, if you're lying about not using weapons, or we find out you harmed someone, the deal is off, understand? That goes for your cohorts, as well, okay?"

After Matt grinned, he nodded. "Yes, of course."

"I'll place a few calls." While walking Matt to the door, Parker said, "I'll phone you tomorrow. By the way, did all your crimes occur in San Diego?"

"No. Some took place out of state or out of the country, but the insurance owners lived in San Diego."

"I'm not sure how that'll fly. I'll do what I can."

Matt stopped. "That shouldn't be a problem. Our deal involves international issues. By the way, the only other person I'll implicate is Luke Percy. That man referred all those who wanted to commit insurance fraud." Matt watched for his reaction, but he had none.

Matt reached for Parker's hand, "It's been a pleasure meeting with you again. I hope we can work something out."

Just as Matt was walking down the hall, he spun around with a large grin. He felt lighter, as if a weight was lifted. Although he was pleased with how things went, he knew not to celebrate until he received his call from Parker.

Once he was home, he scouted through the yellow pages for churches nearby. One had a service that night at seven. He decided to attend.

As he drove to La Jolla to meet with Jack, he was pleased with himself for making some significant steps in the right direction.

He was determined to change, even if it meant doing jail time. When he arrived at the meeting place, Jack was at a table waiting. He quickly stood to greet Matt, "So, tell me. What's going on?"

"What do you mean?"

"You look like the dog that finally caught up with the cat."

While grinning, he said, "Let's order, then talk."

Soon a slightly overweight, middle-aged waitress came to the table. She had brittle red hair and deep facial lines.

"What can I get for you, fellers?"

"Just coffee for now."

Soon she returned with coffee, but her hands shook while filling their cups. Later she returned to take their orders, and slowly moved out of sight.

While Jack listened to Matt giving the updates on the case, he was intrigued that it included a spiritual change as well. He rubbed his temples while saying, "Wow. That's a lot to take in. Talk about a turn-around, it makes me feel dizzy."

As Matt chuckled, he said, "Actually I feel pretty good knowing I'm doing the right thing."

"I'm both surprised and impressed. After listening to you, I can tell you're doing this for yourself, not the woman. That is amazing."

"If I don't change for me, it won't stick -- I know that. It hit me, the only things I have control over are my choices and how I react to my problems. If I continue making the same mistakes, they'll eventually destroy me."

"It's about time you came to your senses," Jack said, while leaning back in his chair with a broad smile.

"Okay. Now, I need to ask you something," Matt whispered. "How did you justify helping me fence stolen goods all those years?"

"Fear, if it wasn't me helping you, you may have ended up with the wrong people. Tell you one thing, it was hard on me."

"You're a solid friend, Jack. I'm sorry for taking advantage of you."

*   *   *

After Matt returned home he called Abigail, but had to leave a message. At that moment, he was energized and decided to clean the house. When he heard himself humming a tune, it surprised him. As he glanced at the clock, he realized he was running late for the seven o'clock church service.

Chapter Thirty-two

While Abigail sat and watched her sister lying hooked up to equipment, she listened to the beep, beep, beep, over and over again. She covered her eyes. *How can Mother stand to watch her like this day after day?*

The pale green walls felt as if they were closing in. She went to the window to look at the ocean. The water lacked its usual sparkle. When she glanced over her shoulder, she saw a book her mother left. She walked over to her sister's bed stand to retrieve it. As she flipped to the marked chapter, she read it out loud hoping her sister could hear and enjoy the story.

After reading several chapters she placed the book on the table, and watched her sister. She wanted to tell her everything and said, "What can I do Alisa? I love him so much. It kills me to end our romance before it begins." As she watched her unresponsive sister, she touched her forehead and started praying for her recovery.

When finished, she said, "I know. A double-minded person shouldn't expect anything from the Lord. Okay, I'll try to stand firm," with a tear filled face she kissed her hand, "I miss you, Sis, and I love you so very much."

On her way to the car, she decided to phone Carry. When she answered, she said, "Boy, do I need a friend right now. Can we get together?"

"When and where?"

"One hour, at the Prado restaurant in Balboa Park."

"Sure."

"You're a good friend. There's no doubt. When I need you most, no questions asked, you're there for me."

"You would do the same for me," Carry said.

While driving though Balboa Park, Abigail enjoyed the beauty of all the trees and flower gardens. Although she parked on the lower level, she enjoyed her walk up the hill and admired the unique architecture of the embassy buildings. She passed the magnificent outdoor stage and the Oriental Gardens. She had never gone through them. *Perhaps I'll take the kids next week.*

Once she reached the restaurant, she sat and waited for Carry. Suddenly she tapped her shoulder.

"Oh, you startled me," she said with a giggle.

They followed their young hostess to a table on the patio.

While searching her friend's face, Carry said, "So, what's up? It's that guy again, right?"

"You rat, you know me too well."

"What's wrong?"

"My head and heart are conflicting," she said while looking away.

"What does your head tell you?"

"Never see him again."

"And your heart?"

"To fall into his arms and never let go."

"Even if he is a thief, you still want him in your life?"

"He won't be one for long." Abigail said leaning forward. "Today he's going to talk to the FBI."

"What do you mean?" Carry put her drink down. "When did he decide to do that?"

"Recently he said in order to have a new start he can't be worrying about his past."

"It might be a ploy to get you. Or, did you even think of that?"

"No, I haven't." Abigail dipped her chip into the hummus.

"Why?"

"Because he didn't call me, I called him, and he had already made that decision. In addition, not once has he tried to convince me to see him."

"Not yet, you mean," she said, with a scornful tone.

"So, tell me, you've never fallen for the wrong guy?" Abigail asked, with a smug face. She sat back in her chair glaring at Carry.

"You know the answer. That's why I'm so cynical," Carry said. "But, going back to you, what changed? You were so firm about your decision. So, why doubt your resolution? Do you want to date him?"

"Believe me, I want more than to date him, my cynical friend, he's great with children, and I enjoy being with him. And, most importantly, he turns me on. And, that's difficult to pass up."

Carry laughed. "Spoken like a true woman." Okay, now tell me what God's saying to you?"

"Not much. So I'm relying on His word, which said to only marry someone with the same beliefs."

"So, what are you going to do?"

"Trust God and try really hard to stop obsessing about the man of my dreams, the man I may never have."

"Now, who's the cynical one?" Carry grinned and patted Abigail's hand. "I know this is difficult for you, but I don't want to see you get hurt or have any regrets."

"I know."

When Abigail returned home, she was utterly exhausted. So she flopped on the couch, placing her feet on the table. She closed her eyes, just for a few minutes. A half-hour later, she woke up and saw the answering machine flashing. After listening to it, she quickly returned Matt's call. Subsequently they conversed with some small talk for awhile. She then asked, "So how did things go at the FBI office?"

"After doing everything I could, it's still up to Special Agent Parker. However, he did show interest and said he'll call me tomorrow."

"I'm happy for you. I hope you get what you want."

"Before you hang up," he said, "I need to thank you."

"What for?"

"Because of you and the children, I now want to settle down and have my own family. When you rejected me, it broke my heart and hurt me deeply. However, I still want to have what is good in life, and to become a better man."

"You're a good person Matt. Don't go selling yourself short."

"So are you, Abigail. It's amazing that you have placed your faith above your heart."

"What do you mean?"

"When we're together I see that you want to be with me, and I feel your body respond to my touch. Yet, you stick to your convictions. That's impressive."

I guess you don't realize I want to yell, TAKE ME! But, she managed to hold her tongue and silently yearned to be with him.

Matt sensed she was vulnerable, and wanted to protect her so he said, "Before I say goodbye, I want to thank you for making me want to become worthy of someone like you."

After their goodbye, she quickly phoned Carry for strength.

"If they don't offer him immunity, what do you think he'll do?" He's a schemer, that's for sure."

"Is that your pessimistic nature, I hear?"

Carry was silent for a minute, yet had to laugh, "You got me, but right now I find it hard to know how to be supportive of you."

"Everything within me wants to see him, but I can't. Although, we're such a good fit in so many ways, my foremost desire has always been to share my faith with my man."

"Do you think we're being too picky?" Carry said.

"What do you mean?" Abigail said as she settled into her chair.

"Look at our ages, neither of us ever married."

"Yes, we're picky," Abigail said. "But look at our friends. Many have been married, had children and are now divorced, raising them alone. The others have remarried and are complaining about having trouble adjusting to a blended family."

"There's a saying that many people get married while they're waiting for the right person to come along. Perhaps, there is truth to that."

On her way to visit her parents and the children, she hoped that Matt was telling the truth and not what she wanted to hear. Like when he said, "It was my first glimpse of God's grace." Although she wanted to believe him, she knew it would take a miracle to turn an Atheistic Thief into a Reformed Christian overnight.

When she pulled into her parents' driveway, she saw her dad sitting on the porch with Danny. The boy ran to the car to greet her with his arms open, saying, "Aunt Abigail!" After hugging, she said, "I missed you so much."

Looking at her father, she waved and yelled, "Hi, Dad!" When she reached him, he stood to give her a bear hug. "Any news about Sis?"

"No," he said, with sadness in his eyes.

"Where's Lisa?"

"She's in the kitchen helping her nana."

"I bet she's talking Mom's ear off."

He grinned and nodded.

While he stood holding the door open, Abigail thought he had aged. Although he was putting on a happy face, it was a feeble attempt. She entered the house and went directly into the kitchen.

"Aunt Abigail. You're here!" the child said while jumping into her arms. "I missed you."

"What are you two up to?" Abigail asked.

"I'm helping make banana bread, Nana's teaching me."

Elizabeth came over and embraced her daughter and kissed her cheek. Quickly, she returned to the sink while clearing her throat.

Soon Abigail came up behind her mother and whispered, "Can I help with anything?"

"Yes, you can reassure me that your sister will come out of her coma."

"With prayer, it is possible Mom."

"Okay. You can tell me about your friend Matt." When Elizabeth turned, her eyes sparkled, and her dimples were showing.

"What do you mean?"

"Lisa talks about him." She said while glancing at Lisa. "Don't you, dear?"

Lisa nodded.

"And, we saw the telescope he bought Danny."

"Yes, he has been very kind to the children."

"Was he kind to you, too, dear?"

"Yes. Very kind to me, as well, Mother!" she said with a bite.

"So, have you been out with him alone?"

"I can't believe this. I'm thirty years old and being interrogated by my mother!" Her face was flush as she stated, "Yes, once for dinner."

"When will you be seeing him again?"

"Never! Now please change the subject." Abigail spun around and marched out of the kitchen. When she reached the living room, she took in a deep breath and let it out slowly. She felt angry. *Why do I let her get to me?*

"Are you okay?"

"Yes, Dad." she said while trying to inhale and exhale on a count of ten. Once she calmed herself, she said, "Have the doctors said anything at all about Alisa's recovery?"

"Same old thing, she can hear us, but can't respond. And, it's anyone's guess if or when she'll come out of her coma."

"Are you satisfied she's getting the best care?"

"Yes. We think so. If the hospital is good enough for John Wayne, it's good enough her. Besides, Scripps Green Hospital is the best in our city."

"How do you know John Wayne was there?"

"I saw him in their elevator wearing a hospital gown. He must have had some tests or X-rays. He was a friendly cuss."

"I liked John Wayne," Danny said. "I have a picture of him."

After smiling, Abigail said, "I saw it, it's a good likeness." Soon she turned to her father, "Have you gone golfing lately?"

"No. Not since your sister's accident."

"That's too bad. Want to go tomorrow? The children can ride with us. It'll be fun."

Danny became animated and his voice rose, "Can we go? I'll drive the golf cart."

"No." John said.

"But why not?"

"I just don't feel up to it Danny."

Abigail reached out to her father and held his hand. "It would be a good change of scenery. It would be good for you too. We can all go while Mother has her Bible study in the morning. I'll call the hospital and ask them to call my cell number if there is a change."

"I don't know."

"I'll call and get a tee time, and if you decide not to go, I'll take the children."

"But, you'll need two carts with two children," John said.

"Yes, that's why we need you."

He let out a loud breath, "Okay. You win."

After dinner, Abigail sat pretending to read a magazine but was thinking of how she might give grace to her mother for snooping. No matter where she went, Matt seemed to be the topic of conversation. She wondered if the woman was curious, worried, or knew she was in love.

Chapter Thirty-Three

While Abigail tried to sleep, she became restless. So, she got up to warm some milk. While sipping it she wondered how Matt was doing with his bargaining for immunity, yet had peace that everything was now in God's hands.

When she returned to bed, she quickly fell into a deep sleep. Matt and she had just married. While at the doorpost of their honeymoon suite, he scooped her up in his arms and carried her across the threshold. After setting her down, he placed his hands on her face while looking into her eyes, saying, "You're such a beautiful bride." As he kissed her, his lips were warm and tender.

Without a warning, he walked away out of sight. When he returned he said, "I hope you like bubbles in your bathwater." When she entered the prepared bathroom, she quickly undressed and slipped into the hot water while letting it cover her tall slender body. With her head resting and eyes closed, she moved to let the jets manipulate her feet and shoulders.

After her bath, she grabbed a towel. While drying she noticed the glorious marble floor, pedestal sink, and ornate vanity. She could see Matt behind her in the mirror carrying a tray of strawberries dipped in chocolate. When he approached, she gladly accepted his pampering. Soon he vanished to turn back their wedding bed. So she quickly slipped into her transparent nightgown.

Suddenly the stupid phone rang. She wanted to toss it into the trash. But instead, she got out of bed and answered.

"Hello Dear, it's Mother. I want to give you some good news."

"What?" Abigail said with a grumpy tone.

"Your sister moved her fingers this morning. It's the first sign she might recover."

"Well that's amazing news, do the kids know?"

"Not yet. They're at home with Dad."

"Oh Mom, I'm so happy. Won't the children be thrilled? I bet Lisa will happily dance around, Danny will have the biggest smile, while Dad will probably cry from happiness."

"I'm still at the hospital. I'll wanted to call you first."

"Let's go celebrate Mother. I'll come take you to breakfast, would you like that?" Abigail said.

"Yes that would be delightful. Do you have any idea, how relieved I feel?"

"Sure do! So am I. It's an answer to all of our prayers."

*   *   *

While showering, Abigail was full of gratitude as she praised God for the news. Soon the warmth of the water brought back memories of her delightful dream. But the shower couldn't compare to the amazing vision of a bath drawn by Matt.

Once she dressed and locked up, she was on her way to the hospital. Within twenty minutes she entered Alisa's room, but to her surprise, Elizabeth was gone. Yet Abigail was pleased to spend time alone with her sister.

"I'm so proud of you Sis. You're such a fighter. I knew you would make it. You had to. The children need you too much."

After her visit, Abigail headed for the cafeteria. When she saw Elizabeth, she quietly walked over and slipped into the bench seat, and kissed her cheek, "Hi Mom."

"Oh hi Honey. I knew the minute I left you'd come." They chatted about what joy they felt over Alisa's milestone.

Later they returned to Alisa's room hoping for more progress, but there was none.

"Ready to eat? I know a nice place nearby."

Elizabeth nodded, and turned to kiss her daughter lying so still, "You're a warrior. You'll get better, I'm sure of it."

While driving slowly down the street to La Jolla cove, they looked for a parking space. Luckily they pulled into a spot without much trouble. Soon they were climbing up the steps to the same restaurant Matt and she visited that overlooked the cove.

After they arrived, there was a slight morning breeze that kicked up. So when their host arrived, Abigail asked, "Is it okay to sit under a heat lamp? It's a little chilly."

The young man smiled and graciously led them to a table. After handing them menus, he explained the daily specials. Soon they ordered Spinach Omelets.

"This is lovely," Elizabeth said while watching the kayakers. "Have you ever done that?"

"Yes once with Carry. We were having a grand time until a sea lion came too close. It freaked her out. So we quickly rowed into the nearest cave."

"That sounds like fun."

"Yes. It was a memorable day. The cave we visited was small with sun shining down through a tiny opening at the top of the rocks. Don't you remember me telling you? I showed you my lump on my head?"

"How did that happen?"

"Well, we decided to take a short cut back…so we thought. But it brought us too close to the current causing the kayak to turn over and hit my forehead. While still in the water, we laughed so much it made it harder to get back into the kayak."

"Yes, I do remember. You acted as if you two went on some fun adventure."

Abigail grinned, "Actually it was. But enough about me, how are the children doing?"

"They're still adjusting. I hear them talking about their past outings with their father. They do miss him."

"Frankly, I can't imagine losing Dad at that age. It must be tough on them. But at least they have good memories."

"When they say their prayers, it is for their mother's recovery. They will be so pleased to hear the good news about their mother," said Elizabeth.

The waiter interrupted their conversation as he bent forward to sit the plates before them. Little talk transferred as they ate. While relaxing with a cup of coffee after their meal, Abigail touched her mother's arm, "I'm sorry about my reaction the other day, I don't know what got into me."

"It's my fault. I pried. If you want me to know something, you'll tell me."

"Well, I'm ready to talk now. The man you asked about, is Matt. We met at the yacht club and were on the yacht together. And yes. As you may have guessed, I'm in love with him. But I have certain reservations, so I told him to only call if he had information about the murder investigation."

"You said you love him, so why are you brushing him off like that?"

"Mom, we don't share the same faith or values. And I don't want my kids to be dropped off at church by their dad."

Elizabeth nodded, "I understand. But why do you think he's such a hopeless case? We always have hope when we include God. Look how your father changed once we found a new church?"

Abigail was shocked that her mother approved of a man she never met.

*   *   *

When Abigail returned home she fixed iced tea and grabbed her book. As she sat reading, the phone rang. At first she was annoyed, but remembered the good news her mother brought.

When she answered it, she heard Matt's voice.

"Oh, hi, Matt, did you hear from the FBI?"

"Yes."

"So what's the verdict?"

"Remember the Iraqi they found?"

"Yes."

"This morning an interpreter made a statement for him. Apparently the man admitted to the murders, but added, that they deserved to die, because they refused to return the smuggled item."

"Wow. That's amazing."

"After our 911 tragedy, we went to war in Iraq. It was at that time that the historical Artifact was taken from their museum."

"Well, now we know who killed them and why." Abigail said.

"One of our American spokesman, also made a statement. He emphatically vowed to return the relic to Iraq the moment it is recovered."

"So have you returned it yet?"

"Yes. I did this morning around the same time the story broke out."

"How did it go?"

"The FBI worked out an agreement with the State Attorney's Office. Once it was returned I would receive immunity for us. The deal is complete. As the song goes, it's signed, sealed and delivered. It states, if any of us ever commits insurance fraud again, the agreement is null and void."

"I'm glad they included that."

"Frankly, so am I," he said.

"Well good for you. They must have seen you as redeemable."

"Yep, but I'm not good enough for you, am I?"

"Stop that," she ordered. "I refuse to let you make me feel guilty."

"It's true. You are too good for me, but don't feel bad about it. It took you years to become you. But for me, I'm just getting started. However, I'm determined to become the best edition of myself possible. That's a commitment I made to myself."

"That's wonderful Matt. Things are looking up for you. I'm glad." Abigail felt warm inside. *Perhaps there is some hope for us after all.* "So what are you going to do?"

"For starters, I found a church near home. I want to meet the pastor and visit their Men's Bible Study. Tomorrow I'll attend Sunday morning service. They're teaching about the book of John."

Suddenly Abigail felt flush as her blood boiled. *At least as a thief, you told the truth,* she wanted to yell. *Why are you lying? No one changes that much over night. I'm not that dense,* but instead of saying anything, she silently bit her tongue.

While talking, he was unaware she had stopped listening.

"I'm actually looking forward to studying about John. It's the book my aunt inscribed in my Bible as a kid."

Abigail was now holding the phone away from her ear. *I don't believe a word you're saying. You're only telling me what I want to hear,* she wanted to yell. Her head was reeling, she wanted desperately to hang up, but couldn't.

Finally he said, "What's going on? You seem preoccupied. Should I call back?"

"No. That won't be necessary! I'm truly happy for you and hope you move forward as planned. But please, never call me again. It's inappropriate now that the case is closed." Her face was red as she slammed the phone into the cradle.

*   *   *

After hanging up he was in shock, *What just happened, why the coldness? Isn't she happy for us?* He repeatedly shook his head in disbelief, not knowing what to think. When he glanced down, he saw a brochure with the phone number of the church. He dialed and spoke with the pastor. After making an appointment for later that evening, Matt tried to make sense of her reaction to the best news he could possible give.

After parking his car, Matt walked to the front door, but it was locked. So he followed the sidewalk around to the parking lot. When he saw a door marked *Administration*, he entered the building. While waiting, he noticed that the furniture was old as if donated. He thought, *Someday, I'll do something about that.* After hearing footsteps, he turned and watched as a grey-haired man came toward him.

"You must be Matt?"

"Yes."

"I'm Pastor Thomas Wright, but call me Pastor Tom." His handshake was firm. His smile was warm and friendly.

"My office is this way." After the man pivoted, Matt followed.

The sparse office had a few old filing cabinets, a desk and three chairs. The opened window blinds let in the flood lights from the parking lot. The tan colored walls held his credentials. There was a painting of Jesus leaning on a large rock while praying.

"What can I help you with, young man?"

Matt slowly gave an overview of his criminal past, his family history and how his relationship with Abigail developed into love.

"When she rejected me last week, I became despondent. After days of agony, it finally came to me that I needed God. So I asked for forgiveness. Afterward, I felt clean inside. Suddenly it came to me to turn myself in and pay restitution. But I did hope that I would get a lighter sentence because I didn't have any priors."

"That was a big step in the right direction young man."

"Well. The next morning, while listening to a T.V. news reporter, I discovered that an Iraqi was found on the Yacht. It was my first glimpse of God's love and help."

"Well good for you. I'm glad you're acknowledging God in this."

"One thing lead to another resulting in working out a deal with the FBI in return for immunity. Part of the deal was if I ever commit insurance fraud again, the agreement is void."

"Good for you young man, I'm happy for you."

"Everything's great for me, except with Abigail."

"So why are you telling me this young man?"

"For one, I plan on attending this church and wanted you to know about my past."

"Son, everyone here has a past. We are all sinners saved by grace. You'll be in good company. I'm proud of you for repenting."

"Repenting?"

"Yes. That means you no longer want to steal, right?"

"Oh yes." Matt said while leaning forward. "I need to understand something."

"What?"

"When I told Abigail about wanting to meet you, and to attend your church, she became distant. She told me to never call again and hung up. Does it offend other Christians when someone becomes a believer?"

The man laughed hardily. When he stopped, he said, "No son. We're elated when someone becomes a believer."

"So why did you laugh?"

"Son, the woman thinks you're conning her, that's all."

"But why? I was telling her the truth. Besides, we hit it off so well and have great chemistry."

"Is she a believer?"

"Yes. She's a strong Christian woman, why?"

"If that's true she would never want a man who didn't share her faith."

Matt sat with his head low as he glanced up, "If that's the case, she should be happy for me and for us."

"She would, if she believed you, but she doesn't."

"I'm confused," Matt said while staring at the pastor.

The man leaned forward, "To her, it's too good to be true. Within a week after rejecting you, you became a Christian and have a clean slate, and want to attend church. She just isn't buying it. It's as simple as that."

Matt slumped further into his chair.

"If the lady thought you were telling the truth she would be elated. If she pulled away, she must have felt manipulated."

"What should I do to convince her?"

"You won't like my answer," he said while leaning back with hands folded."

"Try me."

"Young man you need to adjust to your new life. Forget about her for a while. First you must make some significant changes. Attend church, and our men's group." He looked at Matt for a while. "You must find a new career, and make new friends who support your direction. Those are some tangible signs of a redeemed life. You must stay firm in your faith for months or even a year before dating anyone."

"What should I do about her?"

"Put her on hold. If you're meant to be with her, she'll wait. Are you willing to trust God?"

"Yes. I'm willing to do that. Where do I start?"

"I recommend you get some good Christian Counseling."

After Matt leaned forward he said, "Can you recommend someone?"

"That's the right attitude. Take actions now, don't wait." The man handed him a business card for a therapist.

As Pastor Tom and he were standing and saying goodbye, he leaned forward, and gave Matt a long bear hug. He said, "I'm proud of you son. You're making all the right decisions. If you need help, my door's always open. You're now a child of the living God, so welcome to our family."

"What do you mean family?"

"At the moment you accepted Christ you became part of one big Christian family. We need you as much as you need us. At times you will inspire someone here, and other times a person will encourage you."

As he choked back tears, he said, "Thank You." I have never felt so loved and supported, not even by my own parents.

About the Author

Dr. Mary Gale Hinrichsen

Writer, Speaker and Life Coach

Dr. Hinrichsen is known as, "The Trash Talking Therapist." She specializes in finding our mental trash and helping us to recycle it by accepting a more accurate belief. Our unconscious is unable to determine fact from fiction. It will automatically support what we believe and help it come true. Therefore, if we think we can't, our subconscious will assist that belief. Likewise when we think we can, our subconscious will help us find a way to make that become a reality.

Dr. Hinrichsen is a self-made-millionaire, has a PhD in Christian Counseling, and holds three Master's Degrees. She has co-authored several non-fiction books, and authored *Ethics of a Thief*, which is her favorite. Her hobbies include oil painting, sculpting and golfing, but her passion is spending time with her children and grandchildren.

Visit her author website at
marygalehinrichsen.icrewdigital.com

And **trashtalkingtherapist.com**

19411594R00166

Made in the USA
San Bernardino, CA
26 February 2015